COCKTAILS

COCKTAILS

STANLEY CARTEN

BLUE MOON BOOKS
NEW YORK

COCKTAILS

Copyright © 1991 Stanley Carten

Published by
Blue Moon Books
An Imprint of Avalon Publishing Group Incorporated
161 William Street, 16th Floor
New York, NY 10038

ISBN 1-56201-253-3

9 8 7 6 5 4 3 2 1

Printed in the United States of America
Distributed by Publishers Group West

Contents

1

Shady Lady

Mix

1oz. Tequila
1oz. Melon Liqueur
4oz. Grapefruit Juice

Combine ingredients over ice in a highball glass
Garnish with a lime and a cherry

...tened in the diffuse red and blue cast ...ng Station's neon lighting. Annie da Pheelanupe ...anaged expertly to catch every last drop of semen in a standard size Pump cocktail napkin, leaving only a thin smear across the dick from whence the fountain of spunk had erupted. She'd even added a little cough of her own at just the right moment to mix with the Pump's monotonous background music, the resultant din thereby masking the gasp that issued forth from the slightly overweight businessman to whom the penis belonged.

Annie had cleverly shielded her hand motions with her cocktail tray and the profile of her more than adequate figure. To the casual observer it just looked like Annie was chatting quite intently as she delivered a customer his vodka and tonic. It was early on a Saturday night, and the Pump had not yet hit even one third full. With three waitresses on the floor, it was not unusual for one to spend a little extra time with a customer. It usually meant a bigger tip. And in this case – it really did.

Once the semi-erect penis had been safely stowed away by its satisfied owner, Annie hovered above the businessman with her multi-purpose tray.

'That'll be five dollars for the drink, sir.'

Annie emphasised the 'for the drink' portion of her request.

'Thanks – thanks – so very much.'

Speech was still a little difficult for the businessman as he plopped down his wad of cash.

3

in tips fro...

Annie da Pheelanupe...
when phonetically pronounced...
though she'd spent the the the last ten of her...
California, she was originally born and raised...
Star state of Texas. Annie's great-great-grandmother w...
legendary French-born Kitty de Pheelanupe who ran Fort
Worth's famous 'Madame Kitty's' brothel. That was back
in the days of cowboys, Indians, sheep and long lonely cattle
drives.

Annie retained much of her colourful ancestry, and when
she wanted to she could still drawl out her words Texas style.
Especially when she met someone and told the unsuspecting
victim her name. It wasn't just Annie, it was Annie da
Pheelanupe – which sounded in Texan very much like 'Ah
need a feelin' up.' An introduction no doubt guaranteed to
break the ice at even the most staid of parties.

Not that Annie needed much help in breaking ice. Every
aspect of her five-foot-two-inch body radiated enough heat
to melt the polar icecaps. Take her breasts. Not really that
large – she wore a 36B cup – but combine their delectable
roundness with her small size and, well, the obvious analogies
spring to mind. And to put these lethal weapons in something
as flimsy as a Pumping Station cocktail dress was downright
close to being guilty of inciting a riot. And then there were
her legs. They started somewhere around the floor level with
her perfectly formed ankles and ascended skyward past
superbly tensioned calves, pausing only slightly at exquisitely
trim thighs, leaping immediately to a tightly rounded bottom
that the serious observer could be forgiven for estimating was

4

a good six feet off the ground. It was, of course, just an optical illusion – but one that made Annie appear so much larger than life. Wherever the leers were focused, Annie's body – including her face – outdid itself. Her petite form was capped by an unruly mop of blonde hair that framed big blue eyes and a mouth that gave forth a huge smile only a truly immodest Texan could deliver. And with her little turned up nose she looked perpetually sixteen – not thirty. Attributes that made Annie well equipped to tackle life at the Pumping Station – to its fullest.

Which she did, and very well too. Her extra-cocktailing efforts had all started by accident one very slow night, many years ago. Back then Annie had only been at the Pump for three months, but in that short time she had been propositioned by seemingly legions of men. Tired of making all those same old excuses like 'I have a boyfriend', or 'Sorry, I'm busy tonight', Annie tried a new approach that led her to a whole new world of sexual adventures. Even now, some five years later, she remembered every detail of her initiation into the fine art of selling sex . . .

There were four of them. All very tall. Very blond. Short hair. Blue eyes. All very German. They sat quite rigid, ordering imported German beer. After three rounds they started to loosen their starched collars a little and become more friendly. Annie decided that they were probably on an expense account, so she thought a little conversation would be rewarded.

'Where y'all from?' Annie retained many Texas euphemisms. 'Y'all' was one of them that was particularly difficult to get rid of. It was so convenient – especially when used to address a bunch of people.

'Ve come from Siemens.'

'Oh that's nice.' Annie had no idea that they meant an electronics giant of a company. She thought they were just being rude.

'Y'all here on business – or pleasure?'

'Siemens' business.'

'I see. Can I get you boys anything else to drink?' Annie thought it best to change the subject from what she incorrectly surmised was sex.

'*Ja* – ve all vant another round, *ja*?'

'Yeah – coming right up.'

And Annie had served the Siemens representatives quite a few more rounds throughout the rather slow evening. Despite the language barrier between Texans and Germans, Annie was able to spend enough time with them to learn that they were from the Fatherland, and their names were Hans, Jergen, Wolf and Dieter. It was getting close to last call when the fateful exchange occurred.

'Almost closing time boys – any last requests?'

There followed a brief whispered exchange with many '*ja*'s' and '*Mein Gott*'s' being issued. Finally Hans managed to put together a coherent sentence, despite the beer-induced alcoholic haze that enveloped his blond brain.

'Vhat time do du get off?'

'Why?'

'Ve – Jergen, Wolf, Dieter and I, Hans – vant to – how do you say? – party vith you. Ja?'

Annie was about to use one of the three thousand excuses she'd memorised over the last few months when she decided that attack was perhaps the best form of defence.

'I'll be off in half an hour – but it'll cost ya.'

Annie felt sure that the brazen hussy approach would scare them off. She underestimated the worldliness of the Euro-male, used to state-run brothels – paying for sex was no big deal. Following Annie's offer there followed another huddle.

'It is a deal – how much?'

'Oh wow.' Annie thought fast. She chose a number she thought would discourage them. 'Three hundred dollars.'

Four blond heads nodded their ready assent in eager drunken unison. Annie didn't pay much attention to the business pages of the newspaper. If she had she'd have realised that the dollar hadn't been doing too well against the Deutschmark. $300 wasn't really that much to German engineers on an expense account.

'Aw shit,' mumbled Annie under her breath.

'Pardon you?'

'Oh – er – where shall we meet?'

6

'Ve are at the Ambassador Hotel, right next to you – room 1266. In thirty minutes ve party hardy – *ja?*'

'Yar – in thirty minutes ve party hardy all right.'

And with roaring smiles displaying their perfect teeth, the four German businessmen left the Pump to stumble across the parking lot to the adjacent Ambassador Hotel. Annie was left to contemplate her fate. She could have easily have told them that she was joking, just trying to make an original excuse, but her mischievous nature took hold and decided against playing it safe.

It didn't take her long to rationalise that 'partying hardy' with four Teutonic terrors for $300 was a hell of a lot better money than cocktailing, and they did seem like nice guys. Never once did the term 'hooker' cross her mind. She just looked at the whole situation as a way to make a large tip for being extra nice to a few good customers. Briefly, for a fleeting moment, as she walked across the windswept parking lot, the cold night air of January caused her to pause and consider doing a no-show. It would be so simple to get in her car and drive away, leaving the four Germans to jerk each other off. But she decided against it. She'd snorted a little something in the changing rooms to give her the extra boost she needed to take on four guys, and the drug pulsing through her body really didn't want her to go home and sleep soundly. Without some form of body-draining exertion she would be up for days. The doubts that crept into her mind were quickly banished. And she did feel decidedly randy walking across the parking lot with just a floor-length leather coat covering the lingerie of her Pumping Station uniform. Her high heels clicking on the Ambassador's driveway sounded like the telltale countdown of a timebomb about to explode. There would be no turning back.

'Hello.' It was Hans who opened the door to room 1266.

'Hi.' Little smile. Annie stepped into the room. Jergen, Wolf and Dieter stood politely nodding. Annie swallowed deeply as the door shut behind her and the chain was latched. *Think – think – think*. Annie's brain raced through the possibilities facing her. That she could be so practical with amphetamines dancing around her brain later caused Annie

7

to be quite proud of her self-preservation instincts.

Annie thought back to the late-night movies she had seen. There was a small chance that these guys could be cops putting on fake German accents, so she used a ploy common to hookers everywhere that they always seem to make a point of forgetting to use in the movies, thereby allowing the hero macho vice squad officer to make the bust and keep the streets clean for Mr and Mrs America. She pulled her leather coat tightly around her and made her rapidly prepared statement.

'OK gents, take off all of your clothes. All of you.'

There was more mumbling and a few *neins* and a few more *dumkopfs*, and then a consensus of opinion appeared to be reached. In true Teutonic ceremonial fashion they all began to disrobe rather efficiently. As the last few socks joined the neat piles of clothes, it was clear to Annie that none of them were wearing hidden microphones. A smile crept across her face.

'Well — that's quite a smorgasbord y'all got there.'

Puzzled looks wrinkled the Germans' blond faces.

'Oh never mind — who's first?' It was amazing how wanton the drug in her bloodstream made her feel. Annie had quite an illustrious past, but never as porno movie-like as this. As if a seedy band were playing burlesque music, she tossed her black leather floor-length coat over a chair and strutted over to the bed. As she lay down, legs widely spread, she noticed that four German cocks had leapt to attention in the short space of time that it had taken her to make herself comfortable. Hans, Jergen, Wolf and Dieter stood huddled together like some Olympic swimming team about to tackle the 400 meter relay. Jergen was the first to dive in.

'Come on lover — Annie da Pheelanupe is waiting.'

As Jergen inched himself onto the bed, Annie quickly licked her fingers and inserted them into her pussy. She needed a little extra wetness that the sight of four almost identical naked blond Germans with straining cocks hadn't yet induced. Jergen halted, visibly stunned by the sight of Annie in her Pumping Station uniform of red suspender belt, black fishnet stockings and five inch shiny black high heels replete with ankle straps casually sliding a few fingers inside

8

her fair-haired quim. It didn't take Annie much time to shake him out of his trance.

'Give me that dick, Jerkoff.'

'Jergen.'

'Like I said, give me that dick, Jergen.'

With one hand she grasped the German's taunt penis and with the other she clasped his snowy white buttocks and pulled him to her. As she forced him into her he collapsed onto Annie's ample breasts, squishing the round orbs against him. He tried to kiss her, but again — memories of all those movies counseled Annie in the ways of an impersonal hooker.

'No kissing on the lips sugar — just on the neck. And no biting — don't damage the merchandise.'

'*Ja—ja—ja.*'

The German love of authority revelled in Annie's strong tones. Hans, Dieter and Wolf waited with baited breath and pulsing cocks as Jergen enjoyed the first few strokes of his fuck. Out of the corner of her eye Annie could see the glistenings at the tips of the waiting cocks. They stood like flagpoles ready to honour her bedroom efforts. It had an exciting effect upon her already supercharged system. Like a car shifting into high gear, Annie revved up her engines.

'Aw, come on Jerkoff, ram your big dick up to my throat. Stick your balls in their too, honey. Fill me up — fuck me up — I'm so fucked up.'

'*Ja—ja—ja.*' was all Jergen could manage. He didn't even bother to correct Annie on the pronunciation of his name. He thrust his penis in and out of her with all the rapidity of the pistons of a runaway steam locomotive. In response, Annie was flowing in torrents of cunt juice. She felt like a bottomless fountain. She felt like she could fuck all night long.

Jergen's sweat and juice soaked crotch pounded and rubbed against Annie's cunt, further heightening the feelings of raw lust that drove her to excess.

'You can lick my tits Jerkoff. You can squeeze 'em too — if you want to,' she whispered in his ear as he tickled her neck with his tongue.

'*Ja — ja — arrrrrrrrh.*' Jergen didn't get a chance to latch on to Annie's quivering boobs — his dick just seemed to

9

explode inside her, turning his mind, his body and his resolve into a warm sticky mush.

'Come on honey – give me all that German jism – fill my quim to the brim.' Annie continued bucking wildly, legs wrapped around Jergen's waist, prodding him with her heels as she drained the length of his cock into her.

'OK Jergie baby – off ya get. Don't be a hog.'

Jergen just groaned and remained inert, alcohol and excessive sudden sperm loss taking their toll.

'Hey boys – how about a little help?'

Hans and Dieter lifted the dead weight of Jergen off of Annie. There was a slippery splat of a noise made by Jergen's now flaccid cock exiting the honey-trap of Annie's pussy. Under normal circumstances, Jergen would have been embarrassed. But these were not normal circumstances at all.

'Which one of y'all's next?'

Wolf stepped forward. Annie noticed that his penis was larger than the rest of the Germans' tools, bigger in length and girth. Annie whistled in admiration and anticipation.

'Phew, Wolfey – you're gonna make me howl at the moon tonight with that club of yours.'

'*Ja* – I fuck you good.'

'Oh my – Wolfey – I do so like it when you talk dirty to me. Let me wrap my hands around that cannon.'

Using both her hands she slid the large cock into her well-prepared opening.

'Hmmm – now that's what I call a dick.'

Wolf was easily the most experienced of the group with women. He'd had many prostitutes before. He knew all of their sly ways to make him come quickly. He took grim pleasure in gaining the upper hand. He slid his penis out of Annie's cunt and used his free hand to hold it stationary just at the opening of her slit.

'Wolfey, Wolfey – don't tease me so.'

'I fuck you good. You see, *ja*.'

He moved the tip of his large instrument up and over Annie's pussy, nesting it in her pubic hair. Backwards and forwards he slid his tool, each time sparingly inserting the tip ever so slightly into Annie's quivering hole. Annie tried to thrust forward to take all of his swollen length inside her, but each time Wolf would back away.

'Oh, *ja*, *ja*, Wolfey, you fuck good. Too fucking good. Just stick that hunk of meat into me. I'm dying for it.'

'Like this – you like it like this – *ja*?'

And Wolf rammed the full length of his dick into Annie in one swift movement and let the monster expand inside her to fill every nook and cranny of her shocked cunny. He held it there, at the top of his stroke as Annie writhed on the erect member like some impaled animal in the final agonising throes of death. Just as Annie reached the point where she felt she might lose consciousness, Wolf would slide the intruder out of her cunt and let it sit at the mouth of her swollen cave. She was beyond words. Just heavy, forced breaths, heaving breasts, quivering thighs, craving the release of sexual tensions no normal human being should ever be asked to endure for longer than the instant of orgasm. Every second, every minute seemed like an eternity of coming as Wolf repeated the torture. Each time the split of his cockhead slipped over Annie's budding clitoris she died and was resurrected. She bit furiously at the pillow of the bed, determined not to scream. After all, she was supposed to be in control here. She kept telling herself that this was supposed to be a job – strictly business.

Wave after wave of orgasm rolled through her body, racking every nerve ending already ultra-sensitised by the drugs she had taken just a few moments ago. And yet, in the deep of this ocean of abandoned lust, she somehow fought for sexual supremacy. She could not let Wolf win the war, but she did have to admit that he'd easily won the first few skirmishes. As he plunged his cock deep inside her orgasm-torn pussy, she reached underneath her thighs and gripped his balls with one hand. With the other she had her long red fingernails stroke the delicate space between his balls and his asshole. Annie's nails dragged softly one by one across this 'no-man's-land' that is usually ignored by inexperienced lovers in too much of a hurry. Her other hand kneaded Wolf's balls firmly – almost painfully.

His reaction was sudden – perhaps violent. He wrenched

11

his voluminous cock out of her sopping cunt, but she hung on to him with her hands for all she was worth. Still, as he bucked and writhed to free himself, she fondled him in his most vulnerable of places. With an almighty scream that must surely have woken the whole hotel he thrust his head back, his cock skyward and came in huge off-white lightening bolts like some Norse god of old. The spunk splattered on Annie's chest like heavy summer raindrops clearing the anticipation-filled night air of August in the tropics.

But it wasn't August – it was January. And it wasn't the tropics – it was Silicon Valley. And as far as Annie was concerned it was now two down and two to go.

Once Annie let go of Wolf's throbbing tool, he tumbled off the bed, narrowly missing his head on the bedside table. Hans and Dieter looked on in mortal terror. Both had erections that were turning an ugly shade of purple.

'Would one of y'all kindly fix a lady a drink before we – er – resume. Gin and tonic would be mighty fine,' requested Annie as she wiped the remnants of Wolf's orgasm onto the bed sheet.

Hans quickly fixed a stiff one at the bar and passed it to Dieter to serve.

'I guess that means you're next, Dickter?'

'Dieter.'

'Sure – well let me have a little drink, and then you can soothe that hot boner of yours off in my cooling pussy waters.'

'*Ja – ja – ja.*'

Dieter's knowledge of English was limited to basic phrase book 'where is the post office?' type of stuff. Annie's plea for a little respite was lost on Dieter who only heard the German equivalent of English phrases that translated to 'fuck me now,' no matter what was originally uttered.

And one could hardly blame him after the two prize fucks he'd just witnessed. So it was not surprising that he just leapt right on top of Annie, spilling most of the gin and tonic over the bed. Given the rather large amount of other forms of moisture that emanated from two rapidly spreading spots, the gin and tonic was a minor addition to the dampness of the sheets.

12

But it was something like the straw that broke the camel's back for Annie. After recovering from the momentary shock of being pounced upon, she was damned if she was going to be treated like a fumbled ball on a kick-off return in the Super Bowl. With a strength that not only surprised her but also Dieter, she wrestled the unsuspecting German on to his back, right slap-dab in the middle of the wettest part of the bed.

'Take that, you bastard,' as she drove his purple penis into her to its hilt. Not willing to rest too long on the wet bed for any one moment, she bounced from knee to knee, trampolining on Dieter's hardness. With each slap of her thighs and ass against his body. Annie's breasts jiggled erotically as they too reversed their trajectories. Her mop of blonde hair flew in a million directions as if free-falling in the weightlessness of space. Occasionally, like gravity the spoiler, her sweat would cause a few strands of hair to stick to her face, momentarily defying the lure of bouncing skyward. 'Just take that, you bastard,' she pounded away. Like a boxer with his opponent on the ropes she pummelled relentlessly.

'*Ja – ja – ja*.' Dieter was enjoying himself immensely. So too was Hans, who couldn't help but wonder what might be in store for him. Wolf and Jergen were still out cold. Jergen was snoring loudly.

Dieter was slowly becoming hypnotised by the sight of Annie's hardened nipples describing complex figures of eight in the steamy air of the room. As her tits bounced freely, her nipples seemed to pursue some course of their own, sending almost subliminal messages to the vulnerable Dieter.

'Come, you bastard – come inside me.'

'*Ja – ja – ja*.'

'Not *ja* – come, you motherfucker. Splatter your brains in my cunt.'

Annie was frantic with lust and drugs. Something primal in her had been triggered by Dieter's uninvited mounting, and it wasn't going to be calmed easily.

'Arrrrrgh – ohhh – arrgh.'

Annie didn't stop as Dieter's orgasm shuddered inside and around her as she continued to bounce up and down on the

13

writing form beneath her. Dieter's cock slapped out of her opening and was immediately pounded against his stomach by Annie's bouncing ass.

'Arrrrrgh – ohhh – arrgh.'

Saliva began to trickle out of Dieter's mouth as he faded into never-never land. And still Annie continued to bounce on his battered cock until something told her that she was quite literally flogging a dead horse. Dieter was dead to the world, knowing intimately the abyss of sexual exhaustion and fulfilment. He would never be able to fuck normally again. If Annie had know this she would have been well and truly satisfied.

But she didn't. And she wasn't. Breathing in deep forced gasps, she turned to face Hans. From underneath her matted blonde bangs she hissed, 'Now it's your turn, Hansy.' Pivoting on Dieter's flaccid cock, she swung around and stood, legs apart, all five foot two, breasts heaving, stockings torn and looking like something out of a Wagnerian Opera.

'So how do you want it?'

'Er – er – oh, shit.' Hans panicked and ran for the safety of the bathroom, fearing possible bodily injury. It was not a wise move for a naked man with a throbbing hard-on to attempt. His slapping dick slowed him considerably, giving Annie's amphetamine-charged body ample time to leap after him and head him off at the pass. She grabbed his dick as it swung from left to right.

'So you want to play bathroom games do ya? Well, follow me asshole.'

'Ja – ja – ja.'

And like some unruly child being led by the ear to the headmaster's office for punishment, Hans was tugged by his pole-like penis into the bright and shiny bathroom of room 1266 of the Ambassador Hotel.

'I'm kind of sweaty – and sticky. Why don't we take a shower together?'

This sounded pretty innocuous to Hans who readily nodded his compliance and rapidly adjusted the knobs and controls until a nice steady stream of pulsating 'Micro-Finger' waterjets were issuing forth.

14

'*Ja — ja* — ve take shower.'

'Y'all get right in then.'

Hans looked a little puzzled, not realising that it was standard Texas-speak to use the plural 'y'all' interchangeably with the singular 'y'all'. Even so, he readily hopped into the shower and pulled the plastic curtain across the tub to prevent the creation of a minor flood. No sooner was the curtain closed than it was ripped from its moorings in quite a Psycho-the-movie-type fashion. Somehow the viewer of this sordid scene may have been forgiven for thinking that Hans would have been happier staring at a knife-wielding-Anthony-Perkins-in-drag than the crazed female that stared maniacally at him.

'Y'all not gone shy on me, have ya?' Hans didn't have time to answer as he stumbled back against the coldness of the shower wall. Not wanting to lose the advantage of surprise, Annie grabbed his rock hard penis and hoisted herself into the shower — still wearing the fuck-me-tender outfit of red suspender belt, black fishnet stockings and black five-inch heels replete with ankle straps. She dropped to her knees — the warm water splashing on her back and on her hair — and found herself staring eyeball to slit with a raging hard-on. Annie casually hefted the balls in her hands, kind of like some religious offering. Her hair and what passed for her clothing were soaked through. The high heels, dripping wet, glistened nastily. Still hefting Hans' balls she spoke softly, still staring the hard-on right in the eye. 'Shampoo my hair Hans.'

'*Ja — ja* — shampoo.'

And Hans complied, pouring the whole bottle of Ambassador complimentary shampoo on Annie's blonde hair. He began to massage the shampoo thoroughly into her roots, kneading the scalp. The feeling was sensuously intoxicating, striking some primitive chord deep in his being. It took a few moments for him to realise that as he worked over Annie's head with long, slow rhythmical movements, she too was working over his little head with long, slow rhythmical movements. Annie moved her head backward and forwards guided by the patient motions of Hans' hands.

'*Ja — ja — das ist gut — sehr gut.*' Hans reverted to his

15

Germanic roots as he massaged the lather luxuriously through Annie's tingling mop.

'Hmm – mumble – mumble – hmm.' Annie moaned in stunned ecstasy, unable to speak for the cock presence in her mouth. She was a sucker for anyone who played with her hair – obviously. She felt the all-too-familiar stirrings somewhere in the depths of her stomach. Without losing her rhythm she latched one hand behind Hans' leg and pulled it roughly between her thighs. Hans almost lost his balance but steadied himself with his hands on Annie's head – and still he continued to give her the best shampoo of her life.

Annie suddenly realised that the bend of a man's foot, right where it becomes a leg, roughly around the ankle, on the upper part of the foot was the perfect shape on which to rub her pussy. The nobbly little ridges and bones were better than any dildo – better than any thrusting pelvis she'd ever felt. And so she ground away, sucking Hans' dick while he continued to run his fingers firmly through her hair. The pulsing shower water carried the lather as it was formed in waves of suds down the sucking drain.

The whole imagery of the shower scene was riddled with sexual innuendo.

In time with the gurgling of the suds and water down the drain, Annie felt the rumbling of her own orgasm building. She suddenly wanted Hans to come at the same time as she. It became an immediate obsession with her. She had to make him come in stirring concert with herself. Annie felt the quivering in her thighs begin. It wouldn't be long. Urgently, she built the pressure on the base of his cock with her other hand. In concert with her sucking, she masturbated him. Her body moved in many synchronised motions like some complicated machine. Her legs flexed up and down, causing her pussy to slide along Hans' foot. At the same time her hand and head moved backwards and forwards along the straining arch of Hans' bulging member.

And the machine achieved its designed purpose in grand style. Both Hans and Annie boiled over at the same time, crossing the threshold from the so-called real world into that soft mushiness bounded by the throes of gut-wrenching, mind-tearing orgasms.

They both collapsed into the tub. Hans melted down the wall where he was brought to rest against the curled-up form of Annie. Together they stayed, being gently pounded by the pulsations of the 'Micro-Finger' water jets.

How long she slumbered Annie never knew. Time seemed to stand still as dancing little bursts of water cooled the stinging between her mons veneris. In her mind's eye she pictured the water drops evaporating as they spluttered on her swollen pussy lips in much the same way that a Dallas thunderstorm in July steams off the baked Texas sidewalks. It was a soothing and comforting image.

Careful to turn off the shower so that Hans would not drown in his sexually exhausted stupor, Annie removed all of her clothes and shoes and left them on the floor as souvenirs for the four German Siemens representatives. Wrapping a towel around her head and pulling her leather coat tightly round her she bid the slumbering Hans, Dieter, Wolf and Jergen '*auf Wiedersehen*' and boldly exited the hotel through the main lobby dripping the occasional blob of water and leaving a trail of wet footprints as she went. Luckily, it was still the early hours of the morning and only the janitor seemed to notice the strangely dressed lady. He assumed she was some sort of foreign potentate and went back to mopping the tiled entry of the hotel.

It was only when she was safely back in her apartment and on the verge of falling asleep that Annie suddenly realised that she'd forgotten to pick up her $300. A smile crept across her face as she dozed into an oblivious rest − it was worth it anyway. She'd enjoyed it as much as they. Probably more.

After the kind of deep sleep that only the well and truly fucked know, Annie veritably bounced into the Pump the next evening full of herself. Quickly on to the floor, she eagerly awaited the night's customers − perhaps the Germans would be in again?

'Hey, Annie − some foreign guy dropped this by for you earlier,' droned Arnold the bartender. He handed her a plain white envelope with her name written on it.

'Gee thanks Arnold − did he say anything?' Annie was

17

aware how guys talked – especially to bartenders. She held her breath awaiting Arnold's reply.

'No – he just asked if you were working and I said that you wouldn't be in until eight, so he asked me to give you the envelope because he had to catch a plane and couldn't wait. That's all. Why? A new boyfriend?'

'Oh no, nothing like that.'

She made like the envelope wasn't too important – just put it on her tray and went about with the normal run-of-the-mill cocktail waitress/bartender matter-of-fact conversation. After a few minutes she said that it was about time to see if anyone wanted a drink. So she left Arnold and made her way around the lounge. Sitting at an empty booth out of sight of the bar, Annie tore open the envelope. Stuffed inside were twelve one-hundred dollar bills and a handwritten note on Ambassador Hotel stationery. As might be expected it was brief and to the point.

Dear Miss da Pheelanupe:

You forgot to collect your well-earned reward for last night's 'partying hardy.' Find enclosed $300 from each of us as per our agreement. We are all very sore, but very happy. We shall be sure to visit you on our next trip. We will recommend you to our associates.

See y'all

Hans

P.S. Thank you for the souvenirs.

Annie read the note once more and smiled broadly. Laughing to herself she couldn't help but make a comment that quite baffled the adjacent booth of three geeky electronics engineers drinking away a hard day's programming.

'God damn – I've only been in Silicon Valley for three months and already I'm a fucking entrepreneur.'

By the end of the night the engineers knew exactly what Annie had meant by 'fucking entrepreneur'.

Her great-great-grandmother would have been proud of Annie.

18

2

Eye-Opener

Mix

1 Egg Yolk
½ tsp. Powdered Sugar
1 tsp. Anis
1 tsp. Triple Sec
1 tsp. Creme de Cacao (White)
2 oz. Light Rum

Shake with ice and strain into a whiskey sour glass

S ilicon Valley, California, just forty miles due south of San Francisco on Highway 101. A high-tech promised land where just a few years ago the personal computer was born, and with it the fortunes of many talented entrepreneurs. And now the heady rebellious days of the micro-computer revolution are over. Now, large corporations battle for market share and fortunes are won and lost overnight as stock prices fluctuate according mostly to rumour and sometimes to fact.

Whether jaded electronics executive or bright-eyed computer jockey, there is always the need to wind down after a day-long and sometimes night-long stint in monolithically sterile office buildings and research labs. The bars of Silicon Valley have always existed to provide an oasis of relaxation for these computer soldiers to unwind between the demands of the bosses and the yawnings of the wives. And one bar in particular has seen it all. The Pumping Station Lounge, strategically located at the hub of the Valley, has been there the longest and has witnessed more than its rightful share of the triumphs and disasters of the full spectrum of Silicon Valley inhabitants.

Built on the ruins of a failed full service petrol station, the Pump, as it is affectionately known by its die-hard regulars, symbolises the rags-to-riches attitude that lures so many people to this area from all over the world, from all walks of life. Ask anyone in Silicon Valley where they might want to meet to pump a few drinks, or to pump a competitor for information, or perhaps to meet someone interested in a spot

21

of leg-over pumping and you'll be answered most probably with two words – the Pump.

The reason for this popularity is quite simple. It's not the food – although that is very good and reasonably priced. It's not the drinks – although they are truly strong and excellent value for money. It's not just the location, although being right next to 101 does help with easy access. The Pumping Station's popularity is due, plain and simple, to its waitresses. Seductively dressed, exquisitely attractive and perhaps oh-so willing, they offer the legions of Silicon Valley computer salesmen, engineers and executives the fantasy of a lusty escape from the technologically stuffy confines of their day-to-day lives. And there is always the chance that in Silicon Valley fantasy can easily become reality . . .

It was an exceedingly difficult task for the Pumping Station's junior manager, Bob Vest, to concentrate on the supposedly real reason for the attractive young woman to be seated across from him.

'Well – err – Kerry. Where were we?'

'Uniforms – you were describing the Pumping Station's uniform policy.'

'Ah yes – uniforms. Well, since you worked here last summer as a food waitress you are familiar with what the cocktail waitresses wear here, so I don't have to describe the – er – outfits to you.'

'No – no – I'm quite familiar with what I'm supposed to wear.'

'Yes – well – even so, it is one thing to be aware of the uniforms – it is another to actually be comfortable in such attire. How well you do your job will depend upon how at ease you put your customers – and you can only achieve that feeling of comfort if you're well at ease in almost next to nothing with complete strangers leering after your body.'

Bob Vest's penis was as hard as a rock from his talking to the barely twenty-two-year old Kerry Farnum. It was all he could do to stop his member from beating time on the executive desk behind which he hid his stand.

Kerry Farnum was the quintessential young American

beauty. Shoulder-length auburn hair, peach-like complexion, immaculate athletic figure, pert breasts, long legs, permanently puckered lips, and brains to boot. Bob Vest had wanted to fuck her when she worked as a food waitress at the Pump last year, but he had been just a cook and she had shown no interest in becoming a part of the Pump's ongoing who-slept-with-whom soap opera. Bob Vest, in his chef's uniform, stood little chance of catching the eye of this unusually attractive third-year engineering student from the University of California at Berkeley. He tried everything from a little extra french fries on her orders to making her seafood salads visually stunning – but nothing seemed to work. Deep down inside he thought it was because he wasn't that good-looking. Tall and thin, with short yet unruly brown hair, Bob looked uncoordinated, even clumsy. In his chef's hat he looked downright silly. He'd never drummed up the confidence to say more than 'hi' to her.

That was over a year ago, and Bob had matured quite a bit. He was still tall and thin, but his brown hair was styled more confidently and he didn't have to wear the silly chef's uniform. Now Kerry was back looking for a more lucrative cocktail waitress job and Bob was the junior manager – with all of the privileges such a position commanded. One such privilege was the interviewing of prospective cocktail waitresses and he definitely was enjoying the interviewing process – even if it was difficult to concentrate.

'Yes – well – where was I?'

'Being comfortable in next to nothing.'

'Yes – do you think you can handle it?'

'Oh yes most definitely. I've worn less at the beach.'

I bet you have, thought Bob – and I bet you are very comfortable in next to nothing, his increasingly raging libido added.

'Well, yes – but here at the Pump we've learned that there is no substitute for actually being there, so we like to conduct the rest of the interview with you in the uniform. If I think you can sit here in a fully lit room dressed in almost nothing, being quite comfortable with me, then I'll have the confidence in you that you'll do well on the floor.'

23

'Sure — I have no problem with that.'

'Good — you can use the changing rooms next door. You'll find clothes that should fit you there. Take your time. Remember — in this job appearance is everything. Just knock on the office door when you are ready to resume the interview.'

'No problem — I'll be right back, Bob.'

Bob Vest watched the retreating form of Kerry Farnum leave the office. Even in the conservative business suit she'd worn for the interview she betrayed her youthful sexuality with a playfully teasing swing of her hips. His earlier words, 'you'll do well on the floor,' bounced around his erotically supercharged subconscious, stirring the most lustful of thoughts. He began to visualise the scene before him. There was Kerry pinioned to the floor of his office by his own urgent form. Her trim little dress was up around her waist and Bob had excited her so by tearing out the crotch of her tights with his teeth. Her legs wrapped around his waist and crossed behind his back at her slim nylon-covered ankles. Pushing against the hardness of the floor she rocked to and fro against the equal hardness of his cock. Long, deliciously hard and fast strokes of wet tightness sucked at his straining dick. She was lost to the passion of the moment. 'Fuck me — fuck me — fuck me hard, Bob. Fuck me hard — don't slow down. You fuck me so hard — so well,' Kerry would scream wetly into his ear as she playfully bit his neck. She'd lift her ass ever so slightly off the floor so that his hard dick slid all the more deeply inside her. She fucked well on the floor . . . yes, she would do well on the floor.

It wasn't anywhere near New Year's Eve, but Bob made a resolution to have his cock well and truly inside that beauty before the summer was over. He really couldn't take too many more of these naughty thoughts that seemed to control his being with tantilising visions of gargantuan amounts of steamy sex. He would really have to have her. And soon.

Immediately that Kerry left the room Bob Vest leapt to his feet and locked the office door. In a flash he was back at his desk and typing a few commands on the Pumping Station's automated surveillance system. To ensure security

24

throughout the building, the Pumping Station had installed a video-camera network that monitored strategic parts of the building and the parking lot.

And thanks to the electronic wizardry of Bob Vest, a few simple commands activated hidden cameras in the women's changing rooms. Bob had been a promising electronics student at Silicon Valley Institute of Technology when financial problems had forced him to quit his studies and work full time. One day he intended to continue his education, but for now the Pump paid good money and gave him an opportunity to use some of his talents − albeit covertly.

One of the reasons Bob had risen through the Pump ranks so quickly was because of his electronics skills. He quickly distinguished himself by dealing expertly with all of the 'bugs' that periodically invaded the Pump's computerised sales registers and the software that made them do their magic. Quite unknown to anyone at the Pumping Station, he'd also made a few modifications to the security system that betrayed deeper interests beyond integrated circuits.

After a few sweaty keystrokes the video views of the parking lot were replaced by a wall, ceiling and floor colour views of the women's changing room. Bob quickly slapped a blank video disc into the laser imaging recorder and pressed the 'record' button. He slid back in the chair and watched with heavy anticipation as the door opened and Kerry Farnum entered the room clutching her uniform. Bob's mouth went dry as he continuously licked his lips in a subconscious leering manner. All he needed was a drab raincoat to complete the image he radiated.

Monitor Number One, the floor view, quickly gave Bob his first view of Kerry's usually hidden charms. Looking straight up past her small high heels, Bob could follow the curves of her legs up to the darkened material of the top of Kerry's tights. As she arranged the uniform on clothing hooks, Bob got numerous worm's eye views of Kerry's thighs and buttocks as the business suit swished upward with her movements. A small wet spot began to emerge in Bob's polyester suit. He knew better than to play with himself whilst watching such a display. He'd come too quickly and miss something. It was better to prolong the ecstasy and wank off later to the recorded version.

Monitor Number Two, the wall camera, gave Bob an excellent view of Kerry unzipping her skirt and stepping out of the garment. What a sight. Kerry walked – no, strutted – towards the camera and hung her skirt over the hanger in which the camera eye was hidded. The view was perfectly erotic. Her heels added just the right amount of tension to her nylon encapsulated thighs. Lurking behind the darkened patch of tight material covering Kerry's crotch was an extremely skimpy pair of panties. Bob couldn't quite make out the colour – but it was predictably something light and virginal.

Monitor Number Three, the ceiling camera, gave Bob a bird's eye view of Kerry's tits. After taking off her suit jacket and unbuttoning all too slowly her lacy blouse, she'd reached behind her and unsnapped her white lace bra. It was just as Bob had guessed. Her tits didn't sag one millimetre as she set them free. They were beautifully full and pert. From the ceiling he could easily make out the protuberances of her nipples as the cool air of the changing room hardened them into small bullets fired point blank at his brain.

Bob was sweating buckets. He shifted position every few seconds to free his erection from the confines of his underwear. He pulled at the collar of his shirt, loosening his tie as Kerry continued her unwitting striptease show. It was a bit of an understatement to say that he was getting hot under the collar. With every movement of her supple young body, Kerry was melting Bob Vest as if he were trapped fully clothed in a sauna.

With her back to the wall camera, Kerry hooked her fingers into the elastic of her tights and tugged them down, bending over as she rolled them off her feet. Bob was presented with an exquisite ass shot. Her panties were peach coloured and quite transparent. Pouting between her legs as she bent over, Bob could discern the telltale bulge of Kerry's pussy lips. He had to bite on his clenched fist to prevent himself from screaming in adoration.

She stood in the changing room, naked except for her

peach-coloured diaphanous panties. Three views of loveliness battered Bob's visual senses. As if this wasn't enough, now began the reverse striptease. Before dressing, Kerry fastened the obligatory pearl 'choker' Pumping Station necklace around the base of her delicate neck. Standing facing the mirror, both arms hooked behind her neck as she fastened the choker tightly against her creamy skin, she presented a reflected view of exquisite innocence and beauty. Her breasts thrust forward – superbly erotic without even knowing it, Kerry looked the epitome of a nubile virgin bride preparing for her wedding day.

But no virginal bride ever wore lingerie as whorish as that Kerry now donned. Slowly she hooked the red suspender belt around her waist, and then began the visual torture of putting on the black nylon seamed fishnet stockings. Definitely not standard issue from the bridal boutiques.

'Ohhh –.' Bob couldn't stifle the moan of exquisite agony escaping his lips as Kerry delicately rolled the fishnet stocking slowly up her cocked leg. With her leg still bent in that classic pin-up pose, she hooked the front strap and then stood up to complete the process on the rear. Again, Bob was treated to a full frame view of Kerry's immaculate bottom as she reached behind her to snap the red catch of the suspender belt to the jet-black nylon top of the stocking. And as if that wasn't enough for poor Bob to suffer, she teasingly repeated the process for the other leg. Finally, once the ribbed nylon sheaths hugged their contents, Kerry looked into the mirror and stood tip-toe to make sure her seams were straight. Bob noted with a true voyeur's eye how her calf muscles strained and tensed as she made a few fine adjustments to the seams. He could almost hear the delicate rustling of statically charged nylon-clad thigh against nylon-clad thigh.

And now came the dress. The Pumping Station cocktail waitress dress was the slinkiest piece of black material to be found in the civilised world. The garment was more space held together by a sensual blackness than the standard image of an evening formal cocktail dress popular at all the best charity balls. Backless with two thin straps that held up an extremely low cut halter-like top, the dress flared from a skin-tight middle to a flowing floor length fan of material slit all the way up to the very top of the thigh. The dress left just enough to the imagination to make it highly sexy. Worn correctly by someone with a perfectly flirty nature and most importantly, the appropriate figure, the dress was lethal.

Kerry pulled the dress over her head and shimmered into its glove-like fit. As she smoothed it to her body she stepped into the requisite black high heels. Bob actually gripped his crotch in earnest as Kerry steadied her stocking-covered legs on the changing room bench and fastened the tight black straps of the shoes around her stocking covered ankles. The split of the dress fell away revealing a full profile view of Kerry's delicious legs – from ankle to hip all was revealed. The high definition cameras revealed such detail as the nylon of the stockings rippling delicately under the tension of the strap. First one leg and then another. If Kerry had been a spider, Bob would have come in his pants by the time all eight straps had been fastened.

All that remained to complete the transformation were the finishing touches of brushing her hair and touching up her make-up, which Bob watched in rapt attention. As Kerry puckered her lips to add just the right amount of pale pink lipstick, Bob could imagine those lips sucking his cockhead. He closed his eyes and visualised the figure-of-eight mark she would leave on his dick. The lipstick would smear down the length of his shaft as she swallowed his full length. She'd then take her hands and . . .

Knock – knock – knock.

Bob's daydreaming was disturbed by the knocking on the office door. A quick look-see at the monitors told him that Kerry had left the dressing room and must be at the office door. While typing a few commands into the security system's terminal that restored the normal views of the parking lot, Bob yelled out for Kerry to wait a few moments.

'Be right there.'

He smoothed his somewhat dishevelled appearance and opened the door, his hand carefully covering the damp spot in his trousers. A vision of loveliness, made even the more captivating by his secret knowledge of her dressing and

28

undressing rituals, smiled at him.

'I hope I didn't keep you waiting too long?'

'Oh no – I was busy with some – err – security matters. Please – won't you – sit down.'

Bob steered Kerry to the chair and in quite the gentlemanly manner held the seat for her.

'So, how do you feel?'

'Fine – like I said, I've worn less at the beach. I feel perfectly at ease.'

'Yes – quite. Now, where were we.'

Kerry may have been comfortable, but Bob certainly wasn't. He had a pounding erection that just wouldn't quit. He started to try and force himself to think of three-mile cross country runs and cold showers and playing football with the guys. It made it difficult to conduct an interview.

'The rest of the interview. Bob ... are you all right? You look like you're running a fever.'

'I'm just too hard – I mean – working too hard. It's been really long – I mean – a really long day. I might be going down – I mean – coming – I mean – well, when can you start?'

Kerry regarded Bob quizzically and then continued.

'Now that school is out for the summer I can start right away. The sooner the better – I need the money.'

I bet you do, thought Bob. The sooner the better – uh – well, here's $50 – suck my dick. Bob's mind was rambling.

'Bob – are you ok?'

Kerry's inquiry brought Bob back to the real world.

'Oh yes – yeah. Now – well – ok. You've got the job. You'll start Friday night training with – let me see – Hazel. She'll show you the ropes. I'm sure you'll pick things up in no time. Especially after working all last summer as a food waitress.'

'Great. Thanks so much, Bob. The money I earn this summer is going to help pay for my last year in college. Hopefully I'll be able to put some aside for graduate school.'

'Yes – well – I'm sure you'll do very well in the tip department. You certainly seem ideal for the position.'

'I'll do my best. See you Friday.'

'It's my night off – but maybe I'll come in and be a customer.' As Bob said these seemingly innocuous words his mind once again roamed over the hidden meaning in his earlier comment. '. . . ideal for the position.' The position – yes – Kerry was on her hands and knees on the floor of the changing room. She must have dropped an earring or something. Bob used his master key to sneak into the room and without so much of a 'nice to see ya' mounted Kerry from the rear. It was a simple matter to lift up the long flowing dress and slip aside the skimpy panties. Kerry was already wet in the anticipation of Bob's hardness penetrating her pouting pussy lips. She hadn't really been looking for an earring. No – she'd been waiting on her hands and knees for Bob to have his way with her. She knew what he liked and was willing to give it to him – even if it did mean bruised knees. She rocked backwards and forwards as Bob held on to her like he was riding an unruly horse that had to be broken. In this position there was little she could do but submit to his pounding erection. Bob was driven wild by the red suspender belt vista holding up the magical black stockings. He could feel the metal of the clasps stinging his thighs as he slapped against Kerry's ass. He was rapidly becoming delirious with lust. Strange things began to happen. In between thrusts he noticed that the seams of Kerry's stockings needed straightening. In this position he could see everything. Yes – in this position – the position . . .

Kerry just smiled, completely unaware of Bob's musings and took Bob's comment as her cue to leave.

'Well, Bob – if there's nothing else, I'll go and get changed.'

Bob snapped back from his fantasy position on the changing room floor.

'Yes – I mean no, there's nothing else. Good luck.'

'Thanks Bob – you won't regret it.'

As Kerry closed the door, Bob immediately locked it after her and switched the security system to its ulterior usage mode.

'I bet I won't regret it.'

Kerry entered the changing room all smiles. Clearly she was pumped up by her job acquisition. Bob would have liked to have pumped her up with something else, but he settled for his secret video show.

It was right after Kerry had rolled down one of the black nylon fishnet stockings that Bob decided he couldn't watch any further. His dick felt like bursting. His balls ached from the strain of maintaining an erection for so long. He turned around in the swivel chair and stared out of the office window at the incessant stream of traffic on Highway 101 carrying commuters to and from the many high-tech companies in the Valley. Every few minutes he stole a furtive glance at the screen to check on Kerry's progress. Finally, after much primping and preening, the changing room was empty. Bob breathed a sincere sigh of relief as he popped the video disc into his pocket. Careful to put the system back to normal, Bob quickly left the office.

He joined the traffic on 101 and absent-mindedly fought his way home to his apartment. Before arriving at his destination he stopped at one of those round-the-clock convenience stores that seem to spring up magically at almost every street corner in America. He paid no attention to the exorbitant price they charged for the extra-large giant-size bottle of super-dooper moisturising hand cream. His mind was on other things besides being a smart shopper. Within minutes of being home he had placed the disc in the player and began to relive the whole experience again.

And again, and again, and again, and again . . .

Until he finally ran out of hand cream and fell asleep dreaming of doing much more than undressing Kerry Farnum.

3

Long Island
Iced Tea

Mix

½ oz. Vodka
½ oz. Gin
½ oz. Light Rum
½ oz. Tequila
½ oz. Triple Sec
Juice of ½ Lemon
Cola

Combine ingredients and pour over ice in tall glass. Add a dash of cola for colour. Garnish with a slice of lemon.

*I*t had been one of those nights for Louisa Hampton. She'd been awake for two straight days and nights thanks to the Pumping Station's shortage of waitresses and her own tendency to burn more than the candle at both ends. Now that Kerry had been hired, Louisa rationalised that she might be able to get a night off. She knew though, that no amount of free time away from the Pump would stop her from seeing just how far she could burn the candle of her life down perilously close to nothing.

The night had started out bad. She'd been late for work and received the obligatory management lecture. Immediately as she was out on the floor she'd encountered her worst cocktail waitress nightmare. She'd served a group of ten wafer assembly technicians recently imported from one of the Silicon-slave plants in the Far-East. In halting English they had worked their way through the Pump's 'Speciality Drinks' menu. The drink descriptions artfully displayed in the menu meant little to the fabrication workers whose knowledge of English was limited to 'How much?' and 'What that?'

'What that?'

The fab-worker pointed at a brightly coloured photograph of an extremely large glass full of some yellow concoction.

'Pina Colada.'

'Oh, P-i-n-a C-o-r-a-d-a. How much?'

'Five dollars.'

'Oh – I have Pina Corada.'

And then the menu was passed to another worker who after

35

much deliberation chose the next drink picture – a Ramos Fizz. And on to the next, through all ten of the workers – all asking the same basic questions. And after repeating their order for several rounds in much the same manner, the group of fab-workers had left only a fifty-cent tip.

'Fuck – $200 in drinks – two hours of my time – and a measly fucking fifty cents. Fucking foreigners. Don't they teach these people how to tip before letting them in the country?' Being a cocktail waitress sometimes brought out the ugly racist tendencies hidden deep in everyone. And tonight, Louisa wasn't in too tolerant a mood.

Arnold Rimskikoff, the Pump's senior bartender just rolled his eyes in muted agreement with Louisa's tirade. It hadn't pleased him too much to have to make all of the 'foo-foo' drinks, but he didn't feel like reminding Louisa that she'd had the same complaint about a group of barely twenty-one year-old true-blue, Mom and apple pie, all American college students who had consumed $50 in Budweiser and had tipped even less than the fab-workers. Arnold knew better than to trifle with Louisa when she was on the warpath. He hadn't been a bartender at the Pump for over ten years without learning well the fine art of cocktail waitress diplomacy.

The night didn't get any better for Miss Hampton. It was kind of downhill from the moment she'd walked in the door of the Pump. Louisa worked a full eight hours for a piddling $30 in tips. Not enough to get well and truly drunk or even as high as a kite on. Hardly worth working. And since she'd been the closing waitress she'd had no opportunity even to have a relaxing drink before heading home, or wherever the steering wheel of her precious Ford Mustang took her.

'Here – don't say I don't look after you.'

Arnold handed Louisa a tall glass containing one of the most potent blends of alcohol known to the civilised world – a Long Island Iced Tea.

'Thanks, Arnold – sorry if I'm such a fucking bitch.'

'Well, get out of here and get some rest before I start agreeing with you. And before management sees you with that drink – it's after two a.m. and the bar is officially closed.

If you get caught, you'll be a fucking out of work bitch and so will I.'

'See ya Arnie.'

'See ya Louisa.'

And with a final wave Louisa made her way out of the Pump and through the now barren car park to one of the closest things to her heart – her car. She carefully wedged the Long Island between the seats of the Mustang and lowered the convertible top. The night was quite cool, but Louisa needed the awakening blast of cold air to keep her eyes from complying with gravity's wishes. After several large gulps of almost pure alcohol, Louisa pulled the red Mustang out of the parking lot and off into the general direction of home. She'd decided that after two days of candle-burning, it was time to be a good girl. At least for one night.

Officer Norman Moore was also leaving the Pumping Station. The restaurant at the Pump was a favourite hang-out for Silicon Valley's police force. The food was good, the portions large and the girls – even the food waitresses – much more attractive than the old hags that worked at the plethora of nickel and dime coffee shops littering every intersection of the Valley. The Pumping Station was so popular with the local police that the Chief of Police had enforced a two-car limit at the Pump at any one time. There had been numerous citizen complaints that too many officers were sitting around drinking coffee and ogling waitresses instead of being out on the street doing something useful like stopping crime.

Officer Moore was just radioing into Headquarters that he was leaving the Pump so that another hungry officer could take advantage of the remaining hour of restaurant service when he noticed the red Mustang rapidly leave the lounge parking lot. It didn't take him long to put the police cruiser into drive, switch on the lights and sound the siren. Moore knew that an arrest out of the Pump would be good for public relations – sort of justifying the amount of time the police spent there.

'Fuck – fuck – fuck.' Louisa saw the flashing red, blue and white lights in the Mustang's rear-view mirror. She hadn't heard the siren – she'd had the radio up at maximum volume to help keep her awake. She pulled the car into the parking lot of one of the many electronics companies in the area. Now deserted, it was at least private property and the police probably wouldn't impound her car if she got arrested.

Officer Moore unsnapped his revolver, unclipped his truncheon and walked officiously up to the driver's side door. He immediately recognised Louisa as a waitress at the Pumping Station. He thought it best not to acknowledge the recognition.

'Going a bit fast weren't we, miss?'

'Not as fast as I could have been.' Louisa was not in a good mood. It had been a bad night – and it was rapidly getting worse.

Moore responded officiously.

'Driver's license and vehicle registration, please, miss.' Officer Moore was determined not to be intimidated by the feisty blonde bombshell he'd seen so many times at the Pump. He would act as if he was going to give her ticket and then be quite the gentleman and let her off. Who knows what favours she might do in return?

Louisa fumbled in the glove compartment of the car. She retrieved a mess of papers, some of which may have been the required documents. Officer Moore leaned into the car, ostensibly to take the papers, but his prime purpose was to stare up Louisa's short mini skirt. Louisa was still wearing the Pumping Station regulation red suspender belt and black stockings. She'd been in such a hurry to get out of work that she couldn't have been bothered to change out of her undergarments. She'd just taken off the slinky black dress, pulled on a tight black mini-skirt and thrown her black leather jacket onto her shoulders. Now, seated firmly in the bucket seat of the Mustang, her dress had inched its way to the top of her thighs, revealing by the dim lights of the parking lot not only the suspender belt and the stocking tops so exquisitely held taut, but also the tantalizing vee of white lace panties and the wispy darkness they contained. The zipper of her leather jacket was down low enough to reveal the upper curves of a lovely pair of pert breasts.

Officer Moore's police senses were distracted from the erotic vista of Louisa's thighs by a familiar smell. It took him all of a few seconds of continued staring before it dawned on him what vapours were wafting around his nose. He backed his head out of the car and stared accusingly at Louisa.

'Have you been drinking, miss.'

'Why?'

'Just answer the question – I can smell alcohol on you.'

'No shit, Sherlock Holmes. You know damn well I'm a fucking cocktail waitress at the Pump. So what do you expect me to smell like – fucking pigshit?'

'Just step out of the car, miss.'

Officer Moore was starting to think that maybe this wasn't going to be as easy as he'd thought. This one had a temper as fiery as her red lips.

'Okay – okay – come here – smell my breath – you tell me if you think I've been drinking.'

Louisa knew that the two or three gulps of the Long Island wouldn't make their way past the haze of cigarette smoke and lipstick that laced her breath. Officer Moore leaned forward hoping once more to catch a faint glimpse of Louisa's pussy while overtly trying to smell alcohol on her breath. It was a huge mistake.

Louisa didn't really know why she did it, other than it seemed like the right thing to do at the moment. In one quick movement she took the glass of alcohol given her by Arnie and threw what was left of the Long Island into Moore's face.

'Now can you smell it – asshole? Now can you smell alcohol?' Louisa taunted the shocked officer. He'd expected an eyeful of pussy and got something that stung a whole lot more. He stumbled back rubbing his eyes. When his vision cleared Louisa was propped up against the car smoking a cigarette, smiling in the truly condescending way that only a woman who knows she has the upper hand can do. It was more than any man – even a policeman – could stand. He rushed towards her. What he intended to do once he got there his brain hadn't yet figured out.

Louisa swung her fist at the onrushing cop who ducked just a bit too late. The blow caught him high on the head, but not squarely. The impact forced Moore to bend downwards. Louisa who was by now quite perked up – this was the most fun she'd had all night – decided that a kick in the ass was just what Moore needed. She swung her leg but Moore who was still bent over from the missed blow saw it coming and grabbed her stocking covered calf. It was no great effort for him to spin her around as she pivoted on her five inch spike high-heels. Now, suddenly off balance, Louisa was thrust with all of Moore's might into the side of her Mustang. The impact knocked the breath out of her, who in this position was no match for a much stronger and angrier man. Resorting back to the training he'd received at the Police Academy, it took just a few moments for Moore to handcuff Louisa's hands behind her back and as an added measure of security to handcuff her legs together just above her ankles.

Officer Moore stepped backwards a few paces to catch his breath. Louisa slumped over the Mustang gasping for air. It was then that Norman Moore realised that he possessed the hardest erection he'd ever had the pleasure of being the proud owner of. It was even harder than when the stripper at Captain Will's bachelor party had done that trick with Moore's hand and a cucumber.

The cause of Norman Moore's hardness was the unwitting Louisa. The struggle, the fight, the body contact and of course the distinctly erotic process of handcuffing her arms and long legs had caused his adrenalin and blood pressure to peak beyond its normal limits. These days, working nights, his wife and he didn't enjoy sex so much as go through the motions. And now facing him was an erotic vixen in somewhat of a vulnerable and appealing state. Officer Moore was on the edge of losing control. He may have been able to maintain his professional demeanor if it hadn't been for the sight that met his still alcohol sore eyes.

Rubbing the last few drops of the Long Island from his face, Moore's eyes focused first on the ground and then travelled inevitably and oh, so slowly up Louisa's subjugated form. The silver of the handcuffs glistened against the shimmering darkness of the black nylon stockings that were exquisitely highlighted by the five-inch black high heels held securely to Louisa's ankles by the most delicate of straps. Journeying up the dark seams of the stockings to the even darker stocking tops held taut by the red suspender belt of Louisa's uniform, Moore's gaze halted just a few inches above the splendid sight.

He caught his breath.

'Dear God ...'

In the struggle between them, Louisa's tight mini-skirt had been forced all the way to her waist revealing to Moore the tempting sight of her white-lace-covered bottom framed invitingly by the red suspender belt. Slumped forward over the Mustang, Louisa's ass was thrust towards Moore in a most come-hither manner. His libido took no small note of the erotic effect of having Louisa's wrists handcuffed exactly in the middle of the space framed by the suspender belt. The handcuffs on her ankles were also in perfectly sensual symmetry. As he approached Louisa's gasping form he notice for the first time that her fingernails were long, exceptionally long, and very blood red.

Louisa was quite unaware of her predicament. The force of being thrown against the car had momentarily stunned her senseless. She felt too weak to stand, thankful of her car as a crutch. It was as she started to gain some small feeling of being human once more that she felt two strong hands take her by the waist, and in one swift movement lift her skywards. Her head reeled as she was tossed roughly over Moore's shoulder. He steadied her from falling by spreading his hand over her bottom and pressing her tightly against his uniform. As he marched militarily to his car he rhythmically rubbed her ass cheeks in a squeezing, kneading manner. Small as she was, Louisa's bottom was firm and resilient – perfectly formed – just right for squeezing and pinching.

It was these invading feelings that brought Louisa fully to her senses. She quickly ascertained the situation, remembered what she had done and realised that tonight would be spent in the county jail.

'I guess it's jail for me,' Louisa mumbled as Moore lowered her into the back seat of his police cruiser.

'Not quite, bitch.'

41

'Temper – temper. I was just having a bit of fun.'

At first Moore didn't answer her. He went to the front seat and turned off the flashing lights and the headlights. He turned the ignition of the car off. All was silent except for Louisa's forced breathing.

Moore returned to the back of the car and stepped inside. With a resounding crash he slammed the door shut behind him.

'A bit of fun, was it? Well, I'm going to have a bit of fun now.'

Moore's manner was menacing as he leaned towards Louisa. He stank of alcohol and sweat.

'Don't touch me. I'll scream. I'll scream the fucking windows out you bast ...'

Louisa didn't get to finish the sentence. Moore stuffed his regulation police issue leather gloves into her mouth. The leather, dampened by Louisa's spit, smelled strong and erotic, further exciting Moore. He uncuffed Louisa's wrists and quickly reattached them to the bars on the car window frame. Similarly, he uncuffed her legs, and attached them one by one to the bars on the opposite side of the car. He was careful to separate Louisa's legs just the right amount.

Louisa wrenched and bucked against her restraints but there was no breaking free. It was then that she decided that another strategy would be more effective. No stranger to the more bizarre forms of sexual release, Louisa decided that she would play right along with Officer Moore's bondage fantasy. There was more than one way to skin a cop ...

Moore unzipped his blue police pants and pushed them down around his ankles. His holster and gun now resided there also. It was of little concern to him. There was nothing that the waitress bitch could do, all trussed up like a turkey at Christmas.

Louisa could see Moore was wearing large white underwear – the kind wives buy their husbands to ensure male fidelity. Wifely reasoning was simple and quite logical in a suburban sort of way. Would any self-respecting male really want to have an affair with an attractive someone with him wearing something that looks like it belongs at a campsite or on the mast of a ship? No – plain big whites were sure to embarrass most men into being completely faithful.

Even in the dim light of the police cruiser back seat Louisa could see that Moore's big whites were stained by the tell tale signs of a long straining erection. To fuck Louisa, Officer Norman Moore didn't even push his underwear down, he just pulled his cock out of the side – as if he was going to piss. Likewise he pulled Louisa's white lace panties aside as he urgently rammed his hard dick forcefully into her now quite moist cunt. Louisa was excited by the situation in which she found herself. She didn't particularly relish fucking Norman Moore, but she had to admit that some of her most memorable fucks had been a bit on the rough side.

'I'm going to fuck you senseless, bitch – I'll teach you to play games with me. Now you're playing with the big boys – not those wimps that you flash your ass to at the Pump.'

It was all Louisa could do to stop from writhing with laughter at Moore's macho talk. Luckily the gloves made it somewhat difficult to giggle. Amidst her inner laughter she decided it was time to activate her plan. She began to writhe and squirm her hips forcefully into the pounding crotch of Officer Moore. A calculated arch of her back forced her pussy to rub at Moore's erection making her tighter and much wetter. She closed her eyes and moaned deeply, heaving her chest. In almost a Pavlovian response Moore wasted no time in further unzipping her leather jacket and squeezing Louisa's taut nipples. Louisa moaned and arched her back further as his rough pinching and biting of her breasts inflamed her moist cunt.

'You like it, bitch – you like my dick fucking you. You're enjoying a real man's cock giving it to you hard.'

Unable to talk, Louisa just nodded furiously with wide-open eyes that implied 'oh yes big boy!' It had the desired effect. Moore immediately ungagged her. Louisa responded by playfully nibbling at his hands as he withdrew the gloves.

'Oh yes – oh yes – I've wanted your dick ever since I saw you at the Pump. I didn't think you noticed me. You must have so many women to fuck. You fuck me so well.'

Louisa combined her sultry fuck-talk with expert movements of her body. Her thighs gripped Moore's pelvis as he slid his length inside of her. She held him deep within herself and let her well-trained pussy muscles suck confidently at his penis as if trying to lengthen it further, making it go deeper and deeper. She arched her back, lifting her bottom off the vinyl of the seat to follow the motion of Moore's cock as he reversed his stroke, thereby making him rush all the more quickly down into the abyss of his impending orgasm. Relentlessly, Louisa's pussy chased his hardness until it had no place to hide from her sexual onslaught.

'Ahhh – ohhh – ahhh.'

It had taken Moore just a few minutes to come like a gushing oil well. He wasn't used to this kind of sex. He'd often imagined fucking one of the Pump waitresses, especially when his wife just lay in bed with her legs open and stared at the ceiling while he did his best to maintain an erection. Many times the thought of fucking those long-legged waitresses had brought him to wank off inside his boring wife, but now, faced with the real thing, he'd lost all semblance of control. And like the stereotypical male that he was, he immediately rolled off Louisa and began to pull up his pants. Louisa intervened.

'That was great. I haven't been fucked like that in weeks. Don't stop – I want more.'

'I should get back to duty – they'll be wondering.'

Louisa knew it was just an excuse because Moore couldn't get it up again so quickly. She thought rapidly.

'You know what I want. I want you to fuck me with your big black stick. Take that truncheon and do it to me, Norman – fuck me with that big stick of yours.'

Norman Moore thought he'd died and gone to porno movie heaven. Here was an extremely seductive, long-legged, stocking-clad, mini-skirted, hard-nippled, blonde-haired, high-heeled feisty bitch of a woman handcuffed and spreadeagled in the back of his police cruiser, wanting to be fucked with his truncheon. This was too good to be true.

In a way it was.

But Office Norman Moore wasn't thinking too clearly as he slid the polished black wood of his truncheon into Louisa's

44

wet pussy.

'That feels so good Norman — it feels so good to have that stick up my cunt along with your spunk. Fuck me with the big black stick — in and out. Your dick was better — but this is so good and hard, and black, and shiny and ohhh . . . '

Norman didn't know what to say. He just complied and watched in awe as Louisa squeezed her thighs around the stick and bucked violently on the hardened plastic of the cruiser seat. She added to Norman's thrustings with her own urgent pounding, forcing the stick deeper and deeper.

'Squeeze my titties, Norman — squeeze my tits. Hard, damn you, harder.'

Louisa was well and truly enjoying this part of her plan. Norman may have been incompetent in bed, but he was perfectly capable of following even these most rudimentary of instructions. And even though Louisa was technically in somewhat of a submissive position, it was clear to her that she had Norman exactly where she wanted him.

'Press the stick up and on to my clit — rub it there — around and around — oh that's it — grind it in to me — there — there — don't stop — pinch my tits — ahhh.'

Louisa slumped in a satisfied manner against the car seat as her orgasm subsided. Now she could finish her plan. After a few moments she looked over at Officer Norman Moore and noticed that her writhings and dirty talk had achieved the desired result. His penis was large, angry and erect. Now she moved in for the kill.

'I'll give you the kind of blow job that makes most men weep. I can suck your brains right out of your dick, Norman.'

Louisa added the 'Norman' slowly, almost like a mother talking to a small child.

'Now just undo my arms and legs and get down on the seat and I'm going to send you to cock heaven.'

Norman complied with a speed that betrayed his desires. He had no way of knowing what was in store for him. Louisa was not stretching the truth one little bit in her descriptions of her talents. What she could do with her pussy she could likewise do with her mouth.

She began slowly at first, using her nails lightly to caress the base of Norman's cock, teasing the hairs with her finger-tips, pulling at the throbbing skin whilst licking long lashing strokes of her tongue up and down the shaft. Her lipstick acted like a sealant between her lips and Officer Moore's cockskin. The harder she sucked, the harder he became – to a point where it felt as if his cock would explode with a volcano of sperm. She used her teeth to nibble gently at his sensitised head – as if it was some delicate, tangy tropical fruit. Co-operating with her willing lips, her long red-nailed fingers gently squeezed Norman's cock, and in long slow strokes that exactly opposed the sucking of her mouth, masturbated his throbbing penis to the brink of destruction.

Norman Moore was not at this point human. He was convinced he was nothing but a huge dick. He had no arms, no legs, no head – just a huge dick whose only purpose was to come, and come and come some more. His whole body was on automatic.

It was not surprising then that he didn't quite feel Louisa slip a handcuff over his wrist and around the window frame. He didn't even recognise the sensation of metal on skin as she did likewise to the other arm. And he just felt that she was stroking his legs as she fastened his ankles to the opposite window frame. She continued her ministrations bringing him many times to the brink of orgasm in a manner designed to destroy what little brain cells remained unscathed by rampant desire.

And then she stopped.

It took Officer Moore quite some minutes to acknowledge his predicament. When he came to his full senses and committed the obligatory wrenching of his bonds Louisa couldn't help but laugh.

'How's it feel, big boy?'

'You fucking bitch. Let me out of here – do you know the trouble you'll be in?'

'Let's not talk about how much trouble I'm going to be in with you in that position, Officer Norman Moore. What would the Chief say? What would the wife say? So let's not talk about how much trouble I'm going to be in.'

Louisa twiddled with the truncheon that had most recently

spent quite some time being intimate with her. One end was still soaked with her juices. The aroma was intoxicatingly erotic.

'Hmmm – smells good – wanna sniff?'

Louisa stuck the stick under the distressed officer's nose. He shook his head from side to side to try and avoid smelling the fruits of his labours.

'You've got two choices, Norman. Either you suck on this stick or I make you suck on your gun. Which is it going to be big boy? Name your poison.'

Norman looked horrified at Louisa. She was twiddling his trusty .357 magnum around her fingers like a gunslinger of old. He hoped to God she hadn't taken the safety off. Norman didn't want to die like this.

'Come on – spit it out – which do you want to suck on?'

'The stick.'

'Come on – louder – I can't hear you.'

'The stick.'

'Good choice – it tastes better.'

Louisa forced the truncheon into Norman's mouth, making him gag.

'What's the matter, Norman – never sucked a cock before?'

Norman coughed and spluttered. He hoped desperately that this nightmare was going to end soon.

'Lick it good, Norman. Get it good and wet – it has to be really wet.'

Norman slurped on the stick tasting Louisa's juices at the back of his throat.

'Well, look at that Norman – you like giving head. Your dick is all hard.'

Louisa flicked sharply at Norman's cock. It slapped back at his stomach.

'Well, I think that's wet enough – you can stop now.'

Louisa pulled out the saliva-covered truncheon and examined it closely.

'You know, Norman, you are an asshole. You thought you could rape me and teach me a big lesson about how to behave with the big boys. Well, let me tell you, Norman – I've

47

played with bigger boys than you. You ain't even in my league. You're just an asshole – and you know, judging by how hard you got sucking on that stick, maybe you're gay, Norman. Are you? Are you a fag? Not sure? Well there's one sure way to find out if you are.'

And with a swiftness that gave Norman no time to contemplate his fate Louisa took the truncheon and rammed it full force into Office Norman Moore's asshole.

Norman Moore let out a scream worthy of Henry II's hot-poker-induced deathbed ejaculation. Norman was still whimpering as Louisa got out of the car and headed to her awaiting Mustang. She straightened her clothes in quite a business like fashion, and hesitated before getting in her car. She'd planned on letting the electronics workers find Norman tomorrow morning, but she suddenly had a better and more wicked idea. The bastard deserved it . . .

Walking back to the police cruiser she peered in to see Norman grimacing in pain as he tried desperately not to drive the truncheon deeper into his violated anus. He whimpered at her in a sorry attempt at eliciting compassion. Louisa was not in the mood. She picked up the car's radio headset and depressed the talk switch.

'Car 774 – officer down. Repeat car 774 – officer down.'

She turned off the microphone and stared into Norman's horrified face. Having just delivered the universal police code for officer in distress, the area would be swarming with police, ambulance and press in minutes. Thanks to the wonders of modern technology developed in the very buildings surrounding the Pumping Station, the emergency call would be easily traced to the parking lot location. She didn't have much time to lose.

'See ya Norman – it was fun – we'll have to do it again some time.'

Norman just groaned and closed his eyes in utter humiliation.

It was time to go home. Tonight Louisa would sleep well. She couldn't help but laugh at what had transpired. She'd had a lousy night at work and assaulted a police office and technically was raped as a consequence. But she didn't quite see it that way. And somehow, she smiled, neither did Officer Norman Moore.

As Louisa steered the Mustang away from the parking lot and into the Silicon Valley night, her hysterical laughter mingled with the distant wail of the many sirens rushing to Norman's aid.

It was not music to Norman's ears . . .

4

Bosom Caresser

Mix

1 oz. Brandy
1 oz. Madeira
½ oz. Triple Sec

Stir with cracked ice and strain into cocktail glass

'*K*erry Farnum — meet Hazel Heyes.' The raspy words belonged to Don Palumba, the Pumping Station's extremely cynical and business-like General Manager. He had just completed giving Kerry the standard 'Welcome to the Pumping Station' General Manager indoctrination. Now Kerry was being turned over to the waitress who would be responsible for her training.

After the perfunctory welcomes, Hazel began to break the ice.

'So — did he scare you with that gruff voice and no bullshit tone?'

'Sort of — well yeah. He seems pretty strict.'

'Oh, don't let his formica exterior frighten you too much. Underneath that nastiness there is at least a heart. And Don's fair — which is quite remarkable for this place. If you have a problem with anything, or anyone, you can go to him and he'll tell it to you straight.'

'That's good to know.'

'Yeah.' Hazel put a reassuring arm around Kerry and gave her an affectionate squeeze. Kerry wasn't too sure about the action. For some reason it gave her an uncomfortable feeling that Hazel was being too familiar. It was a feeling that she would know several more times before her first night was over.

Hazel was jokingly referred to by the Pumping Station regulars as the Pump's token ugly waitress. In absolute terms she wasn't really ugly. A little on the heavy side, with boobs

53

that tended to do their very best to leap like falling bowls of jelly out of her dress and onto innocent and unsuspecting customers. She was best described as a cartoon caricature of an overweight beauty queen. Her hair was shoulder length and anonymously brown. Compared to the other overtly attractive waitresses, Hazel was everything they weren't. And it didn't seem to bother her one little bit. Not all men were in desperate need of a Mona Lisa — some were happy with quantity, not quality.

'Now, the first thing you need to know is — well, do you smoke?'

'No, no I don't.'

'Too bad. I was going to give you all of the benefits of my secret ways for prolonging cigarette breaks, but that wouldn't be too helpful to you so I'll explain the table layout.'

They went to the bar which was still quite empty at three 0'clock on a Friday afternoon.

'The rush is going to start about four so I've got enough time to explain the lay of the land. Since you'll be following me around this evening it doesn't matter if you don't get this right away. After a few nights you'll know exactly what I mean.'

The Pumping Station lounge was arranged into groups of plush couches clustered low to the ground around small tables. At the entrance to the lounge was a sunken area with a gas-driven ring of flame shooting rocket-like through a bubbling fountain of water. The lighting was a dull neon collection of reds and blues. The walls were lined with mirrors giving the illusion of spaciousness in a relatively small room. The mirrors also made for some interesting optical experiments by Pump patrons with Snell's Law of Reflection, waitresses' dresses and large quantities of consumed alcohol.

The regular customers of the Pump, who for the most part tended to be girlfriendless and hard-up for female companionship, seated themselves at the bar next to the waitress serving station. Strategically located, the barflys-without-homes could make many lewd comments to the girls whilst desperately trying to one-up the bartenders in the biting insult department. None of the long-serving waitresses ever went out with a regular customer but occasionally a new girl fell prey to their transparently amiable 'everybody's friend' routine.

Hazel was quick to point out this pitfall to Kerry.

'Let's start with the serving station. The seats next to it will always be occupied by the regulars. Don't let them get into your panties. They'll just trade stories about you and do their very best to compare notes. And besides, they don't tip — so don't waste your time. They can be funny and entertaining — especially on slow nights — but never go home with them, or even out with them for that matter. You'll just become a trophy.'

'Yeah — I remember hearing some of those stories last year when I was a food waitress.'

'Oh yeah — I'd forgot that you are not a complete Pumping Station virgin. I guess I don't need to go over the restaurant layout and procedures.'

'No — I can remember most of it — and what I don't will come back pretty quickly.'

'OK. The far corner cluster of couches and tables is known as the "passion pit". The lighting is the darkest in the bar there, and it's the only couch that is hidden from our observations at the serving station — hence you get all the mad passionate couples going at it. We'll probably get quite a few tonight — Friday night fucks and all that stuff. They usually tip pretty good but be prepared to close out a tab fast — once they get the urge to go and fuck their brains out they don't like to be kept waiting.'

'Got it.'

'The fireplace is known as the "firepit". You'll get mostly couples who aren't yet ready for the passion pit. These kind tend to be too into talking — they don't tip too well because most of them are talking about problems and just staring at the fire. Businessmen also like the firepit. I guess it's a male bonding thing to sit around a fire with the buddies and bullshit. Just like in the caveman days. Things haven't changed much.'

'OK.'

A simple 'OK' was all Kerry could manage in response to

Hazel's unexpected philosophising.

'All the other couches just have numbers. You'll be assigned a section and you'll be responsible for it.'

'Seems just like the restaurant.'

'Well, it is and it isn't. When serving food you did your job if you got it to the hungry bastards quickly and with a smile. Here, you are on the menu.'

Kerry raised her eyebrows in apparent shock.

'Not literally – unless of course you want to be – but you've got to show some of that body if you want to get the really big tips. Let me show you how. You go sit down and I'll pretend you're a customer. Watch what I do.'

Kerry sat down on one of the overly stuffed comfy couches. Hazel approached like some well-fed animal about to devour its prey just for the fun of it.

'Notice how I sit down opposite you. Use the slit in the dress wisely. If you're serving a group of men, then sit with the slit facing the one who is paying. If you're not sure who the lucky fella is, then give then all a show in turn. Just watch how easy it is.'

Hazel sat holding the hem of her dress underneath the drinks tray which was propped so very primly on her knees. She rotated slightly and released the hem. Gravity did the rest. The filmy material fell from her legs to meet the spongy carpet below, revealing the milky whiteness of Hazel's thighs above the nylon darkness of the stocking. The red suspender belt strap bit into the plumpness of her upper leg leaving telltale depressions in the landscape of her flesh.

'Now watch carefully. If you really think some guy is on the verge of tipping you big time, but may need a little extra motivation, then you can always use this manoeuver.'

Hazel lifted up her tray as a prelude to leaving. With one five-inch heel of her spiked black shoes she held the hem of the dress riveted to the floor. Apparently unaware of this encumberance she turned to get up. The slit of the skirt pulled tight across her waist and separated immediately above her crotch. The movement lasted but a short instant, a moment in which Kerry, even in the dim neon light, was able to see the vee of Hazel's black panties. Kerry couldn't be sure, but it seemed as though the panties barely covered Hazel's bush. Burned into Kerry's subconscious was the image of a huge furry wild animal barely restrained. As before, when Hazel was overly familiar, the overture didn't make Kerry feel too comfortable in that part of the stomach that was generally referred to as the 'pit'.

'If you aren't in the mood to flash your panties then you can always resort to a boob shot. It's best done standing up when you bring them their drinks. Just lean over ...'

'Whoah – wait a minute – there's a big difference between me and you. I don't really have any boobs to flash.'

'And you an engineering student in college! Don't they teach you about the effects of gravity? It don't matter how big your tits are, honey. When you lean over, the material of your dress will fall forward and your tits will be on show – small or large. Some guys like big ones – some go for the smaller handfuls. But all of the male species likes a peek at a titty – no matter the size.'

'Interesting – it's quite an art. But I do have one question – with all this teasing and flashing – I mean what's it worth? If you don't mind me asking – how much do you make in tips each month?'

'On average about three thousand dollars. I only report a fraction of that to the government. They ain't gonna tax my ass – literally.'

They both laughed raucously.

'Thanks Hazel – you've been a big help.'

'Well, let's put it to the test honey – it's showtime.'

Hazel nodded to the door as the first customers of the evening came pouring in.

Kerry's first night on the floor went extemely well. Even though most new girls usually just observed for the first night, Hazel let Kerry handle a few tables on her own. It meant less tips for Hazel, but the quicker she got Kerry out from underneath her wing, the more time she'd have to concentrate on making more money for herself, rather than looking out for the rookie. Judging by Kerry's rapid progress, Hazel figured it wouldn't be long before Kerry would be flying solo.

Hazel had been occupied serving a cluster of microchip salesmen commiserating each other on a lousy book-to-bill ratio. By now all of the depressed high-rollers were quite drunk, and a few of them were crying on Hazel's shoulder. In fact, they were blubbering quite profusely, as Hazel's wet nipple readily testified. Looking around, Hazel thought it about time to see how Kerry was doing.

Hazel had given Kerry two sections around the firepit to work with. One was occupied by a boss and his secretary drinking martinis and trying to deny what was inevitably going to happen just a few hours from now. The boss was thinking of wifely excuses and the secretary was hoping her period wouldn't start at this incredibly inconvenient time. The other section had been vacant, but now Hazel saw that it was occupied and the occupant was talking earnestly to Kerry.

Hazel thought it best to intervene. Tearing herself away from the weeping microchip salesmen she walked over to where Kerry was engaged in conversation.

'Hi Bob – we don't often see you in here on your night off.'

'I thought I'd come and wish Kerry all the best – and Hazel, what's the matter? Leaking?'

Bob could see the glistening moisture on Hazel's right shoulder trickling down to her breast. It presented a good opportunity to change the subject from Hazel's accusatory tone regarding the real nature of his visit to the Pump tonight.

Hazel wiped herself with cocktail napkins.

'No, no, Bob – just doing my job.'

'Me too. You've done a very good job training Kerry. I was just telling her that she should be ready to work on her own very soon.'

'Isn't that great, Hazel?'

'Yes, quite – but there are a few more things I need to teach her. So if you'll excuse us. –'

'Certainly – good luck Kerry.'

'Thanks Bob – and thanks for the tip.'

'I'm sure that's the first of many.'

Bob excused himself and went upstairs to the office. He

was pleased with the progress he'd made with Kerry, and he now had the honour of being her first tip. With any luck it wouldn't be the only tip she ever got from him.

Back at the waitress station Hazel was just about to give Kerry advice on how to avoid being consumed by all of the rampant employee male hormones running wild at the Pump when one of the depressed microchip salesmen fell headlong into the bubbling waters of the firepit. To his colleagues it seemed like just the thing to do so they proceeded to join him, all blubbering amidst the water, bubbles and flames about the really lousy book-to-bill ratio.

'Oh no,' was all Hazel could say. It was her customers – her station. 'Kerry, go get a manager and I'll try and sort this mess out.'

Hazel went over to try and reason with the soaked salesmen who were by now almost hysterical with grief.

Kerry alerted Don Palumba, who rolled his eyes in an 'oh no not again' manner. She was on her way to assist Hazel when she ran headlong into Lester Byron, one of the bartenders. Lester was young with greased-back hair and leering eyes.

'What's your name? Oh – Kerry – look, the bar needs more fruit in a hurry. Will you go in the store room and get some cucumbers, oranges, pineapple – oh – and don't forget the cherries?'

'But I should help Hazel.'

'You will be. She should be taking care of all this but she and Don are busy fishing out the drunks. You'll be doing her a big favour.'

'OK – I'll be right there.'

Lester turned as if to go back to the bar, but halted in mid-swivel. He watched Kerry disappear into the walk-in storage room. With Don the Manager and Hazel the waitress busy with the drunks, Lester would never get another opportunity like this. He decided to take advantage of the opportunity. He rubbed his hands together with lecherous perverted glee.

As he shut the storage room door quietly behind him, Lester leered in the most perverted manner known to uncivilised man. His lips curled back revealing a set of teeth

59

that an alligator would have been proud of. In the cool of the walk-in, he hissed ever so slightly.

Kerry was bending over a box of fruit, shivering in the cold. The noise of the refrigerator fans overpowered Lester Byron's approaching footsteps. With a hideous laugh he threw the unsuspecting Kerry's dress over her head, reached under her arms, grabbed the dress and pulled it tight to her breasts. Simultaneously he reached inside Kerry's halter top and began to roughly massage her small pert breasts. He continued to laugh hideously in a maniacal manner.

'He – he – ah – oh – he – what nice titties you have.'

Kerry, now thoroughly over the initial shock of being bundled inside of her dress and subsequently fondled, let out a scream. It made Lester all the more hysterical.

'He – he – oh – oh – ah – I like it when you struggle and scream – it's more fun that way – I knew you'd be like that – he he – oh – oh –ah.'

Kerry could feel the hardness of her assailant pressing against her bottom. It was then that she thought of a way out of her predicament. What took her so long to react puzzled her later. She concluded that she wasn't thinking clearly, what with the dress being pulled tight over her head, and she wasn't used to wearing such high heels. That's why she didn't think of it at first. She stood on her tip-toes whilst bending her leg at the knee. Her pointed high heel swung up and caught Lester right in the delicate spot between the balls and the bum. It made him yowl with shock. As he recoiled Kerry was able to break free.

It took her a few moments to get the dress back down to its normal position and gain her bearings. She was startled to see Lester clutching his injury whilst writhing on the floor.

'Lester – what? why?'

Lester stumbled to his feet. Kerry grabbed the nearest thing to her that resembled a weapon. It was a cucumber.

'And what are you going to do with that now? He – he – oh – ah – he – he.'

Lester appeared winded but still quite threatening.

'Just leave me alone Lester – or I'll – or I'll ...'

'You'll do what with the cucumber? Oh, I love it when

you talk dirty, Kerry.'

Kerry didn't have a chance to answer. The door to the walk-in burst open and an enraged Bob Vest flew in and punched Lester once on the chin and then in the stomach.

'Are you all right?'

It was directed at Kerry. Catching her breath and putting down the menacing cucumber she nodded affirmatively.

'Yeah I'm fine – now what the hell . . .' Lester answered.

'I wasn't talking to you Lester.'

Kerry interrupted. 'I'm OK Bob – seriously – just a little scared.'

'Shit – ain't anybody concerned for me? I was just having some fun, you know – welcoming the new girl. Hell, Bob – you've done . . .'

'Shut up Lester – you get back to the bar and we'll talk about this later. If Don finds out, you're history.'

'Likewise Mr. Vest.' Lester leered the threat through clenched teeth.

'Just get to work.'

As the walk-in door shut behind Lester, Kerry let out a sigh of relief which turned into a soft laugh.

'Whoah – some first night.'

'I'm sorry about that – you see some of the girls around here are pretty wild and Lester is a bit of a pervert. Some of the girls indulge him – even like it, I guess. I don't think he really meant any harm – but I'll have a word with him. And if you want him fired – no problem.'

'No – no – I guess it was kind of funny. But how did you know what was going on? These walk-ins are soundproof.'

Bob pointed to the video camera in the corner.

'I was up in the office picking up my paycheck when I just happened to glance at the security monitors. I saw Lester jump you so I ran down here as quick as I could. I guess Lester thought no one would be looking at the monitors, what with all the commotion in the bar. Lucky I came in for a drink.'

'Yeah – I'll say. I'd have hated to have to use this on him.'

Kerry tossed the cucumber end over end.

61

'He'd have probably enjoyed it.'

'Yeah – well, I'd better get back to work.'

'You sure you're all right? Do you want to go home?'

'Nah – I don't think I'll have any more problems with Lester. And after that what more could happen to me?'

'Nothing I guess.'

Neither Bob nor Kerry had any idea of how wrong they both were.

'Well, back to work. I'll get this fruit to the bar and go and make some money.'

'See ya later – you can buy me a drink'

'Certainly – I owe you one.'

And with that Kerry launched herself back to the bar. For a few moments Bob stayed in the walk-in reflecting on his good luck. He was a hero in Kerry's eyes. One day he would have to thank Lester the Molester, as everyone at the Pump called the perverted bartender, for his unintentional favour.

The rest of the evening proceeded quite uneventfully. The almost drowned drunks were put into a taxi to go home and dry off, and the boss and the secretary were still there at midnight when Kerry and Hazel ended their first shift together. As best as Kerry could fathom from catching snippets of conversation, the boss and the secretary were now skirting around the issue of where they might go for their romp. The boss favoured the secretary's place but she wanted to go to a hotel so that her roommates wouldn't find out.

Up in the changing rooms, Kerry and Hazel were laughing about the evening.

'Well – you certainly see life here at the Pump.'

'Yeah – sometimes it gets a bit much.'

'Oh I don't know – as long as you don't take it seriously it's quite funny.'

'Well, I hope you take this seriously.'

Kerry had her back to Hazel. Kerry had undone the zipper on her dress and had let the top fall to her waist in preparing to put on the tee shirt she'd come to work in. Hazel too was in a similar state of undress. As she uttered the last statement she reached around Kerry's waist and clasped her hands firmly on Kerry's tits. Pulling the petite Kerry firmly to her much larger body, Hazel ground her mammoth breasts into Kerry's back.

'Do you like that – isn't this nice?'

Kerry felt Hazel's hot breath on her neck. Hazel bit a kiss on Kerry's shoulder.

'I can make you feel better than you could ever feel with a man.'

Hazel's fingertips were working overtime on Kerry's nipples. She twisted and twirled the small buds into intense points of feeling.

Only it wasn't the right feeling for Kerry.

'Hazel – no, please – I don't want – I'm not that way.'

'We all are, honey. You just have to be shown – and I am training you. Now just you let Hazel show you the way.'

One of Hazel's hands dropped down to the slit in Kerry's skirt. With a familiarity of the female anatomy that only a woman could possess Hazel had her hand on Kerry's clitoris in no time at all. In time with her other hand, she twirled the bud of Kerry's nipple in wanton synchronisation with her clitoral meanderings.

The feeling to Kerry was one of utter disgust. And yet there was something extremely attractive about the sensation. It was like the first time she'd experimented with drugs in high school. She hated to do it, but she'd hated even more to admit that she'd enjoyed it.

The thought of those silly not-so-long-ago days snapped Kerry back into the here and now.

'No, Hazel, let me go.'

'You don't mean that, honey.'

'I do – I do – now let me go – let me go.'

Kerry was screaming at the top of her voice. At which point, seemingly miraculously, Bob Vest burst into the changing room. For the second time tonight he punched somebody once on the jaw and then in the stomach. Hazel flopped with an almighty slap onto the tiles of the changing room floor. She sat bare breasted rubbing her chin. Kerry pulled her halter top up to her chin to cover her breasts.

'Are you all right?'

The question was directed at Kerry.

'No, I'm not – I'm going to sue you for assault and battery,' Hazel responded before Kerry could get a word out. Kerry was in a dulled state of shock.

'Shut up Hazel and get out of here. No one is going to be suing anyone – least of all you.'

Still rubbing her chin, Hazel lifted herself up, her heavy pendulous breasts dangling obscenely earthward. She pulled on a sweater, and without a further word left the room. Kerry was still in a state of shock.

'Are you all right?'

'What – oh – yeah – I mean no. What is it with this place? Is everyone a raving sex maniac around here'

It took all of Bob's truth-stretching abilities to answer with a straight face.

'No – no – Lester is a pervert and Hazel is a dyke. You were unlucky enough to run into both of them on your first night.'

The admission 'and I'm a peeping Tom' ran around Bob's brain eagerly trying to leap out.

'But why me – what did I do?'

'Probably nothing – but like I told you with Lester, so many of the girls around here are a bit wild, maybe Hazel just got her signals crossed.'

'I never encouraged her at all'

Kerry was indignant.

'Whoah – time out. I didn't say she was right – I was just trying to explain how weird life around here can get. Cocktailing isn't all just fun and games and making money. You work long hours when most normal people are asleep. Booze is so readily available that you look for other excesses to keep you going. Drugs – sex – it's all part of this business. Ever notice how much people smoke around here? Most people who are done with their shifts still hang around here socializing. At the end of the night the partying just moves from the bar to the parking lot where the inevitable is just postponed until it's time to do it all again the next day. This business is a drug – and it's perhaps the most addictive. Few people who stay around cocktailing for a while ever really have a life outside of the bar business. You don't have to be part of it – but be aware that it is there and don't put down the people who are. It's just their way of coping.'

'Yeah, I sort of understand, but twice in one night is a bit much, you've got to admit. Don't you worry though – I'll be fine. I think I just need to sleep off this night. Do you think Hazel will be mad at me?'

'She won't even mention it to you again. And if you're smart you won't say a thing.'

'I guess I won't. It's all best forgotten.'

'Yeah – well – I'll let you get changed and off home. But just to be safe I'll walk you out to your car. With your luck, who knows who'll be lurking in the bushes.'

They both laughed the kind of nervous laugh that people do when they are trying to gloss over deeper thoughts.

As Bob walked Kerry to her car she stopped and casually asked Bob the obvious question.

'I'm curious – how did you know what was going on in the changing rooms? How did you know Hazel was trying to have her way with me?'

Bob hesitated for a telling moment.

'I was trying to find you to see if you wanted that drink now that you were off the clock, when I heard you yelling to stop. I thought Lester may have gotten out of hand again so that's why I burst in.'

'Oh – well, thank you, my knight in shining armour. I hope you don't have to come to my rescue again soon.'

'And with that she kissed Bob on the cheek and said goodnight, apparently satisfied with Bob's explanation. Bob smiled a somewhat guilty smile to himself that betrayed the knowledge that he knew he would have to come to Kerry's rescue at least one more time tonight. Burning a hole in his coat pocket was the coil wire from Kerry's car. Without it the car would just turnover and splutter. There would be no spark of ignition – and of course Bob would be there to rescue her and perhaps get more of a kiss on the cheek in return?

It was all part of a master plan that took full advantage of the chance advances of Lester and Hazel. Of course Bob hadn't been just casually passing by the changing rooms looking for Kerry. As soon as he'd seen Kerry and Hazel finish their shifts he'd hotfooted it to the office, which was luckily unoccupied. Don was busy satisfying a group of customers who felt as though they'd had lousy service. Some people just didn't understand that tipping helped improve the dedication of the server quite remarkably.

Bob had quickly switched the parking lot monitors to the changing rooms and slipped in a disc to record what transpired. He'd never have guessed in advance that Hazel would put the make on Kerry so quickly, but upon reflection it was to be expected. Kerry had that young, appealing and innocent look that said 'do it to me.' And he had both Lester the Molester's and Hazel the Dyke's seduction efforts on video disc. And while Kerry had been recovering from Hazel's pawing hands, Bob had been out in the parking lot disabling the unsuspecting girl's car.

Bob reflected that Kerry really didn't have a chance with all of the perverts that lurked at the Pump. Someone, somehow was certain to get to her – he reasoned it may as well be him. Bob was the ultimate wolf in sheep's clothing – pretending to be Mr Nice Guy while waiting to pounce on the poor unsuspecting Kerry. In keeping with his act, he turned to walk away as if heading to his car. He kept walking as the old Cadillac kept grinding its starter motor in a futile attempt to start. Bob waited a few more moments before turning and walking back to Kerry's car.

'Got a problem?'

Kerry was almost in tears.

'The damn thing won't start.' (Sob.) 'I borrowed my parent's old car because mine was at the garage being fixed, and now this heap of junk won't start.' (Sniffle.) 'That's all I need.' (Big sob.)

'Oh don't worry, I'll get it going. Sometimes it's just a loose connection. These older cars are a bit temperamental. Pop the hood for me, will you?'

Bob didn't bother to add that he knew how to pop the hood without using the hood release inside the car, as he had done just a few moments before. With the latch released, Bob lifted up the hood and began fiddling knowingly with the car's innards.

'Try it now.'

The Cadillac just made the same old grinding noise.

'Hmmm. Might be in the ignition system – let me try something.'

Luckily the erected hood made it impossible for Kerry to see Bob attach the coil wire.

'Try it now.'

This time the Cadillac roared into life after one splutter. Bob walked triumphantly to the car door beaming from ear to ear.

'Thank you once again, my knight in shining armour.' (Little sob.)

'Don't mention it – a coil wire had come loose. I'd just better check to see if the battery is still fully charged.'

Bob leaned through the open window of the car, ostensibly to look at the voltage indicator.

It was fully charged. And so was he. He turned to face Kerry. Their eyes were level. Their lips just inches apart. As far as Bob was concerned it was now or never. He pressed closer. He could feel Kerry's breath on his face. He was afraid to breath that he might disturb the seemingly passive trance she was in. Kerry let out a small sob left over from her earlier upset. It was Bob's signal to proceed. Their lips met.

And they didn't come apart for quite some time. Looking to the casual observer like the oversized prey of some huge tropical snake being devoured, Bob inched himself through the window of the Cadillac as Kerry slid down onto the mammoth front bench seat of the car. And still their lips stayed locked. Their tongues slid inquiringly around each other's mouth performing a ritualistic mating dance as tried, true and tested as time immemorial. The spell of their first passionate kiss was not to be broken by the mere inconvenience of a closed car door.

Luckily for Bob and Kerry the Cadillac front seat was larger than most small couches, giving the newly amorous couple plenty of room for passionate embraces. As Bob's feet finally made it through the window he was able to place his full weight onto Kerry's petite form. As tongue touched tongue, Kerry moaned deep within herself as Bob's erect hardness pressed against her jean-covered thigh. Inching upward Bob positioned himself between Kerry's legs. Denim-covered-cock rubbing against her denim-covered pussy, both betraying the urgency and wetness beneath.

Their lips finally parted.

'Bob – Bob. I want to . . .'

She didn't finish the sentence. Nature has a way of obviating the need for words in moments like these. Bob took his weight off Kerry so they could remove their jeans. Kerry moaned in erotic anticipation as she unbuttoned the fly that held the tough denim together. They were tight and difficult to remove. As she pulled them down, her red satin panties slid down her legs, pulled along the silkiness of her skin by the tightness of her jeans.

'Oh,' was all that Bob could manage as he caught an enticing glimpse of paradise by the dim light of the parking lot. He too struggled with his jeans. He hoped he'd worn some decent looking underwear. He hadn't really planned on this sequence of events when he dressed earlier in the evening. He needn't have worried. Kerry was too occupied with her own passion to notice such small details as Bob struggled to free himself from the confinements of his undergarments.

Kerry had been lucky. She had been wearing only some slip-on shoes that were easily kicked off. Bob had to sit back and take off shoes – then socks. It somehow didn't seem right to keep them on. His cock bobbed in the air as he sat back on the car seat free of the offending objects. In a movement that took Bob quite by surprise, Kerry sat up and quickly kneeled down and planted her face in his lap. The willing mouth that had most recently kissed Bob's lips, now encompassed his cock.

Kerry's strokes were hurried and urgent, almost as if she felt she had to suck his cock as a prelude to sex. Bob was in no position to object. He hoped there would be plenty of time in the months ahead for experimentation, refinement, even enjoyment. Now was the moment for urgency. The front seat of a Cadillac in the back of the Pump parking lot in the early hours of the morning was no place suddenly to become a perfectionist.

Almost as quickly as she began licking Bob's cock, Kerry stopped and fell back on to the seat, saliva coating the fine surface of her mouth and cheeks. Albeit not the most exquisite of blow jobs that Bob had received, Kerry's quick oral ministrations had excited him to fever pitch. She too felt the pressing need to be fucked. Without words, she reached forward and took Bob's erect cock and guided it towards her glistening cunt. Thanks to her brief lickings of his cock, the tip was still wet and slippery and easily penetrated her moist opening. Both Bob and Kerry gasped in unison as flesh entered flesh and lovemaking began.

Lips sought lips in a vain attempt to stifle moans of ecstacy as they fucked each other senseless underneath the faint glow of the Cadillac's dashboard lights. Their passion was both forceful and soft. Bob's thrusts were matched perfectly by Kerry's gyrations as the tip of his cock danced inside her pussy. Their frenzied coupling held his member tightly inside at the bottom of each stroke, prolonging the sensation of something large, something wild, something alive inside of her being. She felt its every twitching. She felt its velvety head tickle the insides of her pussy, and she felt her own juices flow in torrents in response.

It was difficult for Bob to hold back his orgasm. The pausing after each entry helped him regain some semblance of control, but each delicious stroke felt like the length of his penis was being massaged by a thousand tiny hands. In his state of high expectancy it was not long before his toes arched inward, making temporary depressions in the car seat, as his back arched skyward and his cock strained fully inside Kerry's pussy, showering her insides with hot sperm. Tightly he gripped her shoulders and held her to him as if the explosion might forever separate their lust.

Once Bob's moan had subsided and his arms had collapsed, Kerry took control of the situation.

'Don't – don't stop.'

'No – no – yes – yes, I won't,' was all Bob could manage as the thrusts of his orgasm-sensitised cock continued to batter at his swirling mind.

Kerry's body maintained her and Bob's fucking momentum as her hips propelled Bob in an out, in and out, in long slithery strokes.

'Please Bob, feel my tits – please.'

In their haste to get undressed neither had bothered to take off their shirts, but it wasn't too difficult for Bob to slide his hand underneath the brightly coloured tee-shirt and into the cup of Kerry's bra. Her nipple was like a little button that invited the fondler to press, to squeeze, to pinch, just to see what were the consequences of pushing on such an inviting target.

Kerry responded as if a dam had broken deep inside her. A swollen river of passion flooded her pussy and streamed down over Bob's cock and on to her legs, sweeping aside the last vestiges of control her body and mind held.

Still Bob kept thrusting deep inside her, like a robot who had been given the single command 'fuck'. Her orgasm continued to roll through her, through him, until its draining demands caused both to collapse exhausted onto the soft leather seat of the old Cadillac.

It may have been minutes, or possibly hours later when they both came to. The parking lot was luckily deserted. In a stunned silence they dressed and exchanged slight kisses of affection. Bob didn't know whether to invite Kerry back to his apartment, so instead he settled for the easy way out.

'Would you like to get some breakfast, somewhere? Lenny's is open twenty-four hours.'

'That would be nice.'

And on the way there amidst the darkened streets of Silicon Valley, Bob Vest couldn't help but feel a tinge of guilt creeping through his system at the way he'd tricked Kerry. He quickly dismissed the feeling as too sentimental. But still, strange new emotions dogged him.

And after quite a nice breakfast Bob did ask Kerry to go home with him.

And she did.

5

Martini

Mix

1½ oz. Gin
¾ oz. Dry Vermouth

*Stir vermouth and gin over ice cubes in a mixing glass. Strain into cocktail glass.
Serve with twist of lemon peel or olive.*

*T*o most ordinary women it would have been a waking nightmare. To Annie da Pheelanupe it was just another night's work. With perhaps the exception of the unusual occurrence of Annie having to purchase additional condoms from the overpriced vending machines in the Pump's bathrooms. Annie always thought of herself as well prepared with at least a dozen of Durex's best, but after tonight's precedent-setting fucking she would have to raise her allotment if she didn't want to buy extra johnnies at exorbitant prices.

Or be willing to turn away business ...

Never. Not Annie.

Sunday night was usually morbidly slow, but this normally quiet evening turned out to be an exception to the rule. Definitely one for the record books. Annie had resigned herself to a not-too-profitable early night alone in bed when local wheeler-dealer Arnold Wize and twenty Korean businessmen had descended upon the unsuspecting cocktail bar.

Arthur Wize displayed the Pumping Station's interior to his guests with an orchestral sweep of his arm, ending his stately pirouette, palm open-faced and extended towards Annie in a manner uncomfortably reminiscent of a maniacal butcher displaying sides of questionable meat to a group of starving refugees.

'Annie,' announced Mr Wize ingratiatingly.

'Why Mistar Wize. How narce tah see yew – and all y'all little friends.' Annie emphasised her Texan accent to the point of being a comical parody of the quintessential southern belle.

Annie was greeted by twenty-one pairs of eyes taking in her lusciously available beauty, all doing what such male visual organs usually do when confronted with a truly striking woman: undressing and fucking her in their mind's eyes. Annie could feel their stares, their imaginations, probing her all the way from the top of her tousled blonde hair to the bottoms of her stocking-clad high-heel adorned feet. Annie, no stranger to being visually fucked, responded with a well-tried look that left no misunderstanding in the ogler's eyes. With a delightful little flutter of her eyelids and a sly pout of her moistened red lips, Annie telegraphed each and every male libido the announcement that for the right amount of money they could do a hell of a lot more than look. They could fuck.

With this not-so-subtle invitation in mind the Korean businessmen began to occupy the booths, all jockeying for the most strategic locations. Arthur Wize stepped forward with what to Annie appeared to be the Big Cheese.

'Annie da Pheelanupe – I'd like you to meet Mr Phuc Yu.'

The Korean stepped forward, bowed and took Annie's hand in his. In a romantically gentlemanlike fashion he planted a warm and welcoming kiss on Annie's delicate hand. Still holding her jewelled fingers by the very tips he stared into her eyes.

'I am charmed to make your acquaintance, Miss da Pheelanupe.'

He spoke perfect English with just a hint of Oriental mystique.

'Oh my,' was all Annie could utter as he gently released her hand.

'Say, Phuc – why don't you go over to that booth over there in the corner, and I'll be right over just as soon as I've taken care of a few arrangements with Annie here.'

Phuc Yu nodded slightly, pausing ever so momentarily in Annie's direction before pivoting ceremoniously towards the Passion Pit.

Arthur Wize didn't waste any time.

'Look Annie — there's twenty of them. Will five grand cover that — you know — twenty quick ones?'

'Fuck you.'

'Hey, that's his name — but it's pronounced more like *fook* — so be careful when you fook him — he's kind of sensitive about it.' Arthur Wize chuckled at his mastery of the English language.

'I know what his name is, thank you very much, I'm not stupid as I'm sure y'all know by now. Jesus, Arthur, what do y'all think I am — a bitch in heat for Christ's sake? A dumb cocktail waitress perhaps? Who for a little white powder will suck your dick? Give me a break.'

'Okay — $7500.'

'$10,000.'

'$8000.'

'$10,000.'

'$9000.'

'$10,000.'

'Deal.'

'Deal — give me your platinum American Express card.'

'Don't you trust me?'

'No.'

'Ah — Annie — you are as good at business as I.'

'Coming from you that's quite a compliment.'

'Yes — we both know how to screw people and get paid for it.'

Annie smiled at Arthur as she graciously accepted the double-edged compliment and pocketed his credit card.

'The new girl is on call — we'll drag her in so she can help with the drinks while I see that your guests are accommodated.'

'Thank you, Annie. Make sure they are happy. They are so close to signing on the dotted line. Pulling this deal off means a lot to me.'

Under her breath Annie muttered 'no shit,' as the six-foot-two-inch frame of Mr Wize turned to join his prospective clients. Wize was best described as a big man. As he sat down in the booth the comfy cushions folded around his two hundred and fifty pound frame, causing the much lighter

75

Koreans to be elevated that much closer to the red and blue glow of the Pump's neon lighting. Arthur Wize was one of the perpetual hustlers of Silicon Valley. In today's enlightened age he was known as an entrepreneur. He'd dabbled in every aspect of Silicon Valley business, including some of the more illegal ones. He always had an uncanny knack of being in on a deal before it could legitimately be called the ground floor. It was the standing Silicon Valley joke that Arthur Wize was the one pushing a soft drink called 6-Up and got out of it before they made the changes that made it 7-Up. Probably more legend than truth, that was the kind of luck that usually dogged Arthur Wize. Now he was into real estate and had a fair amount of success building and selling buildings for the burgeoning electronics industry. What he was doing with twenty Korean businessmen would no doubt be the cause of much speculation in the business sections of the local rags.

After processing the credit card Annie had to get back to the reality of cocktailing. She asked Arnold to have the manager on duty, Don Palumba, call in Kerry while Annie quickly made her first round of the booths, ostensibly taking drink orders, but covertly sizing up her customers for the fucking to come. They all seemed eager and ready to pop at the smallest slide of a pussy. Arthur informed her that she should follow protocol and service Phuc Yu first – to do otherwise would be a mortal insult that none of his assistants would dare, no matter how randy they were, to make.

With one round of drinks delivered Annie walked over to Mr Yu and whispered in his ear.

'Sugar – in a few minutes get up and go into the parking lot. Walk around the building until you reach the big garbage dumpster – I'll be waiting behind it for you.'

Mr Yu just smiled and nodded knowingly. Arthur Wize winked a beady little eyeball at Yu who didn't return the compliment.

Annie excused herself with Arnold by pretending to go to the staff bathroom with a loud 'gotta pee' typical of Annie at her flippant best. Instead of answering one call of nature she got ready for another by grabbing a Durex form-fitting condom from her purse. Making sure no one was looking she

76

snuck out of the kitchen and stationed herself behind the dumpster. Not the most romantic of settings but certainly convenient and oh, so discreet with the blackest of black shadows that the lumbering metal can cast.

'Aw shit.'

Annie recognised the accent. It was Phuc Yu, who must have walked into the dumpster whilst trying to find his 'date'.

'Over here, sugar.'

'Ah – Miss Annie – you are positively radiant here in the darkness. I can see my way to you.'

And feel no doubt, thought Annie as Phuc Yu's eager hands latched onto her boobs. He certainly didn't waste any time. His hands displayed an experienced touch that was not lost on Annie's rapidly accelerating desire for a mad passionate fucking. The rings on his fingers were cold to Annie's tits. Every squeeze hardened her nipples and drew out of her an urgency that wanted more. In contrast to the rings, his hands were warm. Cold and warm. Fire and ice. Annie's 36B boobs were seemingly melted and frozen over and over, again and again. The way he kneaded her flesh into some misshapen form and then miraculously formed it into a delicious pair of breasts topped with two extremely hard nipples reminded her of a potter working with clay on one of those rotating wheels. Like ice-cream sundaes topped with bright red cherries, her tits oozed forward waiting to be licked, to be eaten.

Pressed with her back against the dumpster, Annie wedged her legs against the nearby kitchen wall, fully off the ground, and encircled Yu's waist with her lovely gams. The unusual position gave her sex perfect leverage. By flexing her superbly taut thighs she rubbed her tender panty-covered pussy on Yu's hardness whilst he juggled her breasts loosely out of her straining halter top. The milkiness of Annie's tits gleamed in the dancing shadows of the night as the cocktail waitress's breasts were pulled, pushed and squeezed unforgivingly. As Yu fought to contain those delectable orbs in his pawing hands Annie ground her crotch into Phuc's boner. Protected by only the silkiest of fabrics, Annie's cuntlips spread around the lump in the Korean's trousers and slid up and down its

77

wool and cashmere covered length. At the climax of each lovely journey Annie's silk-encapsulated clitoris smashed against the hidden end of Yu's hard dick. Pressing herself against his cockhead she would remain deliciously poised there until she would slide off, descending rapturously down his trouser-covered pole.

Annie always marvelled how ideal the Pumping Station cocktail waitress uniform was for fucking in. In the position that she was in, with her ass off the ground, the dress, slit all the way to her thigh, easily fell away fully baring her legs. And as Mr Yu had so quickly discovered, it took little effort to free her breasts from their not too restrictive confines. Her fishnet stockings and suspender belt were definitely not an inconvenience, and when coupled with the irresistible sight of high heels and ankle straps, the whole combination was definitely conducive to mountains of sex in really strange positions at the drop of the proverbial hat.

And this wrestling match was one of the more unusual ones, to be sure. Although hers was not the most comfortable of positions, Annie's legs were strong enough to support her gyrating bottom long enough to ensure that Phuc Yu was primed for fucking. With him eagerly biting at her nipples with snappy little yapping motions, she reached around her ass and unzipped his suit trousers. Reaching in to his boxer shorts she held his cock in one hand and attempted to slip the condom over the already leaking cockhead with the other. It was then she realised just how big the Korean's dick was. Big — it was huge! The condom stranded itself on the fattest cockhead she'd ever felt. It took all her strength in two hands to force the monster into its protective sheath. The motion, the squeezing, the pinching only served to drive Yu into a fever pitch.

'One size don't most definitely fit all in your case, honey.' Yu breathed hard.

'Yes — I've been told — by many women — yes — I'm quite well endowed.'

'Well, don't just brag about it — show me what you can do with that club y'all got down there. Fuck my little cunny with your big stick.'

Annie slid her panties to one side and let the rubber-covered gargantuan throbber penetrate her. In her squatting position it was easy for her to let her body weight do all of the work. She just let her one hundred and five pounds of fucking pleasure sink earthward, impaling herself on Yu's straining member. Still, it was no easy matter to fit the huge dick inside herself. Her opening had seen many cocks over the years and was used to accommodating all sizes, but this one was perhaps the biggest. The slight pain she felt was exquisite in its piercing intensity. Rapidly she juiced over the sheath, sliding her body up and down in concert with Yu's continually upward thrustings.

Phuc Yu more than lived up to his name, bucking Annie hard against the kitchen wall whilst restraining her from the full impact of such blows by pulling tightly on her nipples, thereby causing her to rebound towards him. This was one fuck Annie thought she should be paying for. At least going halves on. Splitting, perhaps. The thought made Annie realise just how big his dick was. With each deliciously long thrust his penis seemed to grow larger and larger. His girth, doing its very best to ram its blood-engorged way to her throat – the hard way – felt as if it would rent her asunder. Uncharacteristically for Annie whilst on the job, she orgasmed first and quickly. Her juices flowed in a torrential, gushing stream that drained the life out of her. Her legs lost their strength and she collapsed forward like a rag doll around Yu's shoulders. Still the Korean fucked away until each stroke threatened to rip Annie apart with its insistence. Grimly she fought against the blackness that claimed her and once again wrapped her legs tightly around his waist. Her soaked thighs squatted around Yu's dick – her pussy sucked hard at the quivering cock, masturbating it to the brink far better than any hand could ever do. It took but two such small squeezes of her come-drenched thighs to ignite Mr Yu's rocket.

'Wwwwwaaaaahhhhhoooooooorrrrr,' emitted Phu in a low gutteral way.

'Phew,' commented Annie with relief. 'That was one bronco that almost bucked me over the moon. Whoo-wee.' She dismounted and began the courtesy of removing the

79

spunk filled johnny. It was only recently that Annie had starting using condoms, but with the threat of AIDS she was taking no chances. The safety they provided was worth some of the inconveniences – the worst of which was trying to get the damn things off. Yu was still hard so it was no small task to free him from the condom. It took a few moments in which she could tell Yu winched in agony as her fingernails did their best not to pinch his tender cockskin. In the darkness behind the dumpster it was difficult to be careful. Finally the cock splattered free and Annie made a motion to throw the distended condom into the dumpster. Yu interrupted her and took the condom from her.

'No – no Miss Annie da Pheelanupe – I wish this collection of our love juices to keep as a souvenir of a most memorable coupling.'

Annie wrinkled her nose at the thought of Yu having a collection of used condoms, but like the consummate professional she was she took it in her stride.

'Why sure, sugar – now y'all get back to the lounge and I'll be right by with a drink for y'all.'

Within moments Annie was back at the bar fully groomed and ready to serve drinks. The whole episode had taken just six minutes. Annie was inwardly complimenting herself on her skills when Arthur said something that stopped her in her tracks.

'Did you get your hair wet?'

'What? – no – uhh?' Annie consciously stroked her full head of blonde hair worrying that perhaps she'd sweated too much in all the fucking. Or had Arthur been watching? She felt suddenly very guilty. Arthur laughed loudly at her discomfort.

'Oh, I see. Peed through a straw did you?'

Suddenly the joke dawned on Annie as she remembered her bathroom excuse.

'Arthur Rimskikoff, y'all are a vile and disgusting low-down sidewinder to ask a lady such a thing.'

Arthur just kept on laughing. Annie giggled too, glad that her secret was still safe.

'Kerry will be in shortly – looks like you're going to need

the help.'

Annie looked up to see forty-two thirsty and wanting eyes.

'I'd better do another round.' Annie didn't just mean drinks.

Kerry was a little overwhelmed by the pressure of such a hectic night. It didn't seem to make matters any better that Annie kept disappearing every few minutes.

'Keeping up?' Annie appeared after another six-minute absence.

'Barely — are you all right?'

'Sure — why?'

'Only you keep disappearing into the bathroom every few minutes, and so I wondered.'

'Well don't. I'm just a little hung over — I'll be fine. And besides, it'll do y'all good to get slammed. You're only a real cocktail waitress once you've been slammed past the point where y'all can't keep up — but y'all manage — and if y'all can't hack it then y'all ain't gonna make a cocktail waitress. And besides think of the tips y'all be making.'

'Yeah — well — I'll try to remember that.'

Kerry didn't mention it to Annie but Kerry was feeling a little under the weather also. After breakfast with Bob she'd gone back to his place and well, one thing led to another as they often do in such situations, and several other things led to each other and there was lots of tequila and no sleep, until she dragged herself back to her apartment, only to be woken up a few hours later by the call of duty.

'Oh well fifteen down — five more to go,' Annie mumbled as she walked quite gingerly from the bar, supposedly to the bathroom one more time. The line from some fancy book she'd once read in school came to mind. 'Once more unto the breech, dear friends — once more unto the breech.' She wasn't sure where it came from but she certainly had sympathy for the fella who'd said it.

'Beautiful — beautiful — where are you?'

Annie rolled her eyes. The more the Koreans had to drink the more poetic they became — and the more difficulty they had in finding their way around the building.

81

'Oh, where are you, my sweet?'

Annie decided she should put a stop to the drunken Romeo's musings before he attracted too much undue attention. After fifteen 'dates' Annie was in no mood for small talk, so she just reached out from behind the dumpster and grabbed the wandering Korean by the scruff of his neck and hoisted him into position.

'Oh, you are so lovely – my heart pounds for you.'

The words were slurred and drunken. Annie thought it best to act quickly before he passed out and became an embarrassment. And after one exceptional fuck and fourteen rather mediocre shags, she decided to do things a little different.

'OK, honey, you're gonna get the best blow job of your life.' Annie just couldn't stand all that effort of putting a dick inside her for a meagre ten seconds. It wasn't even fair to use the slang term 'in and out' to describe the way most of her fucks had gone this evening. More like 'in and waggle and squirt.'

'Oh, that's good – I never had a blow job before.'

'No kidding. Well, close your eyes and say hello to cock heaven.'

Annie dropped to her knees and unzipped the talkative chap's trousers. Immediately he began moaning. Even before Annie had touched his throbbing penis he was acting as if he was overcome with the emotions of orgasm. He wore extremely tight blue bikini underpants that were sticky with oodles of that funny liquid that paves the way for the fountain of sperm soon to follow. As Annie pulled the waistband of the blue panties aside, the thin and pencil-hard cock sprang out like a coiled snake striking its victim.

After recovering from the shock of being attacked by an angry one-eyed trouser snake, Annie gripped the ersatz reptile and shook it tightly where the beastie emerged from its nest.

'Whhoooooooo . . .'

Years of experience couldn't have prepared Annie for what happened next. Her ever-watchful eyes noticed that large amounts of smegma had formed a rather sticky and unappetising blob right at the business end of the Korean's penis.

Not really being in the mood for such delicacies, Annie attempted to remove the mess by applying a gentle cooling breeze from her already puckered lips.

'Whhoooooooooo...'

And without so much as a shudder or a yell — just that continual low guttural moan — the rigid snake spit its venom right into Annie's face. A full load of steaming hot spunk right between the eyes.

'Jesus Christ,' Annie spluttered. She grabbed the nearest piece of material, which happened to be the Korean's shirt, and used it to wipe off the dripping semen.

'Ah, — now I can truly say I have had a great American blow job.'

'That was your first, wasn't it?'

'Ah, yes — first of many, I hope.'

Annie didn't have the heart to tell him just how much he'd missed out on. He seemed satisfied enough as he stumbled off around the building to join his associates back in the bar.

Only he didn't make it. He took a wrong turn and ended up asleep behind an ornamental bush, only to be found the next morning by the Pumping Station's gardener. The Korean Romeo still had a smile on his face, comfortable with the apparent knowledge that he was no longer a blow-job virgin.

The last four behind-the-dumpster visits Annie got off easily — and so did her dates — in a manner of speaking. All she had to do was reach in the various Koreans' undergarments, take a few quick wanks of the raging hard weenies, and the overprimed, alcohol-nourished, sex-starved Korean businessmen shot their eager loads into Annie's oscillating hand. That the whole sordid experience lasted but a few seconds didn't seem to bother the clients who were unanimous in their praise of how good it was.

Annie was exhausted. Albeit that the last few had been rather easy marks, the sheer mental and physical effort of sneaking outside and expending so much energy in such a short space of time, twenty times over, did take its toll. Back in the bar, as all of the Koreans were filing out, Annie was greeted by a mountain of used bottles and dirty glasses. The expression on her face was one of utter disgust. Usually the barbacks took the empties out, but since it had looked like it was going to be slow, the barbacks had been let go early. Thus, the responsibility for tearing down fell on the weary shoulders of the cocktail waitresses.

'Don't worry — I'll take them out,' offered Kerry. She had made over $300 in drinks tips, so she was feeling quite magnanimous. And besides, Annie looked like she'd been to hell and back.

'Thanks Kerry — I couldn't stand another trip to the dumpster.'

'What?'

'Oh, nothing. I meant the bathroom. I'm not feeling too good — not thinking too clearly.' Annie made a mental note to be more careful in the future. Careless slips could ruin her nice little situation.

As Kerry dragged the sacks of bottles out to the dumpster Arthur Wize came up to Annie and thanked her for a job well done.

'Well, Annie — once again everyone was well and truly satisfied.' His fat face, his slicked back hair, his beady eyes, his little close cropped moustache all leered knowingly.

'I aim to please.'

'Mr Yu was very pleased. He is a very powerful man, Annie . . .'

'Tell me about it.'

'He is going to be a key player here in Silicon Valley.'

'So?'

'So how about one more time — goodwill and all that.'

'No way Arthur — no way. Have you any idea how sore I am?'

'Oh, come on, Annie.'

'No — and that's final.'

'More money?'

'No — I'm exhausted'

'Oh, come on — I've already told him you would'

'Well, you can just go and tell him I won't'

'Oh, come on, will you? He's waiting outside for you now.'

'He's what?'

'He's outback now.'

'By the dumpster?'

'Yeah.'

'Oh, shit.'

'Oh shit,' was exactly what Kerry said as she felt her dress being lifted behind her. She'd been bending down behind the dumpster in the pitch darkness of its shadow trying to pick up the over stuffed garbage bags full of bottles and bar trash. Her racing mind scanned through the possibilities and optimistically concluded that the hand that was becoming most familiar with her undergarments must be owned by Bob Vest. He'd joked that he'd come by and surprise her since she'd had to work unexpectedly, and since Lester wasn't working, then it must be Bob. The chances of her being attacked one more time at The Pump on her first weekend of working there were just too remote. It had to be Bob playing a joke. Wedged behind the dumpster in the pitch blackness of its shadow she was unable to turn around and see her admirer. It must be Bob. He'd have waited until closing time and watched her take the trash out and then snook up behind her. Yes – it must be Bob.

'Bob – is that you?' In retrospect it was probably a dumb thing to say to someone sticking their hand up a girl's dress. What's the owner of the hand to say – 'No, it's not Bob. Surprise!'? Heck no. Phuc Yu was several martinis past answering coherently any question so he just groaned as his hand fought valiantly with Kerry's knicker elastic to get at the juicy lips within.

'Hmmmm-mmmmm-mmmmm...'

'When you said you'd surprise me, Bob, I had no idea. What if someone comes?'

'Hmmmm-mmmmm-mmmmm ...'

'Oh Bob – you animal – you just can't get enough, can you?'

'Hmmmm-mmmmm-mmmmm...'

Phuc Yu had Kerry held firmly by the neck whilst his other hand was rapidly finger-fucking Kerry's tight and juicy opening. It had taken Mr Yu very little effort to tug Kerry's panties down below her bottom and subsequently slide his fat finger in and out of her rapidly creaming pussy. In the darkness behind the dumpster it was impossible for the drunken Korean to tell it was not Annie. Perhaps if he'd been sober and there had been a little more light he may have noticed that Kerry was a little taller and had different colour hair, but one could hardly blame him for not paying attention to unnecessary details at a time like this.

For Kerry's part she was enjoying the feeling of being finger-fucked so rudely. As the dicklike finger slid in and out of her tight cunt she rocked backwards and forwards on her five inch heels, adding sensually to the finger's penetration.

'Bob – Bob – give me your dick. I want the real thing. I want to come on the real dick – not your finger.'

It is amazing how even in the depths of drunken stupor certain key phrases are always understood. 'Give me your dick,' was one of them. Phuc Yu was only too happy to oblige. Removing his finger from Kerry's cunt with a nice slurping sound he unzipped his trousers and took out his club. It stood proudly to attention and zeroed in on its prey like some heat-seeking missile up the exhaust of a fleeing jet fighter. Kerry was wet enough to ease its entry, but still Mr Yu had to force his way inside her opening, such was the enormous girth of his cock. Uncomfortably inside he began to lick Kerry's juices from his dick-substitute finger.

'Hmmmm-mmmmm-mmmmm...'

'Hmmmm-mmmmm-mmmmm...'

'Oh Bob – Bob – you feel so big – so huge – fuck me – fuck me.'

'Hmmmm-mmmmm-mmmmm...'

Kerry was unable to rock backwards and forwards any more. Yu's cock was so large she was impaled almost motionless on its length like some wild beast speared in the frantic hunt. Yu tried harder to move her up and down his length with the hand he'd restrained her neck with.

'Oh God, Bob, you're going to tear me apart. Bob – you're so big – you're so hard – you're – you're not Bob.'

Kerry screamed the last words at high volume. Yu's hand had slid over her shoulder as he tried to force her to and fro on his dick, and his fat ring-covered fingers caught Kerry's eye. She knew Bob didn't have fingers that fat and wear that much jewellery. Suddenly the awful realization dawned on her like the proverbial ton of bricks. She struggled to free herself but to no great avail. She was trapped behind the dumpster and pinioned by Phuc Yu.

'Hmmmm-mmmmm-mmmmm...'

Phuc Yu had no idea of the reluctance of the young woman in whose body his dick resided and was partaking itself of the pleasures of her flesh. He thought the struggling was all part of the fun. It did make him squirm a bit as her ass cheeks jiggled so against his big furry bush of a cocknest.

'Hmmmm-mmmmm-mmmmm...'

Enough was enough for Kerry as she figured that the best thing to do was to try and straighten up her back and stand up. With all of her strength she arched her back and thrust her head skyward, momentarily breaking free from Yu's piston-like hand grip, and collided with the overhanging metal lid of the dumpster. She immediately fell back down into her submissive position, unconscious.

'Hmmmm-mmmmm-mmmmm...'

Mr Yu had no idea anything was amiss until he was staring eye to eye with the not-so-smiley face of Annie and the somewhat embarrassed visage of Arthur Wize. It was then that he realised that he'd made a bit of a mistake. Suddenly the darkness behind the dumpster was flooded with the illumination of a bright flashlight.

'Hmmmm-mmmmm-mmmmmm...'

'What the fuck are you doing to that poor girl?'

Talk about asking the obvious. Annie was just a little upset. How the hell was she going to explain this? How the hell was she going to stop Kerry filing rape charges? The police investigation would surely uncover her own antics.

'Hmmmm-mmmmm-mmmmmm...'

'Stop it. Let her go.'

This must have been another one of those phrases that make it through temporary alcohol-induced lack of awareness. It also helped that it was uttered in his face by the woman whom he thought he was fucking. He relaxed his grip and poor Kerry slid off his rapidly softening cock. She lay sprawled over the bag of bottles, out cold. Phuc Yu was nothing if not mightily confused.

'Arthur, get him out of here – I'll handle this.'

'Sure – sure Annie. Whatever it takes.'

'Oh, it'll take plenty Arthur – plenty to keep this one quiet.'

'Whatever Annie – whatever.'

Arthur Wize helped the inebriated and thoroughly dazed Korean back to his limousine with Mr Wize hoping that the amnesiatic effect of alcohol would save him from having to explain anything in the cold hard light of day.

Faced with an unconscious Kerry who might wake at any instant, Annie thought fast. She ran into the kitchen, picked up a pitcher of iced water and a bar rag. With the bar rag she wiped the insides of Kerry's thighs to remove all traces of Mr Yu's advances. Thankfully, she'd got there before he'd shot his copious load or she'd have needed a few towels to soak up the mess. Annie then carefully rearranged Kerry's panties and smoothed down her dress. Then she splashed iced water on Kerry's face in an effort to revitalise her.

'What – what – I'm – I'm being...' Kerry was understandably disoriented.

'Whoah – calm down. You hit your head on the dumpster. You've been out cold for several minutes. Take it easy.'

'But – I could have sworn...'

'Don't say a word, just take it easy. You've had a nasty shock. Shall I call an ambulance?'

'No – no – I must have been dreaming while I was unconscious – I thought I was being raped.'

'No such luck, honey. I saw y'all bump your head as I was coming to give y'all a hand with the bags. Nothing but us girls here.'

'Wow – really weird. It was so real.'

'Y'all have had a nasty accident. It's not surprising y'all were hallucinating.'

Kerry, with Annie's help, stumbled to her feet.

'Y'all sure you don't need a doctor?'

'No – no – I just need to sit down and take a few aspirin. I have one hell of a headache.'

'I can imagine, dear. Just like the one I just got rid of...'

Kerry didn't notice Annie's guilty smile as the resourceful Texas beauty helped the injured cocktail waitress back into the kitchen. Once more, her great-great-grandmother would have been proud of Annie's guile.

'What a night,' moaned Kerry.

'What a night indeed,' replied Annie. 'All in a night's work, Kerry — all in a night's work. Just think of the big tips you made off of those Koreans.'

'Yeah,' was all Kerry could say. She didn't know it, but she'd had enough of big Korean tips for one night, thank you very much.

6

Zombie

Mix

1 oz. Unsweetened Pineapple Juice
Juice of 1 Lime
Juice of 1 Small Orange
1 tsp. Powdered Sugar
½ oz. Apricot-Flavoured Brandy
2½ oz. Light Rum
1 oz. Jamaica Rum
1 oz. Passion Fruit Syrup
½ oz. 151-Proof Rum

Mix all ingredients with half a cup of ice into an electric blender. Blend at low speed for one minute and strain into a big glass. Garnish with fruit.

It's the same all the drinking world over. Every bar, restaurant, nightclub and pub has them. Regulars. Wayward souls who seem to have no life other than the hours upon hours that they spend in their favourite drinking establishment nursing the occasional drink. Their cocktail of choice is usually something weak – like American beer – to allow these lonesome barflys the ability to drink bottle after bottle without getting too drunk, for nightly inebriation is not the reason for their occupation. Oh, no – the barflys take up residence because they are lonely, and the employees of the bar become a surrogate family. The bartender becomes a brother. The manager assumes a bit of a parental role, and the waitresses are treated like sisters.

And we all know that even in the best of families incest sometimes rears its ugly head – or at least the thought of it does. And behind every regular's chummy 'little pals' routine there lurks a sheep in wolf's clothing dying to do a little fucking of his sisterly waitress.

The Pumping Station is no exception to this rule, although its regulars are somewhat more on the eccentric side. There's Fred who is a car salesman for the local Cadillac dealer, only he hasn't sold a car in over four years. Then there's Larry the computer salesman who tries to act like a playboy but ends up looking like a boy playing. And we can't forget Basil. No one is really sure what Basil officially does for a living. Some say he owns his own fax machine company. Some say he is independently wealthy. Some say he is an art dealer.

And everyone guesses he is the local neighbourhood friendly drug dealer. Basil can get anyone anything, and he's found it quite convenient to set up shop at the Pump where his clientele range from bored executives to trendy yuppies to desperate assembly workers. And don't forget the Pump's employees who have contributed enough business to Basil's little empire to have sent him on at least two of the round-the-world cruises he maintains he has enjoyed.

And some say he was just inventing the stories about the cruises to cover the stretch of time he did being busted for dealing by two undercover cops posing as Hells Angels in need of something to keep them up on an all-night bike binge.

Any way you cut it, you do see life's rich tapestry being woven whilst hanging out at the corner of the bar at the Pumping Station. This is where the regulars strategically situate themselves, permanently-lit cigarettes dangling from their hands – and sometimes their mouths – located at the corner of the bar that just happens to be the waitress serving station. Here the regulars sit talking about nothing and expecting everything whilst slyly looking down the waitresses' dresses as the women bend to pick up bar supplies and fallen napkins.

Some waitresses pretend they don't notice.

Not Louisa.

'Haven't you ever seen a pair of tits before? Or was the last time you saw a nipple when your mommy let you have a suck to stop you from crying?'

Three pairs of eyes immediately rotated one hundred and eighty degrees in a futile attempt not to get caught. Finally, it was Larry who chirped up.

'We can't help it if you're so beautiful, Louisa. You distract us from our important business.'

'Important business, my ass.'

'As a matter of fact that's what our important business was – we were just discussing that you have the best ass of all the waitresses here.'

'Yeah – I'll say.' It was Lester the Molester the bartender.

A loud guffaw of laughter erupted from the corner of the bar. Loudest of all was Louisa who took the comments as flattery. As soon as she was out of earshot, attempting to take drink orders from a cheap rowdy group around the fireplace, Fred began to pontificate.

'Do you think she'd go out with me if I asked her?'

'Nah. None of the waitresses will go out with you – with any of us,' Basil waxed philosophically as he thumbed his glass in the palms of his hands.

'Well, I don't really want to go out with her. I just want to fuck her.'

Another loud guffaw of hysteria emanated from the corner of the bar.

'Your best bet would be to get her really drunk and do it while she wasn't looking.'

Everyone looked at Larry with sneering visages.

'No, really. She gets pretty wasted when she gets off work, and people buy her drink after drink. We should try it sometime. She almost kissed me once when she was really blasted.'

'Larry may have a point – I may be able to procure a substance easily dissolved in a drink that shall we say reduces inhibitions, moistens cunts and opens legs.'

'A*wright*!' The yell belonged to Lester.

'Talking about me again?' Louisa waltzed back to the bar with a tray full of empties and a lack of orders. It was a slow night.

Four voices answered in unison. 'No,' and then 'Yes.'

'What were you saying this time – how nice my legs are?'

Without giving them time to answer Louisa planted her leg on Fred's chair, right at his crotch and let the split skirt fall gently away to reveal her black fishnet stocking covered limb. All of the Regulars' eyes were glued to the black high heel only inches from Fred's pride and joy.

'Louisa – you can get off early tonight. Hazel can handle everything. It's not busy enough for two waitresses,' a voice from the slightly cracked door leading to the kitchen echoed into the bar, breaking the spell of Louisa's long legs.

Bob Vest's head followed his voice. He surveyed the strange scene transpiring and thought it best not to ask what Louisa's leg was doing in Fred the Regular's crotch. Somehow, nothing at the Pump surprised Bob Vest anymore. Especially after his escapades with Kerry.

'O.K. Bob.' Louisa retracted her leg to the dismay of the immediate audience. They all sighed.

'You guys owe me a drink for that. One good look at one of my legs should be worth at least a couple of zombies.' Louisa disappeared into the changing rooms to shed her cocktail waitress skin.

'It's now or never.' Larry was sweating.'

'Do or die.' Fred was determined.

'I'll be right back with reinforcements.' Basil left quickly on his mysterious mission.

'A*wright*!' Lester was unwittingly salivating spittle into someone's gin and tonic which he was trying carelessly to mix.

Within minutes Basil was back with a small vial containing a potent-looking chemical. 'Lester – you heard the young lady. She wanted a zombie. Zombies all around.'

'Coming right up, master.' Lester didn't have to try very hard to imitate the mad scientist's assistant as he poured all manner of liquor into gigantic goldfish-bowl-sized glasses. A space at the bar was cleared for Louisa. Her drink was placed at the counter and Basil slyly emptied a portion of the vial into the mess of alcohol. Like naughty schoolboys playing a prank on the teacher the Regulars sat, clutching their own unadulterated zombies, eagerly awaiting the arrival of the unsuspecting Louisa.

She arrived all smiles and cigarette smoke just a few minutes later.

'I'm wearing my shortest mini skirt just for you guys.'

There were greedy nods of approval from the Regulars. The skirt appeared to be nothing more than a super-wide white belt held together by completely see-through black fishnet material running from the hem to the waist on each thigh. Underneath the skirt Louisa wore sheer-to-the-waist tan tights that made her long legs look skyscraper tall as she slumped in the chair next to the bar and guzzled her drink.

'With legs like these, don't you guys think I deserve another zombie?'

Basil, Larry and Fred stared in amazement. They had

managed but a few sips of their potent drinks. Louisa had slammed hers down in but a few seconds. Not to mention that her zombie had contained a few extra ingredients making it even more of a lethal concoction.

'Coming right up.' Even Lester was amazed. 'This one's on me'

The Regulars felt obliged to keep up with Louisa and sucked down their drinks as she started on her second.

'Another round Lester — and one for Louisa.'

'Well — I'll have to show you my legs more often if this is how you respond.'

'Show us your tits and I'll buy you the most expensive bottle of champagne that the Pump has.' Fred was starting to slur his words.

'Really — well, don't blink.' And as Louisa stood up to go to the bathroom she lifted up the hem of her cut-off white shirt and in a flash of lighting exposed her lovely full tits. The vista lasted but a fraction of a second. Not really enough time even to discern the small nuances of Louisa's tanned orbs, but what the Regular's eyes failed to capture, their willing imaginations were quick to fill in the blanks. Louisa's raucous laugh haunted them as she flitted to the bathroom.

The Regulars were awe struck.

'Ddddid you see those ttttits?' Larry was stuttering.

'I think I died and went to heaven.' Fred was philosophical. 'I never thought she'd do it. Lester — get us the most expensive bottle of champagne you've got.'

'Awright.' Lester was really enjoying this. Even from behind the bar he'd been able to catch a great silhouette of Louisa's breasts. He could hardly wait to have a quick wank. Perhaps while he was fetching the champagne from the wine cellar ...

'Our plan certainly seems to be working,' posed Basil. 'I think I'll empty the rest of this little pick-me-up into the champagne to make doubly sure that nothing goes wrong.'

A chorus of knowing laughs greeted Louisa as she returned from 'powdering her nose.'

'So where's my champagne, Fred?' she asked ignoring what appeared to her a private joke. Probably at her expense she surmised. To get even with the jokers she crossed her legs quite slowly, giving Fred a telling glimpse of the nylon-covered vee between her legs. As much as he tried he could not avert his eyes from the holy grail that beckoned him. Where the hell was that champagne? What was taking Lester so long? Please God let Larry's plan work. Please. Please. All these thoughts bounced around Fred's zombie-stunned brain as Louisa's legs performed their sensuous dance, just like some crafty magician's trick — now you see it, now you don't.

Louisa was enjoying teasing the Regulars. She knew they enjoyed it and she enjoyed the attention. But somehow, tonight, she felt different. She couldn't quite put her finger on it, although she could definitely do with putting her finger on something. That something was what was pulsing between her legs, being rubbed delicately as she crossed her thighs. Deep inside her she could feel the beginnings of incredibly naughty thoughts. She'd only had a few zombies, so that shouldn't be doing it. She felt a pressing need to have sex, only there wasn't anyone in range that could even remotely satisfy her cravings.

'I need my champagne,' Louisa announced. Perhaps that would help her anticipation. Calm her down. Then again, probably not.

Finally Lester, looking quite flushed, returned with the champagne and after much cork-popping and sleight of Basil's hand, Louisa was guzzling 1984 Dom Perignon — turbocharged.

'Aren't you guys going to join me'

'Oh no, Louisa. We'll stick to zombies. Never mix drinks.'

'Suit yourself — all the more for me.'

'Oh yes — there'll be all the more for you. Just you wait.'

Except for Louisa, everyone's words were slurring out of the corner of their mouths so that sentences became really just one big long word. And inevitably that word involved sex. After many double, triple and quadruple entendres, whilst Louisa was once more powdering her nose, the final phase of the plan was hatched.

'So how do we make our move? She doesn't seem too out of it yet. We're almost as bombed as her.' Fred was concerned. The anticipation was killing him.

'It takes a little while for the drug to work. About another hour and she'll be craving sex' Basil tried to appear calm, but inside he too was amazed at Louisa's tolerance for alcohol and drugs.

'I heard on a talk show the other day that if you want to get a girl into bed you should take her to see a porno movie. It makes them hot – the sight of all those cocks fucking cunts. Why don't we make a dare of going to that sleazy theatre on the El Camino. It's dark enough in there that we could fuck her while the movie's playing.' Larry winked knowingly as he spoke. Basil and Fred were amazed at his mental prowess.

'Good idea,' they echoed to a clinking of glasses.

Louisa returned from the bathroom to be greeted by three grinning faces.

'Jeez – what got into you guys?'

Suddenly Larry had a flash of inspiration.

'Fred was telling us about a movie he'd just seen.'

'Comedy, was it?'

'No, not quite – but say, Louisa, what did you do before you worked at the Pump?'

'I worked in an office. Why?'

'Have you ever modelled – or been in the movies?'

'No, never. Well, there have been a few small things but nothing major – why?'

This time the 'why' was getting heavily emphasised. Louisa was getting altogether too curious about the direction the questioning was taking. She'd let a few guys take the occasional photograph of her in a compromising position – but that had been for strictly personal use. But what if the pictures had fallen into the wrong hands? What if these guys had seen the one of her sucking off her last boyfriend? He did sometimes come into the Pump for a drink, just to piss her off. What if he'd passed the glossy evidence around to spite her? Louisa's mind was racing not only with drugs and alcohol, but also fear. Larry broke the spell for her. It was with some relief that she realised she'd worried for no apparent reason.

'Fred says that you were in this movie he caught just last night. He swears it was you – don't you, Fred?'

'Er, yeah. Sure – either you or your twin.' Fred really didn't know what to say. He was feeling pretty drunk. He was starting to be not so sure that this bedding of Louisa was such a good idea.

'Na – arh. No way. What movie was it?'

Fred looked confuse and stalled for time by taking a long swig of his zombie. Larry came to the rescue.

'We'll take you to see it – and you can see for youself what a big star you are.'

'When?'

'How about now. Fred's got his big Caddy, and the theatre is just up on the El Camino. How about it?'

'Sure – only let's stop and get a bottle of Bacardi so we can have rum and coke in the theatre. It'll be a laugh. You guys are crazy.'

And so they all filed out of the Pump and into Fred's Caddy. After stopping at a small liquor store to purchase their refreshments Louisa thought to ask a telling question.

'So which theatre was this movie playing at?'

'Oh – The Towne.'

'The Towne – that's a porno movie place. I'm not going there with you perverts.'

Louisa screamed the words in mock disgust. Fred swerved and fought to regain control of the car and his zombie-blasted vision. Basil concentrated on his shoelaces, trying hard to prevent his stomach from expelling all of the alcohol he'd consumed in his quest to seduce Louisa. Only Larry seemed up for the challenge.

'Oh, not so fast, Louisa. It was you in the movie, and you just don't want us to see you sucking some big guy's dong do ya?'

'I've never been in one of those movies. Fred was probably drunk and imagined it was me. The dirty bastard.'

'(Hic) – oh no – I was sober and it was you. I'd recognise your tits anywhere.'

Louisa hit Fred on the arm which caused the car to swerve once more.

'All right – but you guys will owe me big time once you see it's not me.'

'Sure – anything you want'

'Ha – you're going to regret this.'

Louisa took a big gulp of the 151-proof rum and laughed raucously. She passed the bottle around. The regulars drank gingerly. They had reached their limits but dared not stop with victory almost in sight. Louisa really didn't seem too buzzed. She hid it well. Inside she could feel the telltale signs of too much of a good thing going to work, but her well-trained exterior didn't let on.

'Ladies get in free – that'll be $21 for the men.' The slimy counter clerk didn't look up as he pocketed the money and pressed the buzzer to admit Louisa and the Regulars. They passed a brightly-lit area that sold soft drinks, candy and a variety of pornographic merchandise euphemistically labelled as 'Marital Aids.' How exactly a plastic blow-up sheep could help a marriage caused Louisa's extremely drunk and drugged mind to boggle.

The theatre was dark, and as their eyes adjusted to the blackness, appeared to be quite empty. On the screen a giant pair of red lips was devouring a not too hard cock to a roaring chorus of slurping, gurgling and sucking noises. Louisa sat down flanked on one side by Larry and on the other by Basil and Fred. All their eyes were riveted to the screen and the goings on displayed on it, not because of the exquisite camera work or the award winning acting. Oh, no – they were just a little too self-conscious to look at each other.

Except for Louisa. She noticed that the girl on the screen bore little resemblance to her. There was no way that Fred could have mistaken the girl in the movie for her. She was about to turn and say so when she noticed the lumps in Basil, Fred and Larry's pants. She also noticed the dazed drunken looks on their faces. All three of the Regulars were close to passing out. Fred looked close to throwing up. Louisa was extremely buzzed and definitely randy. It slowly dawned on her that this whole escapade had probably been some sort of plot to get into her panties. Typical, she though. Fucking typical. Still, it was kind of amusing – and randy in a funny

101

sort of way. And although not the most erotic stimulus she'd ever had, the sordid sex on the screen was, in her current over-stimulated state, a really dirty turn-on.

They won't remember a thing in the morning, went through Louisa's sex-crazed mind as she considered the naughty actions she was about to instigate. Why not give them what they've been dying for, she rationalised. Without taking her eyes off the screen she reached over and unzipped Larry's trousers. In one quick yanking movement she pulled his cock out of his baggy boxer shorts and began tugging at the hardened knob with her fingers. Larry moaned and reached over to kiss Louisa. Louisa was having none of it. With her free hand she pushed him down into the seat and advised him that there would be none of that.

'But if it's kissing you want I can do better than her on the screen.'

Larry nodded weakly. Louisa got off her seat and crouched between Larry's legs. From the corner of her eye she could see Basil staring at her bobbing mouth. He was frantically tapping Fred, who seemed to be soundly asleep, on the shoulder.

Larry's cock was, as Louisa expected, of completely average stature. Still, it jutted proudly out of his underwear as Louisa sucked its length, her actions exactly mirroring those of the actress on the screen. Larry dared not breath as if the mere expulsion of his breath would destroy the moment he had so longed and schemed for. For her part Louisa enjoyed the cocksucking she delivered. It pleased her to feel the minute ridges of Larry's cock slide over her lipsticked-covered lips, smearing the red colour around her face. Gently she nibbled the dick's skin with her teeth pulling the shaft this way and that. Her long nails forced open the little slit at the top of Larry's cock so that her tongue could tickle that most delicate of spots as she blew a soft warm breeze over his throbbing cock.

Louisa's hair fell forward as she sucked harder and harder, entangling itself around the hardened stem. The sensation that Larry felt could best be described as if someone was lashing his sensitised dick with a thousand velvety whips that

102

wrapped themselves around his shaft and were pulled oh so softly along its length in a sweetly teasing motion. He squirmed his ass cheeks into the cushion of the cheap chair in a vain attempt to free himself from Louisa's sucking mouth. As much as he squirmed and moaned and begged for relief, Larry sincerely hoped that such a rescue wouldn't be forthcoming. He needn't have worried. Nothing could have convinced Louisa to stop her sucking. Larry's ears pounded with the sucking noises of the girl on the screen being echoed by the guttural noises of Louisa devouring his cock. Somewhere deep inside he felt that if not stopped she would bite off his cock, such was the force of her fellatio.

Louisa had entered the state that only good, true cocksuckers know. It resembles a sheer blindness to anything other than the dick on which the mouth is focused. It is almost as if to stop sucking would be to lose a source of vital oxygen, like a deep-sea diver robbed of his air hose by an attacking shark. Larry's squirming only deepened her trance as her saliva trickled down his cock and onto her rapidly vibrating hand. In concert her hands worked with her mouth, alternating pressure on different parts of his shaft. Hard here – softer there – pinch at that spot – bite the skin – blow underneath the head – a finger there – just a little lower – use the tongue all the way up the shaft – separate the cocklips – taste the juices – get drunk on cock – dive deeper – deeper – drown – drown – down – down …

Thoughts randomly entered Louisa's pounding head like some bizzare commentary. Larry, for his part, was experiencing the effects of a continual orgasm. It had started minutes ago and would not quit. It would not reach climax. The orgasm just rolled through his body, racking every nerve. He desperately wanted it to end. Blackness threatened to claim him when Louisa took her lips from his cock and stuffed his balls into her mouth whilst violently jerking his cock with her hands. She chewed on the swollen glands with delicious nibbling bites that she was careful to direct occasionally at the really sensitive part of the balls right adjacent to the anus. Larry's head fell backwards as he fainted, completely oblivious to the stream of come that shot

103

skywards and splattered on the movie screen at poetically the same moment that the guy in the film shot his wad right into the girl's face.

Larry was out cold, cock flopping in the breeze as Louisa turned to Basil. He was sweating profusely having had a ring side seat at Louisa's cocksucking demonstration. Throughout the bout he had been guzzling down rum and coke, hardly believing his eyes. He had no idea that the drug worked so well. He promised himself that he'd buy more. If only he'd known that the drug was just a small part of the reason why Louisa was acting so wantonly. The major reason was that sex was just Louisa's way to beat men at their own game. She knew the Regulars wouldn't remember anything of this in the morning – so why not have fun?

'Okay Basil – take out that dick of yours.'

'Oh yes, Louisa.' Basil slurred his words so that they were unintelligible over the soundtrack of the movie and the snoring of Fred and Larry. Basil felt somewhat cheated that none of his friends would get to see his moment of triumph, but he comforted himself with the knowledge that it was their loss.

Louisa positioned herself between Basil's legs and turned to face the screen. The girl was now being fucked from the rear by what resembled a Norse god of old. Not a bad idea, thought Louisa who immediately hiked up her short white mini skirt and pulled down her tan tights and lacy panties to reveal a plump set of pouting pussy lips to the waiting Basil. Even in the darkness he could make out the tender nature of Louisa's sex – or was it just that her odour created that impression for him? The senses can be deceptive at moments like these.

'Ohh – hhh – hhmm.' There was no deception in the feel of an almost juicy cunt forcibly sliding its way down the length of a waiting cock. Not fully moist, Louisa's pussy gripped Basil's cock in a vice like grip. The sensation was not quite painful to Basil who enjoyed the rapid transition to the feel of a velvety skin tight glove that Louisa's pussy underwent as she flexed her ass up and down on his lap. Gripping the chair in front of her with her hands, Louisa rocked backwards and forwards, her tights and panties around her knees — her dress hiked above her waist — revealing to Basil the delectable sight of her creamy ass shuddering under the light of the movie as she squatted on his cock.

'Basil — you're a fucking bastard,' hissed Louisa through gritted teeth as she bit on the chair in front of her to stop herself from screaming. Basil's dick was large in girth, if not in length, and so as Louisa sat back fully it forced her cunt lips wide as the engorged dick penetrated until it seemed to be filling her throat. Louisa was definitely enjoying this fuck. Just like the girl on the screen she was lost to the lust of the moment, and so, it seems, was Basil who began to retch from the copious amounts of alcohol he'd consumed and the violence with which his body was being pounded. Luckily he had the manners not to spew up all over Louisa's pumping ass, but instead turned his head sideways and sprayed all over the sleeping Fred. In testimony to the drinks that had levelled him, Fred remained in a completely zombie-like state, totally oblivious to the vomit that covered his sleeping form.

So lost in her fucking gyrations, Louisa had no idea that this disgusting scene was transpiring behind her jiggling ass. She thought the gasping for breath sounds were simply moans of ecstacy and Basil's frantic tapping on her back were just his inducements to pump harder. She had no idea he wanted to quit. And even if she had have known of his plight, she probably wouldn't have let him go.

It was time to bring herself off, she reasoned. Reaching underneath her dripping cunt she grabbed for Basil's balls and pulled them up and around her cunt. Rubbing the sacks against her clitoris she kept trying to bounce up and down pulling the testicles almost to what Basil felt like was their breaking point. The ripe little globes felt exquisite against Louisa's erect clit as they bounced across its sensitive profile. Louisa pinched her clitoris with Basil's balls and rapidly frigged herself to orgasm like some desperate schoolboy jacking off behind the girl's changing rooms.

As she came Louisa bit through the vinyl of the chair in front of her and tore at the foam-rubber lining. The taste was vile, but of little discomfort compared to the intensity with which her pussy shook her whole body. Basil too had managed to come, although the pain from having his balls squeezed had caused him to black out just before coming and just after having been sick, this time all over Larry's zombie-like form.

It was a real mess in the theatre, much more so than on the screen, which just goes to prove that real life can be a hell of a lot more bizarre than fantasy, reflected Louisa as she stepped carefully over the three spew-covered, zombied Regulars. Pausing briefly to make herself look presentable, Louisa stopped by the bathroom to freshen up. It was while she was adding the finishing touch of red lipstick to her aching mouth that she was struck with a flash of brilliance that would ensure the complicity of Basil, Larry and Fred. It was doubtful that any one of them would remember the events of the evening, thinking that it was all part of the movie, but just in case Louisa wanted a little blackmail insurance.

It took but a few moments to purchase the necessary objects from the bored cashier and tip toe into the theatre where the movie's credits were rolling, and the Regulars were still out cold. Luckily, the blow-up sheep wasn't too big so Louisa was able to inflate it rather quickly and position it on Larry's floppy cock. Careful not to get Basil's vomit over her just cleansed hands, she then placed Basil's hand on Fred's cock and Fred's hand on Basil's thoroughly beaten peter. Using the handy-dandy instant camera she'd just bought from the porno theatre's Marital Aids department she snapped off a whole roll of pictures as glossy reminders of the event, should they ever be needed.

Laughing to herself, Louisa used the lobby phone to call a cab and then to place one more call. A sleepy male voice answered the phone. Louisa wasted no time on small talk.

'I'll be there in a few minutes. I want to have sex.'

Basil's drug was just starting to take effect. Louisa was in the mood to fuck all night long.

The last few hours had simply been foreplay.

7

Beer Buster

Mix

1½ oz. 100 Proof Vodka
Ice-Cold Beer
2 dashes Tabasco Sauce

Put Vodka in highball glass and fill with beer.
Add Tabasco and stir lightly.

'*A*nd he pumped a couple of times then he thrust it right up the middle at his tight end to score ...'

'Beautiful ball handling ...'

'That's what I call a muffed punt ...'

'But did you see the way he dived on that muff..?'

'That's the longest hang time I've seen so far ...'

To the casual observer catching but a mere snippet of the television commentary surrounding the average American football game, the mistaken impression that something vaguely sexual was going on could be easily be conveyed. Even the names of some of the teams – the Rams, the Redskins, the Packers – all have a slight sexual innuendo that isn't lost on some of the game's afficionados. And on the nights when national television is dominated by the weekly Monday night football game, every bar in America is crowded with fans rooting for their teams, and the real die-hards who are willing to do a little post game rooting of another kind.

And at the Pumping Station much Monday night rooting of both kinds goes on. So much so that Monday night football was unofficially renamed Monday Night Fuckball by those lucky enough to be in the know. And this Monday's game was a special one. The local favourites, the San Francisco 49ers were playing the much hated Los Angeles Raiders. The Pump was crowded and blood was running high. All of the wait-resses were on duty. The bar was hot, sweaty and full of the excitement that can only come when four hours of football are mixed with numerous cheap drinks, fan loyalty and extremely gorgeous cocktail waitresses.

'That guy over there just offered me fifty dollars to give him a hand job.' Kerry seemed a little shocked.

'Which one?' Annie was more than mildy curious.

After pointing the rather large gent in the 49er sweatshirt out to Annie, Kerry felt a little safer for what she thought was Annie's offer of protection.

'Don't worry – I'll take care of him.'

Annie disappeared into the crowd – only her bobbing drinks tray held high above her head told her of her progress through the crush. Kerry thought that maybe Annie was going to spill a glass of iced water all over his crotch, or something equally lust-dampening. After her last few experiences Kerry had become a little bit paranoid at the Pump. Everywhere she turned someone seemed to be trying to fuck her, but there was little time right now to dwell on her past misfortunes as drink order after drink order came deluging in from hundreds of thirsty, noisy, randy and drunk football fans. The special of the evening was a particularly obnoxious concoction known as a beer buster – for just $1 hundreds of them were being consumed in short order.

'Eight beer busters.' Hazel muscled her way to the serving station and made small talk with Kerry whilst waiting for her order.

'It's going to be wild in here when this game gets over.'

'It seems pretty active right now.'

'Oh no – I don't mean the crowd and the noise. I guess somebody should warn you. You don't know, do you?

'What?' Kerry was still suspicious of Hazel after her uninvited advances.

'Well it's like this – you see most people in here have bets of one kind or another going. They're making them all the time – and not just for money. The drunker they get the wilder the bets. You see that table of four guys over there – they're not bad looking, but they just bet that booth of girls – who happen to be Raider fans and aren't that good-looking, well, the one in the corner has a nice pair of tits – well, those guys bet those girls that they'd be their slaves for the evening if the Niners lost.'

'And if the Niners win?'

'The girls have to be the guys' slaves. Anyway, it'll be a wild time at the Pump tonight. So watch yourself – and don't take any sucker bets.'

Hazel used her tits as battering rams to clear a path through the crowd. Kerry followed behind with her drink order. She made a mental note to thank Annie for taking care of the rude fat guy. As the crowd parted Kerry caught sight of Annie rapidly wiping off the guy's lap with a towel. Kerry smiled. Annie had probably spilled a drink all over him. Then the crowd closed again, and Kerry didn't see the guy hand Annie a fifty dollar bill and smile his thanks for a great hand job.

Louisa was not in the best of moods because she was extremely tired having been up all night and most of the day fucking. She was sore in just about every possible place that one who has tried to experiment in one evening with every conceivable position in the *Kama Sutra* could be. Her only consolation was the way Basil, Fred and Larry were sitting apart from each other doing their respective bests to be as manly as possible. Each time one of them caught the other's eye, their gazes were quickly averted and Lester's repeated questions went ignored.

'So what did happen last night, Louisa?'

'Fuck off and die, Lester.'

'That good, uh?'

'No, it was boring. I didn't look anything like the girl in the movie and these guys all passed out – so I got a cab and went home. What they did after I left you'll have to ask them.'

'They ain't speaking – even to each other.'

'Well, don't keep bothering me – now get me my fucking drink order.'

'Yes, ma'am.' Lester was at his subservient best. He was determined to uncover the truth – by hook or by crook.

It had been a bit of a boring first half. Mostly a defensive battle with the Niners leading the Raiders 7-3. While an equally boring half-time display of high school marching bands dominated the television, punctuated by telling commentary by the football experts, there erupted a huge cheer from the Passion Pit. Suddenly, the whole room seemed to pivot and surround the secluded corner. Hazel who was caught in the middle of the crush had no choice but to use her natural assets to force her way to the front of the crowd. She was greeted by the degrading sight of two women engaged in a wrestling match. The crowd was cheering, there was much screaming from the fighting women, and the more enterprising punters were placing bets on the likely outcome.

The one woman who seemed to be getting the worst of the action was petite and dressed in a business suit. She was probably an office worker who had stopped in for a drink with some friends after work and had got caught in the football crowd. The other combatant was a hefty chick wearing a Raider tee shirt, scraggly bell bottom jeans and army boots. The term 'motorcycle mama' would not have been out of place at all in describing the heavy marauding female.

She had used her weight to pinion the smaller woman underneath her and was tearing at her blouse. A huge cheer erupted from the male portion of the audience as the smaller woman's bra was torn asunder and her breasts were exposed. As small as the woman was, her tits were equally tiny, almost like prepubescent teenage girl's budding boobs. The crowd hooted as the big woman slapped the little woman's breasts. The slapping sound she made as she hit the little titties was rudely indecent. The big woman's friends were screaming 'Kill her Marge,' whilst the smaller woman's friends were asking someone – anyone – to get help. Large Marge, as it turned out she was known, had turned the little woman now face down and was twisting her long ponytail around and around in an attempt to simultaneously twist off her head and grind it into the cushions of the Passion Pit. Another huge cheer erupted as in her struggles to try and free herself, the little woman whose name it turned out was Janet Hodges, caused her business-suit skirt to rip, revealing a deliciously small pantyhose covered bottom. The tights were all-in-one designer type – both tights and panties in one garment, cut

112

quite demurely to simulate high french-cut underwear and sheer tights in a lovely charcoal grey. Perfect for the office, Hazel thought. Large Marge didn't seem too impressed with them as she pulled back Janet's head by her blonde ponytail and proceeded to slap the smaller woman's charcoal nylon covered bottom with fat stubby hands.

Through the crush of roaring spectators Hazel could see Don Palumba and Bob Vest trying to force their way through to put a stop to the surprise entertainment that the drunken crowd was enjoying so. It was then that she acted, feeling a sudden maternally protective instinct for the petite Janet. The sight of those small tits and that taut bottom also had something to do with her heroic response. Hazel gave Marge an almighty push with all the strength that her not-too-small upper body could muster. Precariously poised on top of the smaller woman, Large Marge topped backwards and to the cheers of the crowd lodged herself between the couches of the Passion Pit. Like some huge beast stranded on its back, her legs waved in the air and her arms fought for leverage. Marge's friends advanced menacingly towards Hazel who was busy helping the distraught Janet to her feet. Bob and Don arrived just in time.

'What the hell is going on here?'

Approximately thirty-five people all spoke at once.

'All right – all right,' Don held up his hands, 'go back to your drinks. The game is about to start.'

Chuckling to itself the crowd turned to face the huge television screen as the ball was kicked high into the air to start the second half. The half-time fight seemed but a distant memory to most of the crowd as its cheers, jeers and bets now turned to the usual subject of Monday night's entertainment.

'Now what's the story here?'

Again everyone started talking at once. Don held up his hands and turned to Hazel.

'Hazel – what was going on? – And everyone else shut up.'

'I don't know what started it, but the big woman was beating up the little one, so I stopped the big bruiser from doing any serious damage.'

'O.K.' Don turned to the Raider fans and zeroed in on Marge. 'Why were you beating up this woman? She could have hardly been picking on you, could she?'

'She called Barney a fag.' Marge spoke with a deep gravelly voice. Barney was a short, fat, beady eyed little man dressed identically to Marge except that his Raider tee shirt was partially covered by a black leather waistcoat. Barney nodded along with the rest of the group. 'That's right – she called me a fag.' Barney spoke with a high-pitched whine. He was no doubt a truly sensitive man of the nineties.

'What's your story?' Don turned to the sobbing Janet who Hazel was holding quite protectively.

'I just turned to them and asked if they had a fag. I'd just run out and couldn't force my way through the crowd to the bar so I thought I'd ask them.' Sob.

Janet spoke with a thoroughly prim English accent of the kind that Audrey Hepburn had made famous. Hazel held the quivering woman closer to her.

'A fag?' Don was a little confused.

'Yeah, see – she admits she called Barney a queer.' Marge loomed forward, threatening once more.

'Perhaps I can help.' It was one of Janet's friends. 'Janet is over here on business from England where the term "fag" is used to mean a cigarette. It was all a simple misunderstanding that these people seem to have overreacted to.'

'How would you like to have your old man called a fag?'

'I don't have an "old man", thank you very much.'

The situation was about to turn hostile again, when Don acted like a manager.

'Hazel – take this lady upstairs to the changing rooms and see that she gets any attention she needs. Now as far as you lot are concerned, if you so much as step out of line the rest of the evening I'll call the police and have you thrown in jail. Just calm down and don't say another word. Even if someone calls your mother a bull-dyke. Got it?'

Hazel shepherded Janet away whilst Marge, Barney and the rest of their Raider fan cohorts sat down and grumped to each other.

114

Upstairs in the Pump's changing rooms Hazel tended to Janet's wounds. With a damp cloth she dabbed away the smeared make-up from the petite Englishwoman's sobbing face. Carefully Hazel soothed the scratches on Janet's body. Starting first at the neck, she softly, tentatively, apprehensively worked down the distraught woman's chest until her hands were making ever increasing circles of soothing strokes.

Janet did not resist. Her tear-stained eyes looked up into Hazel's, and without much ceremony the two women kissed. Not an intensely passionate kiss, but more an expression of willingness to succumb to each other's desires.

'Let me just lock the door.'

Janet sobbed. From downstairs the television commentary on the game reminded her of her recent experience. There was no way of shutting it out. The cheers, the shouts, the screams — even though they were for the twenty-two modern-day gladiators doing battle for football superiority — reminded her of the crowd's reaction to her own battle. How they cheered when her small breasts had been stripped bare. How they encouraged the fat woman to slap her bottom. How humiliating. Again she started to cry. Huge heavy sobs as the dam inside her broke.

'There, there — let it all out.'

Hazel stood naked in front of the sobbing Janet. Hazel had shed her waitress uniform silently and quickly. Compared to the petiteness of Janet, Hazel seemed grotesquely large. Everything about Hazel was magnified by the smallness of Janet, but the Englishwoman was not afraid. She sensed Hazel's desires and was secretly warmed that they matched her own. Janet's teary eyes stared at the huge heaving milky white breasts and the large dark circles surrounding the reddening nipples that were now just inches away from her face. Quickly she buried her sobbing frame amidst the soft flesh. They were so warm and comforting. Hazel's tits enclosed the small woman's head, muffling the sounds of the bar below. Releasing all of the hurt she felt, she sobbed hard against Hazel's tits, her torrential tears gradually dripping down Hazel's belly to finally rest amidst her furry black bush. Like a field covered with morning dew, Hazel's tear-soaked pubic hair glistened under the fluorescent lights of the Pump's changing room.

'AND THE BALL IS ON THE FIFTEEN YARD LINE OF THE NINERS – THE RAIDERS ARE THREATENING WITH A FIRST DOWN – LINING UP WITH FOUR WIDE OUTS – THE BALL IS SNAPPED – THEY GO WITH ALLEN WHO TAKES IT UP THE MIDDLE.'

Doing her best to shut out the din of the football commentary Janet pulled her face out of Hazel's massive breasts and looked into the cocktail waitress's eyes. She reached up and kissed her once more. This time it was a passionate kiss, as if somewhere inside her body she had decided to channel the hurt she felt into lust rather than tears. Slipping her arms from around Hazel's neck she dropped to her bruised knees and stared at the tear-soaked black bush. Breathing heavily she watched her tear drops trickle down through the mass of Hazel's dark pubic hair. Once there, the tears rested briefly and then made their way to the collection of hairs curled together below Hazel's cunt lips. At this resting place the tears gathered into a large spherical drop, until a sufficiently big enough ball was formed to force itself free from the pubic nest and fall to the tiled floor, splashing into a pool right between Hazel's spread legs and Janet's bruised knees.

'IT'S THIRD AND LONG FOR THE RAIDERS AS THE NINERS STAND FIRM ON THEIR OWN TWELVE-YARD LINE. SCHROEDER DROPS BACK AND PUMPS – THE NINERS PUT THE BLITZ ON . . .'

Janet slid her tongue out of her mouth like a lizard sensing for a juicy insect. With her eyes closed, she leaned forward until her tongue met the curl of Hazel's pubic hairs where the tear drops were forming. She tasted her own salty emissions, which as she licked them to her, mingled with Hazel's cunt juice. Janet's tongue darted over the cocktail waitress's pulsing little button flicking the swollen clit to and fro. The big woman's legs shuddered and slapped against Janet's tiny breasts. To stop herself from falling Hazel gripped the Englishwoman's head and steadied herself by grinding Janet's head into her steaming black bush. Janet responded by attaching her lips to Hazel's clitoris and sucking for all she was worth – as if Hazel's clitoris was a small cock – Janet sucked, trying hard to force the miniature dick to shoot forth its hidden load. Hazel moaned and gripped Janet's body tightly with her legs. Janet reached around and grabbed Hazel's ass with her small hands and dug her nails deep into the fleshy cheeks.

'IT LOOKS LIKE A FUMBLE ON THE GOAL-LINE. JACKSON WAS GOING OVER THE TOP WHEN HE WAS HIT HARD BY LOTT. THE BALL POPPED OUT AND IT'S ANYBODY'S GUESS WHO HAS IT. THE OFFICIALS ARE TRYING TO SEPARATE THE PLAYERS TO FIND WHO HAS GOT THE PIGSKIN. IT'S THE NINERS BALL – THE NINERS HAVE RECOVERED ON THEIR OWN ONE-YARD LINE. WHAT A GOAL-LINE STAND!'

Hazel was lying on the floor on top of Janet. The larger woman toppled forward as she came, folding over the kneeling petiteness of Janet. Underneath the much larger writhing form of Hazel, Janet kept on licking – not as hard as before – but with more of a probing motion. With Hazel now fully moist it was a simple matter for Janet to slide her nimble tongue fully inside the big woman's cunt, tasting the dripping muskiness at its source. In gyrating circles she moved her tongue around the pulsing walls of Hazel's cunt, producing wave after wave of orgasmic delight. Purposefully she took the largest of her small fingers and slid it straight up Hazel's quivering bottom. The effect was electric. As if a shock was reverberating through her body Hazel bucked and writhed, desperate in all of her actions not to end the intense feeling that consumed her. Janet could feel with her tongue her finger probing up Hazel's ass – she could feel it move through the skin against her tongue as she licked inside the heaving woman's cunt. Finger touched tongue through a thin membrane of skin separating one orifice from another. Like opposite poles of a magnet they attracted each other, performing a magic dance of intimacy inside Hazel's body. With an almighty shove Janet forced her finger deeper and withdrew her tongue, careful to suck on Hazel's clitoris as she withdrew. Hazel arched her back skyward and screamed a banshee wail of orgasmic release. Exhausted, she flopped down on the cold tile of the floor, breasts oozing to the sides of her heaving body.

'TOUCHDOWN – TOUCHDOWN – MONTANA TO RICE – DEEP IN HIS OWN ENDZONE HE FIRED A ROCKET OF A PASS STRAIGHT UP THE MIDDLE TO RICE WHO WAS RUNNING A CROSSING PATTERN. RICE BEAT OFF TWO DEFENDERS AND WAS THEN CLEARED TO THE RAIDER'S END-ZONE BY SOME UNSELFISH BLOCKING BY FELLOW WIDE RECEIVER JOHN TAYLOR. A 99 YARD TOUCHDOWN PASS AND RUN. THE NINERS LEAD IT 14-3 WITH JUST FIVE MINUTES LEFT TO PLAY.'

Hazel's blurred vision cleared to see Janet sitting demurely on the changing room bench facing her with her legs primly touching together, uncrossed. Crawling on her hands and knees, Hazel's big pendulous breasts swung like a cow's udders to and fro as she advanced to the waiting Janet. There she sat in her torn dress and laddered tights, small breasts peeking invitingly through the shreds of her blouse, delicate skin marred by the scratches and bruises inflicted by Large Marge. Janet looked nothing if not appealing.

Hazel inched her way up Janet's charcoal grey nylon-covered thighs. Parting them gently she traced the run of a ladder all the way from the knee, past the thigh to the re-inforced darker material that barely covered Janet's pussy. In the fight the crotch of the pantyhose had been ripped through, providing a very convenient access hole for Hazel's probing tongue. Briefly, Hazel caught sight of wispy blonde hairs between Janet's legs that exactly matched the blonde of her ponytail. She inched forward on the bench and placed her legs over Hazel's shoulders, forcing her swollen cunt right into Hazel's face. Hazel was anesthetised by the scent of sex between Janet's legs. She forced her face and her protruding tongue further into Janet's golden bush. It was as if Janet's petite form was supported solely by the flicking naughtiness of Hazel's plump tongue. Janet was already soaked between her thighs. The nylon pantyhose was sodden with the

Englishwoman's odour. It clung to Hazel's face rubbing the small woman's juices deeper and deeper into Hazel's skin. As rapidly as she licked, Hazel could not keep up with the torrent of emissions that came from Janet's cunt. It was not a stream nor a trickle but more of a swollen river of lust that poured forth from the broken banks of her womb. Hazel gasped for air but had her face forced back into Janet's crotch by the small woman's insistent hands and a pleadingly polite insistence to 'don't stop – please – please – don't stop – keep eating me – don't stop.' Hazel would have gladly smothered herself, such was the intoxicating sound that Janet's prim little voice with its very proper English accent produced.

'THE RAIDERS NEEDING TWO TOUCHDOWNS ARE THROWING CAUTION TO THE WIND. DROPPING BACK IN THE FACE OF A 49er BLITZ, SCHROEDER AIRS A BIG ONE OUT DEEP. AND ... AND ... IT'S INTERCEPTED BY RONNIE LOTT WHO RETURNS IT TO THE RAIDER FORTY-YARD LINE WHERE MONTANA AND CO. WILL TAKE OVER. WITH THE TWO MINUTE WARNING JUST A FEW SECONDS AWAY THAT SURELY MUST BE IT FOR THE RAIDERS.'

Hazel thought her head would pop, so tightly did Janet grip her as the petite woman shook to the throes of a momentous orgasm. It was not one of those simple releases of pent-up emotion but a continuously rising crescendo of desire bursting higher and higher with every little ripple of Hazel's tongue on Janet's engorged clitoris. Finally, Janet slumped forward, exhausted, her ponytail tickling the sweaty back of an equally drained Hazel.

'Stay here and rest – I'll be back later once I've finished my shift. You'll be all right in here, I'll lock the door, and since I'm first off there will be no one up here until I get off,' Hazel apologised as she rapidly donned her waitress uniform so she could help Annie, Louisa and Kerry to cope with the rush of drink orders that would deluge the bar now that the game was almost over. Janet nodded sleepily and tucked her clothes into a pillow and curled up on the changing room bench.

'I'll be back soon and we can take a shower together,' Hazel kissed the dozing Janet on the lips and left the room to assume her waitress duties. As Janet was drifting in and out of the waking world, she couldn't but help hear the last few gasps of the commentary that had punctuated her and Hazel's lovemaking.

'THAT'S IT – IT'S ALL OVER – MONTANA SIMPLY DOWNS THE BALL AND THE CLOCK RUNS OUT – THE NINERS HAVE BEATEN THE RAIDERS 14-3 IN AN AWESOME DISPLAY OF DEFENSIVE POWER AND OFFENSIVE SUBTLETY . . .'

The words drifted in and out of Janet's brain as some wakening part of her consciousness concluded what a strange country America was, and what an even stranger game was American football. She had come to this bar in the hope that she'd meet some big American woman to service her needs, and that strategy had seemed to backfire with Large Marge's aggression. But Hazel had come to the rescue in more ways than one. It had been ages since she'd left her lover in England, and Janet was thoroughly tired of fucking American men. Now that she had a special friend in America the rest of her stay wouldn't be so bad. As she dozed she knew she would always have a fondness for Monday Night Fuckball at the Pumping Station, Silicon Valley, California.

And so too would Bob Vest later that night when he got home and watched the video disc of Hazel's and Janet's escapades in the changing room. He'd set the 'security system' to record thinking that Hazel looked altogether too protective of the smaller woman. He knew Hazel's predatory instincts well. It was too bad he didn't have a camera in the shower because Hazel and Janet were in there for a real long time, and Janet did some truly amazing things with the hard sponge . . .

8

Screwdriver

Mix

1½ oz. Vodka
5 oz. Orange Juice (preferably fresh)

*Pour into highball glass over ice cubes
and stir well.*

*T*here was something vaguely familiar about the Oriental gentleman seated at the fireplace. He was conversing animatedly with the prim-looking woman in the business suit. His mannerisms, his clothes, his proper accent, his build: it was all too unsettling. He and the woman had been sitting there for about five minutes, and Kerry really should have gotten their drink order, but for some unfathomable reason she felt apprehensive. Kerry couldn't put her finger on what exactly was troubling her but she had that uncanny feeling that she and this mysterious Oriental had met somewhere, sometime.

Putting her professional concerns above her personal worries, Kerry approached the couple.

'Good evening. Would either of you care for a cocktail?'

'Ah, Kerry – how are you tonight?'

He did know her – but from where? Kerry thought fast – better play along with him in case he tipped her well in the past. Good-tipping customers hate to be forgotten – why else do they tip so well?

'I'm fine, thank you – and you?'

Kerry did her best to act friendly, but she thought it would be stretching things to ask if he wanted his 'usual.'

'I think we'll have a bottle of – hmmm – shall we say a nice California Chardonnay. Something a little dry. You choose – you did such a good job the other night, under such difficult circumstances, too.'

Kerry smiled and offered her thanks for the compliment

whilst beating a hasty retreat to the bar to place her order. It was then that Hazel returned from her dinner break. Kerry thought she'd ask Hazel if she recognised the mild-mannered gent.

'You see the couple by the fireplace – do you know that guy? He seems to know me, but I don't ...?'

Hazel stared for a few moments while her eyes adjusted to the darkness of the bar. With a yell of surprise and pleasure, Hazel interrupted Kerry's musings and ran over to the couple. This further flustered the already confused Kerry to the point where she was about to swear off alcohol for good. Since starting work at the Pump, Kerry had been drinking much more than she usually would. Large amounts of booze were supposed to destroy brain cells and make a person forget things. Perhaps her inability to recognise the Oriental gentleman was a by-product of one too many shot glasses of tequila?

'Janet – how are you? What a surprise – I didn't expect to see you here. You're looking so good.'

After a more than friendly hug Janet began the introductions just as Kerry arrived with the wine.

'How nice to see you Hazel. I really must thank you for the other evening. You were quite the heroine. I don't know what I would have done without you. But forgive me, let me introduce you to my boss – Mr Yu. Mr Yu, this is a new friend of mine, Hazel.'

Phuc Yu took Hazel's hand and kissed the top of it very gently.

'I am charmed to make your acquaintance, Miss Hazel. A friend of Janet's is always welcome. Would you care to join us?'

'I'd love to, but I'm working right now. Perhaps when I get off in about an hour?'

'Oh yes – please do,' invited Janet.

'Your wine, sir.'

'Oh – Kerry, I'd like you to meet some friends of mine. This is Janet and this is Mr Yu.'

'We've already met.' Kerry didn't sound too convincing. She was still trying to put the pieces together. 'Yu,' – that name did sound awfully familiar.

'Oh – well – I'll be back shortly. Enjoy your wine.' Hazel bid her adieus and made a round of the lounge looking for drink orders. Kerry poured two glasses of wine while Mr Yu and Janet went back to their lively discussion about first options, lease versus buy and Eurodollars versus Yen leverages. As Kerry straightened to leave, Mr Yu handed her his credit card.

'Please run a tab for me?'

'Certainly Mr Yu.'

It was as she ran his credit card through the computer reader that she remembered where she'd met him before. He was one of the Koreans that had been in on that Sunday that she'd been called in after getting almost no sleep, and Annie had no help and to top it off she'd knocked herself unconscious on the damn dumpster. No wonder she didn't remember him. Slowly it came back to her. He was the big boss and he'd tipped her really well. How could she have forgotten? She made a mental note to go and see the doctor about that bump on the head. To think the things it could make her forget.

On her next round she made a point of checking that everything was well with Mr Yu and his guest and made an extra special point of thanking him for remembering her humble service on Sunday. Ever the gracious dignitary, Mr Yu was quick to direct his thanks to Kerry. 'The pleasure was all mine.'

Indeed it was.

Hazel joined Phuc and Janet just in time to help drain the second bottle of wine.

'What shall we have now, ladies?'

'Would you like another bottle of wine? That particular vintage is remarkable good for a Californian, don't you think?' Kerry was doing her best to be the model cocktail waitress in the hope of receiving yet another big tip.

'Yes it is, but I'm in the mood for something a little, a little . . .' Janet was searching for the right word.

'Harder, perhaps?' Mr Yu had found it.

There followed much tittering until Hazel regained composure and ordered for everyone.

'Let's have a round of screwdrivers – I think that would be appropriate, don't you?'

'Indeed.' Phuc Yu was positively brimming as he stared at Hazel's mammoth mammaries shaking and jiggling seemingly uncontrollably as she laughed to the extremely gay banter bouncing back and forth.

'And make them doubles,' specified Mr Yu authoritatively. There were no prizes for guessing where the inspiration for that order came from.

After several rounds of double screwdrivers and many more veiled innuendoes, the witching hour of two a.m. was rapidly approaching. It was time for last call. Phuc, Janet and Hazel were the last ones left in the Pumping Station.

'I'm afraid it's time for last call. Will there be anything else, Mr Yu?'

'I think we can manage one more round – doubles – again.'

'Certainly, Mr Yu.'

'And Kerry, Hazel tells me you are studying engineering.'

'That's right – this will be my final year at U.C. Berkeley. Electrical engineering and computer science are my specialities.'

'Ah – a fine school – a wise choice of subjects.'

'Yes – this is the place for it, Silicon Valley you know.'

'Quite. Please accept my card. I own several engineering companies and will soon be establishing myself here in Silicon Valley. Should you need employment, I would be most honoured to be your employer.'

'Why, thank you, Mr Yu. I'll get those drinks.'

Kerry didn't know what to think. Was he for real or was he just after her body? He certainly seemed like he was after Hazel's, and for that matter it seemed like he'd already had Janet's. Kerry didn't want to become just another notch on his dick. Then again, there was no harm in being nice to someone who might end up owning half the Valley. And so what if he was interested in more than her educational assets? After her first few nights' experiences at the Pump she had

126

confidence in her ability to handle almost any situation.

As Kerry was waiting for the drink orders to be filled, Hazel tumbled back from the bathroom.

'Say, Kerry, Phuc is having a big party in his penthouse suite at the Regency – tonight – right now. Seems he just signed some major deal and they'll be partying all night long. I'm sure he wouldn't mind if you came. Do you want to come? I'll ask him if you like?'

'No Hazel, but thanks. I'm pretty tired, and...'

'And but nothing. You'll never get another chance like this. Just think of the people you'll meet and Phuc already has offered you a job. You don't want to blow that.'

Kerry thought for a few moments.

'Well OK. Just for a short while, but I really mustn't stay long because I promised Bo ...somebody, that I'd be somewhere after work.'

'OK. I'll ask him.' Hazel disappeared back to the fireplace to join Janet and Phuc in a deep conversation. Kerry was thankful that Hazel was diplomatic enough not to let on that she'd noticed Kerry's mental slip in starting to mention Bob West's name. Bob was paranoid about people finding out about their relationship. He said it was bad for employee morale.

Kerry delivered the drinks and Mr Yu signed his credit card, giving Kerry a $200 tip which she graciously accepted.

'It has been a pleasure serving you.'

'The pleasure has been ours, and may we repay the compliment by inviting you to a small celebration I'm hosting at the penthouse suite of the Regency tonight.'

'Why, I'd be honoured, but it will be at least another forty-five minutes before I can get out of here.'

'That will be no problem. After the deal I signed today, how do you say in America, we'll be partying all night long, baby.' There were laughs all round.

'Well, I'll be there.'

'It will be my pleasure.'

Indeed it was.

Kerry was a little worried that she was dressed too casually for her debut at a high-tech-high-flyer party. She hadn't intended to go out this evening so she'd gone to work in her old sweater, leggings and cowboy boots. In the lift on the way up to the penthouse suite she'd taken the time to add a little make-up to accent her naturally pretty features. With a quick brush of her auburn hair she peered into the lift's shiny doors and gave herself a quick boost of confidence.

'You'll have to do, Kerry Farnum.'

She wasn't quite sure what to expect of this party, but she kept telling herself that she'd stay no more than half an hour, an hour, tops. Bob would be waiting for her. She paused at the door. It didn't sound too noisy, but she could hear a little laughter and what sounded like opera. She knocked on the door and waited. No one came – the laughter continued – an aria was reaching its climax. Again she knocked. Muffled through the sound of a very solid door she heard Mr Yu's unmistakable tones.

'Coming,' he said, his words followed by quite a bit of giggling.

Mr Yu opened the door, startling Kerry. She just wasn't prepared to see her host and prospective employer open the door with a glass of champagne in one hand, a towel in the other, dressed only in the shortest of Japanese silk robes.

'Ah, welcome Kerry. So glad you could join us. Have some champagne.'

He handed Kerry the glass which she took hesitantly. As he shut the door behind her and chained it shut she felt obliged to offer her apologies for disturbing him. It appeared as if he were ready for bed.

'I'm sorry if I'm late, or if I'm disturbing you, but . . .'

'Not at all. We were just taking a jacuzzi and admiring the view of my prospective kingdom. Won't you join us?'

'Oh – I don't have a bathing suit with me.'

'Not to worry. We can accommodate you.'

What that exactly meant caused Kerry no small concern as she followed the Korean into the suite. Her concern was amplified by a brief flutter of Mr Yu's light silk robe as he turned to lead her to the jacuzzi. She hoped it was his leg that she caught a glimpse of. It had to be his leg. No one

.s a willy that big, she kept telling herself as she followed
1 into the splendour of the suite.

'Wow!' Immediately that she had uttered the superfluous
perlative, Kerry felt slightly stupid. In her defence, even
e most experienced of commentators or jaded of travellers
ould have been at a loss for words when confronted with
e sight of the Regency penthouse suite.

The room was mostly dark except for the ambient lights
the Valley and a few well-placed candles. Some tragic
alian opera reverberated around the room. Floor-to-ceiling
indows over twenty feet tall arched almost a full three
undred and sixty degrees around the suite revealing a
vinkling wonderland of lights that was the high-tech play-
ound of Silicon Valley. Far in the distance lay San
rancisco, with all of its diversity and perversity, shimmering
ke a far-off jewel. Kerry, like a small child peering hopefully
a toy store window at Christmas-time, walked to the centre
indow and pressed her hands and face to the glass.
lesmerised, she stared at everything, not really seeing
lything but a blur of sensory overload.

It was a loud splash heard somewhere between a lull in the
opranos agonising and the rising of the heart-stretching
rings of the orchestra that disturbed Kerry's silent musings.
uickly she turned around to see that the centre of the room
as occupied by a huge circular sunken jacuzzi barely
uminated by hanging candelabras. The impression was one
' Roman decadence. From her vantage point at the windows
ie could barely make out three smiling faces staring at her.

'It is rather breathtaking isn't it?' The voice was Janet's.
'I've lived here all my life – I never really realised how
eautiful ...'

'Yes – it is, isn't it?' This time it was Phuc Yu.

'Come on in, Kerry – the water's fine.' Hazel was
oullient.

Kerry advanced the jacuzzi sipping her champagne as she
ent. Her cowboy boots clicked sensually on the marble floor.

'Where shall I get changed?' Kerry felt bold about her
resence in the room and the prospect of entering the jacuzzi.
omewhere in the back of her mind she wondered where the

other guests were, but the sights and sounds surrounding he[r]
made all concerns pale in comparison.

'My dear, we have no bathing suits. We are naked und[er]
the water, but have no fear — in the cloak of darkness you[r]
modesty will be protected.'

'Oh, I'm not worried . . .'

Kerry couldn't believe her mouth. She didn't really wa[nt]
to take off her clothes in front of Phuc Yu, let alone Haz[el]
and her wandering hands and her friend Janet, but he[r]
inhibitions seemed so childish, so meaningless in the[se]
surroundings. A part of her brain kept yelling that Bob wa[s]
nowhere near to protect her, so be careful. Bob — Bob[,]
oh yes — she was supposed to see him this evening, but a[ll]
thoughts of her commitment to him seemed to fall away wit[h]
her panties as they dropped to the cool marble floor like [a]
falling leaf commemorating the end of summer. Witho[ut]
further ceremony she stepped naked into the hot bubbli[ng]
water.

'Indeed, quite beautiful.' Yu was deliberately ambiguou[s.]

'Yes — the view is overwhelming.' Kerry sat opposite Y[u]
and adjacent to Janet and Hazel. She shrank down in th[e]
water to cover her breasts from anyone's gaze. Kerry couldn[']
help but notice that Hazel's tits floated on the surface an[d]
were bounced around by the hot water jets. The sight of th[e]
milky white globes dancing like some drunken deep se[a]
creatures was repulsively hypnotic to Kerry. It was Janet wh[o]
broke the spell.

'More champagne, Kerry?'

'Oh — certainly.' Janet was standing intimately close [to]
Kerry as she poured the champagne. Their legs brushe[d.]
Kerry pretended not to notice the feeling of flesh on fles[h,]
skin on skin.

Phuc Yu began to pontificate.

'Kerry my dear, I must propose a toast. A toast to Silico[n]
Valley and its beauty. The beauty of the money to be ma[de]
here, and the beauty of its women.'

The clink of champagne glasses could hardly be heard ov[er]
the bubbling water and the opera.

'Mr Yu is too modest to brag, Kerry, but as of today h[e]

owns a vast portion of those lights. Although not yet public knowledge, Mr Yu has purchased Integrated Machines, Levity Software, All Purpose Electronics and Floppy Devices with options on four other companies. I think we should toast the new King of Silicon Valley – Phuc Yu.'

Janet and Hazel stood up to toast the Korean entrepreneur, so without thinking Kerry followed suit. What a sight greeted the Oriental. Three women of varying degrees of beauty, completely naked, standing before him holding champagne glasses erect in his honour. This is what I work so hard for, he told himself. Before him he could see the boyish small tits of his European assistant, the mammoth jugs (no other word would come to mind) of the plentiful American waitress and the pertness of the young Berkeley student's full breasts. And tantalisingly revealed by the varying level of the bubbling water he could see the silhouettes of their pubic mounds and their furry bushes outlined by the lights of his Valley and the flickering of the candles overhead.

Deep down below the water his huge cock stirred at the sight of these three eminently fuckable women toasting his achievements. As he stood to clink glasses with them his hardness broke forth from the water like some huge torpedo homing in on a defenceless ship. Kerry gasped at the sight of the monster not realising that she had taken the behemoth once inside her. The champagne dulled her sense of shock and heightened her curiosity. It was the largest cock she had ever seen. She began to wonder . . .

Little did she know that she already knew the answer.

And for his part, Phuc Yu had no idea that it was the delectable young student that he now desired so that he had pinioned behind the Pump's dumpster just a few days ago. He had slept heavily that night, waking late in the afternoon, the previous evening somewhat of a mystery. Even a cold and clammy used condom in his pocket didn't jog his alcohol- and sex-bashed memory into remembering the intimate details of the night before. And his Oriental reserve prevented him from asking the crude Mr Wize for the full story that the 'Ugly American' would no doubt readily convey, replete with grins, winks and nudges.

131

He had put the Sunday's escapades completely out of his mind and successfully closed the deals. And this – these three women – were his reward. It was time, Yu reasoned, for the special part of his celebration to begin. By now it should be ready.

'Please sit down, my lovelies. I have something special for you. Make yourselves comfortable amongst the bubbles. Let the hot water ooze over you.'

Down amongst the hot water, her body once more hidden by the bubbling foam, Kerry glanced at Hazel who looked at Janet who looked at both of them with an air of expectancy. Mr Yu reached behind the taps of the jacuzzi to a small cabinet and retrieved an urn from which a pale smoke gradually escaped.

'I have for you a special gift from the Far East. It is very expensive and available only to the most privileged. In my hour of triumph here, I wish to share it with you. Please accept this delicacy with my compliments.'

From the urn he retrieved four long-stemmed pipes and handed them to the three ladies, retaining one for himself.

'Please be careful not to get the pipe wet. We do not want the burning embers to be dampened. At your convenience please suck deeply on the pipe. Hold in the vapors. Let them permeate your very being. As the warmth flows through you, breath out. The pipe will last about thirty minutes, by which time we shall all be in a sensual heaven.'

Janet began inhaling right away. Hazel looked at Kerry, shrugged her shoulders and did likewise. Kerry looked up from the pipe to see Phuc staring at her as he consumed the pipe's contents. For a series of moments he did not break eye contact with her until he began to exhale. As he did so he closed his eyes and spoke as if residing in a far-off place.

'You have nothing to fear, my dear. Neither the pipe nor its contents will harm you. You will find a true peace – an ecstasy that you can never know through any other means. Please join me there.'

'What is it?'

'It is an extremely rare form of opium. It is quite mild and certainly not addictive at this dosage. It is farmed only in a remote area of Thailand known to my family and controlled by a small religious sect to which we belong. It's used on rare occasions to commemorate events of great importance. As I said before, do not worry – it is not addictive in small quantities, but I do warn you that you will experience pleasures that even your most personal of moments must pale in comparison to.'

Yu's warning served to excite and entice Kerry. She glanced around the jacuzzi. Both Janet and Hazel looked completely out of it. They had their arms around each other, gently stroking each other's skin and hair as the pipe's smoke permeated their brains. Their eyes were closed, yet they appeared to be looking at each other with a deeper vision.

Opium – the word bounced around Kerry's mind and rolled around her mouth, drooling out of her lips, forming an ideal receptacle for the pipe she held in her hand. Apprehensively, Kerry touched the pipe to her lips but did not inhale. The vapours rose through the pipe without her assistance, titillating her throat. In reaction she breathed deep, taking in a gulp of acrid smoke. It was not distasteful, but it was not truly pleasurable. Kerry had never been much of a dope smoker – only twice during high-school parties had she ever joined in. It had done nothing for her then, but this was not like that. The smoke stayed with her, bringing a peace that only the dead should have the pleasure of knowing. Time stood still. She never even remembered taking another drag of the pipe. Instead of inhaling air she felt as if she was breathing constantly the smoke – as if the air in the room had been replaced by the penetrating vapours.

The bubbles in the jacuzzi seemed to engulf her, encapsulating parts of her body, floating her above the jacuzzi and around the room. Her eyes perceived movement, like shadows in a darkened room that disappeared once looked at carefully. Her senses deceived her. She could not tell reality from the cotton-wool that seemed to surround her swimming brain.

She was sure that she stepped out of the jacuzzi at Yu's invitation, taking his outstretched hand, but she could not swear to it. She was sure that Janet and Hazel swamped her in extremely soft towels drying her sodden skin, but she could have been mistaken. She was sure that she enjoyed the feeling of their muffled hands rubbing dry her pert breasts, and she was sure she even parted her legs ever so slightly so that Janet could stroke her pussy to dry it from the waters of the jacuzzi just so her cunt could get wet again, this time from her own juices. But it could have been wishful thinking.

But it wasn't. The opium smoke, the champagne, the earlier cocktails and wine all mixed together in the bubbling cauldron of the jacuzzi, warmed by the lights of the Valley and stirred with four sexually charged bodies to create a potion guaranteed to conjure up an orgy of lustful excess.

After a festival of drying each other with large, soft and warm towels, Yu led the three women to a huge semi-circular bed that looked out over the sprawling lights below. With his outstretched hand he invited the women to lie down on the bed. Janet guided Kerry into the middle of the bed and motioned for Hazel to take up a position flanking Kerry. Surrounded by female flesh that had already begun to explore the intimate details of her throbbing sex, Kerry felt completely submissive, as if she was watching this orgy unfold from a distance. The swirling tones of the opera added to the illusion telling her hazy brain that this wasn't reality.

In unison both Hazel and Janet each took one of Kerry's breasts and began to lick the nipples with soft languorous strokes. It was as if Janet and Hazel divided Kerry's body down the middle like some gourmet delicacy and feasted on their respective portions. Hazel's and Janet's hands met on Kerry's pussy, providing the placid girl with ten rhythmically massaging fingers. Together, their fingers would pressure and squeeze Kerry's clit while occasionally a lone finger would slide softly inside her quim, teasing and coaxing her juices deep from within.

To Kerry this felt like an extremely randy and nasty dream. It was as if she was floating above the Valley on a passing cloud, being fucked by naughty angels who just happened to be Janet and Hazel. At the very edge of the cloud, right above what she thought was the Pumping Station, floated a huge and angry dick belonging to the leering Mr Yu. Phuc stroked his cock in eager anticipation. As if speaking in slow motion, like a tape recorder with failing batteries, Phuc Yu moved his lips and Kerry thought she heard him ask, 'Is she ready for my tool?'

Janet took her finger from Kerry's quivering pussy and licked the full length of her cunt juice coated finger. 'Hmmmm – she is ripe for the fucking.' Janet and Hazel reached out and took the club like cock of Mr Yu and guided it to Kerry's opening. For the second time in just a few days, the massive cockhead forced its way into Kerry's tight cunt. This time, Kerry did not struggle but gladly accepted the dick within her, sliding her body down its mammoth length and gently squirming as her juices melted around the dick's throbbing shaft. Yu rocked backwards and forwards while Hazel and Janet squeezed each one of his pendulous hanging balls, actually providing the thrusts that fucked Kerry into obliviousness.

Something inside Kerry told her not to be completely submissive. Her mouth sought Yu's lips but he resisted, preferring to see the three women kiss each other beneath him as he fucked the young cocktail waitress. Still, Hazel and Janet continued to fondle Kerry's breasts, pinching the tight little nipples into points for Yu to bite and snap at. In Kerry's mouth she could feel her own tongue being massaged by the enfolding tongues of Janet and Hazel. Lips encircled lips in an orgy of kissing, as Yu's gigantic cock threatened to burst through Kerry's ecstasy-racked body and join the entwined tongues to be sucked as well as fucked.

As Yu's massive cock cycled through its pendulous journey in and out of Kerry's come-drenched opening, her body was forced to and fro on the silky sheets of the huge bed. Janet and Hazel, surrounding the younger woman with their bodies, gripped Kerry's hips with their pubic mounds. As Yu fucked Kerry and she slid around, her hips rubbed the other women's cunts as she became an extension of Yu's gigantic dick. The effect he was having on the three women did not escape his all-seeing eyes. The high it gave him to feel the power of fucking three women at once – actually to be fucking them – using one as a giant dildo attached to his already massive dong – was a feeling of power even better than the charge he got from closing a deal.

In Yu's mind the two – business and sex – were almost identical. As he fucked Kerry, Janet and Hazel he glanced over his shoulder to see what he regarded as his domain, and he smiled a wicked grin. He had fucked the American companies with his ruthless competition, and now he fucked their women. Just as he had done some years ago in Europe in which Janet had become his personal assistant in charge of European operations, he wondered at what the future offered for the young engineering student in which his dick was readying to unleash its load of come. As he came Yu was thinking of all these things. Of the tight cunt in which he was squirting and his desire to possess the body and brain of its owner, just as he had taken control of the Valley's major companies.

Such complicated power trips were far from the minds of the women surrounding Yu's cock. As he arched his back in orgasm, Janet reached around and stroked the back of his balls with her finger, just below the anus. Yu emitted a small moan in perfect key with the rising opera music that was the orgy's unwitting soundtrack.

The throws of Yu's orgasm provided the catalyst that initiated Kerry's release. It began not in her pussy but in her breasts under the ministrations of Janet and Hazel's lips. Her nipples felt as if they were melting under the heat of the other women's breath. As the hot saliva of the two tit-suckers dripped down Kerry's boobs, she began to come. She was convinced her tits were showering out come like ornamental fountains into the faces of Janet and Hazel. As Janet stroked Yu's balls, Hazel slipped her hand between Kerry's pussy and Yu's thrusting pelvis. Adding her own pressure to that of Yu's body, Hazel inserted the final critical energy into Kerry's near-boiling cunt. In waves of rolling intensity Kerry was shocked by a feeling of total and unequivocal release. It was as if she had popped like a balloon with all her juices flowing out of every exploded opening.

Kerry's come-induced writhings sympathetically ignited first Hazel and then Janet. Kerry could feel their cunts oozing over her hips as they too joined in the communal climax. Together they bit hard on her tits as they released their pent-up tensions over Kerry's hips. In wanton lust, Hazel had begun to hump Kerry's hip, slowly at first and then violently, threatening to destroy the intimate coupling of the four bodies with her thrashing motions. Gasping for breath, lying on her side, Hazel's large tits slumped onto Kerry's and covered the smaller woman's body. The sight of such large breasts moving beneath him gave Yu further desires. He had barely finished coming inside Kerry as he withdrew his dick and began to direct the next phase of his celebratory fuck.

Yu gave the women little time to rest. In their drugged state they really didn't need much of anything other than direction. To the come-drenched Kerry, Janet and Hazel life seemed to be moving at half speed. The opera music slurred about the room – their words stumbled into incoherence – and their bodies felt like no effort was required to do anything. They were willing puppets of Yu's imagination and desires. He, being that much more used to the effects of the mild opium smoke, was definitely in control. There was no resistance or reluctance whatsoever from the women as Yu motioned for Hazel to take Kerry's position in the middle, and for Kerry to take Hazel's place.

Phuc Yu was already hard from looking at the awaiting sight of Hazel's huge tits falling to the side of her chest. Now there were a pair of tits worthy of his dick. On none of his travels, and certainly not in his homeland of Korea had he ever had a really delicious tit-fuck. Women had tried. He had tried. He'd even come a few times on several womens' tits, but it had never been as good as he'd imagined. Then he'd seen Hazel's breasts – he'd stared at them thinking how good it would be to wrap them around his meat and jack off into her face. And now he had the opportunity to do just that.

From the bedside table he retrieved a bottle of hand cream courtesy of the Regency Hotel. The women paid him little attention, satisfied enough to touch each other's bodies lazily in a slow dance of sexual patience. As Janet and Kerry made random finger motions on Hazel's boobs, Yu emptied the hand cream on to the tits. Quickly Kerry and Janet coated the expansive flesh with the slippery liquid. As if mounting one of his polo ponies. Yu leaped onto Hazel and straddled her waist with his legs. His throbbing boner slapped right between Hazel's tits and was caught between the globes as Kerry and Janet entrapped it between each tit by pushing the boob over and around Yu's dick, forming a cunt-like tunnel for him to fuck.

Yu let out his trademark moan. 'Hmmmm-mmmmm-mmmmm . . .'

Somewhere deep in Kerry's opium-laced brain that sound registered as having been heard before – somewhere – but there were more pressing matters to attend to. The brain said, 'later'. Kerry complied with her brain's request and concentrated on forcing Hazel's pliant flesh around Yu's hardness. Hazel's tit was doing its best to escape from Kerry's grasp, so she found it best to use two hands to ensure that the full length of Yu's cock was immersed in the soft warm tightness of milky white tit-flesh. Janet was doing the same, having the time of her life squeezing the adorably huge tit of Hazel's around her darling Mr Yu's dick. This fucking was a cornu-copia of minor sensations cascading into a massive overdose of sexual feelings. Every so often Janet's hand would graze Hazel's hardened nipple as she brushed against the delectable Kerry. Beneath the oozing breasts Janet and Kerry could feel the hard ridges of Yu's cock sliding back and forth, and Hazel's hips – somewhat larger than Kerry's, bumped into their pubic mounds after each thrust of Yu's dick with a firm and exciting slap.

Hazel could see the purple swollen head of Yu's dick forcing its way with each stroke through the compress of her tits. As it burst through the supple barrier of Hazel's tits, the dick's skin was pulled back causing its slit to open and slimy liquid to ooze out and trickle down to join the lubri-cating mess of sweat and hand cream. If Yu thrust as hard as he could Hazel was able to flick the sensitive purple head with her fat tongue driving Phuc Yu into convulsions. On a few thrusts Hazel was able to get her lips attached to Yu's dick head sucking on him like a vampire desperate for blood. To Phuc it was like being fucked and sucked at the same time.

This was everything that Yu imagined fucking the big tits of the American cocktail waitress would be. He decided very early on in this tit-fucking session that it was better than fucking cunts, for these tits were bigger than any cunt could ever be and just as tight as the tightest pussy he'd ever had. Under the urgent control of his helpmates Janet and Kerry, Hazel's tits gripped his full length like no cunt ever could. And it wasn't only his cock that was getting the full treatment. Under the pressure of his weight, Yu's balls were being squeezed against Hazel's stomach and subsequently between her tits, giving the bucking Korean the sensation that his gonads were being held in the tightest of grips. As he stroked his cock in and out of Hazel's tit-trench, his balls slid up and down her rib cage to smear cream all over her stomach. His soggy pubic hairs left slimy little trails all over her belly that gradually worked their way down to Hazel's dark furry bush to mingle with her own rapidly approaching wetness.

Hazel was approaching oblivion. She moaned from deep within as if she was experiencing an extremely lewd dream, 'I want a good tit-fucking. Feed my tits with your come, Phuc Yu. Grease me up like a stuck pig with that big dick of yours. Squirt on my titties – please. I've never been tit-fucked like this before. Such a big, big dick...'

Such filthy talk was too much for Yu to take, given the sensations he was feeling. Half of him wishing it wouldn't happen just yet, and the rest of him screaming for release, he felt an eruption of come beginning to travel upward from the throbbing base of his cock. He stopped thrusting and forced Janet and Kerry to encapsulate completely his dick with Hazel's tits. To bring him off he motioned for the two women to squeeze his dick through Hazel's tits. He didn't last long as he came into the tight breast cavern, squirting copious amounts of semen into every nook and cranny. The pressure was too much to bear – come squirted between Kerry's and Janet's hand's and all over the room, splattering even on the floor to ceiling windows.

To Yu it felt as if his dick had exploded, such was the force with which his orgasm had burst the fleshy seals of Hazel's tits. He collapsed off her and on to the floor, writhing in exquisite agony. Janet and Kerry paid him little attention, content to feed each other with sticky little drops of his come that had stuck to their fingers. Hazel was sound asleep, snoring ever so slightly. Looking into each other's eyes, Janet and Kerry continued to feed each other Yu's juices off of the slumbering Hazel's tits. It was an extremely decadent thing to do – but it fitted right in with the mood of the night. At that moment, under those circumstances, it was, in both their minds, the perfect thing to do.

As Hazel slept, Kerry and Janet fed on her tits like ravenous savages until every last drop of Yu's come had been eaten. They finished their feeding nose to nose, eye to eye, with their lips fastened on one of Hazel's nipples. They paused, staring at each other's wild-eyed gaze. Finally, Janet broke the silence of their heavy breathing.

'I want to fuck you.'

She spoke the words in her very proper English accent. No one could have refused her. Kerry didn't want to. Having sex with this petite and prim young Englishwoman seemed the wickedly erotic thing to do. With her boyish good looks and long blonde pony tail she carried an androgynous air about her that intrigued Kerry so. The opera was reaching a climax – far above the hills the first rays of the morning's sun were peeking like a crazed voyeur into the room – she wanted to feel this woman's mouth on her cunt, and she wanted to do likewise to her. It amazed her that before this night she had never done such a thing – and now it seemed so natural. Perhaps Hazel had been right that first night at the Pumping Station ...'

'And I want to fuck you.'

'Please, be my guest.'

Janet climbed over Hazel's slumbering form and pivoted completely around so that her head was facing the foot of the bed and Kerry's feet. She gripped Kerry's ankles and buried her face deep into the American girl's sodden bush. It tasted salty with sweat and spunk. Janet thrust her bottom into Kerry's face. Her odour was intense as Kerry stuck her tongue forward for Janet to fuck madly. Kerry reached around and held Janet tightly around the waist, pressing each of their bodies together. They rolled around bumping into Hazel, but not waking her. Their bodies became as one – a blur of sex consuming sex with an intensity of passion rarely found. Neither woman remembered distinctly coming at any particular moment so much as always feeling like they were melting over each other's faces.

They dared not separate from each other lest the sensation stop. Long after they had finished actively tonguing each other they still remained locked in the classic position, sleeping soundly, their bodies racked from too much pleasure. Kerry was briefly disturbed – at least she thought she was, she might have been dreaming – by the bed creaking under the weight of Phuc Yu pounding his dick into the sleeping Hazel's cunt. Kerry smiled and began to drift off back into a deep slumber scented by the aroma of Janet's still dripping cunt. Before she was completely asleep her eyes focused on Phuc Yu's hands gripping the sleeping Hazel's shoulders to steady himself as he pounded away.

There was something very familiar about those pudgy fingers and those rings. Where had she seen those rings before? It was recently she was sure . . .

Her brain was tired of all this effort. It had exhausted itself this evening with too many new sensations. It didn't need a puzzle right now.

'Later,' said her slumbering consciousness. 'Much later.'

9

Chocolate Banana

Mix

1 large spoonful of Vanilla Ice Cream
Banana
½ oz. Creme de Cacao
4 oz. half and half (or milk)
1 oz. Rum
2 oz. Chocolate Syrup

Mix all the ingredients in a blender and blend on high speed until completely liquid. Pour into a tall glass and serve with a straw or tall spoon.

Louisa was feeling very randy. The kind of stomach-pounding hollow feeling that can only be filled, in her case, by the biggest cock she could get her hands, lips and mouth on. Unfortunately it was Wednesday and being right on the hump of the week it was an incredibly slow night. She'd placed several strategic calls and received no response. All of her regular fucks were either out of town, busy, or still recovering from their last encounter with her. Things were looking pretty grim. The only human beings – and Louisa applied the term loosely in these instances – that had been in the Pumping Station this dull and frustrating evening were Fred the Regular who had been unable to look Louisa in the face and had soon left without finishing his beer, and her working companion for the night – Lester 'the Molester' Byron. In either case she wasn't about to stoop so low as to have sex with them. She'd gotten away with her little scene at the theatre, but she didn't want to press her luck. Teasing yes, fucking no. Even in her present state she still had standards. Her own skilled hands, for example.

Just when Louisa had resigned herself to an evening with her favourite dildo and her long fingers, salvation came walking through the Pump's door in the form of the Sacrabento State College basketball team. They were exceptionally tall, very dark and as far as Louisa was concerned, fuckably handsome. They were dressed in coordinated red, yellow and black fluorescent training suits that accentuated their size – in more ways than one.

143

'Can I get you a cocktail?' Louisa really dragged out the first syllable of the last word of her introductory sentence with her lips and emphasised the second with a slight wiggle of her perfect ass.

'Where's the action in this place?'

'Pardon me?'

'Where is everyone?'

'It's been pretty slow tonight – midweek, nothing going on.'

'That's for damn sure. Nobody was at the game tonight.'

'Game? What do you guys play?'

Louisa didn't want to appear to presume that this collection of gigantic men belonged to a basketball team. She'd heard that all tall black men were sensitive to people automatically thinking that they were basketball players.

'We're part of the Sacrabento State basketball team. We're in town to play Silicon Valley State. We wupped their ass.'

'Yeah – and nobody was there to see us do it.'

'That's too bad. Maybe a few cocktails will make the night a little better.'

'Man – only a little pussy could do that.'

'You shut your mouth, Malcolm. There's a lady present. Pay no attention to him, miss. He's frustrated and got no manners.'

'Yo mama.'

Ignoring Malcolm's jive jibes the leader of the team continued.

'I'm Charles – you've met Malcolm – this is Lance, Akim, Watson and Roger. And who are you?' They all nodded except Malcolm, who strutted. Everyone ignored him.

'I'm Louisa.'

'Louisa – pleased to meet you. Now what shall we have to drink?'

Everyone ignored Malcolm's muttering of something that sounded like 'pussy', opting for a round of Chivas Regal cognacs. As she walked away to place their orders Louisa wiggled her hips playfully, knowing full well that there were six pairs of eyes burning holes in her clothes.

Munching on the free peanuts that the Pump provided its patrons, a heated discussion ensued amongst the Sacrabento State College basketball team.

'You're full of shit, Charles. Yo said that this place would be crawling with babes – and the only one here is working. This place is dead.'

'Stop thinking with your dick, Malcolm. Use your brains – what little your mama gave you. I can tell that cocktail waitress is as horny as a big old toad. And if I'm not mistaken she fancies a little dark meat tonight. And I bet she has a few friends too.'

'You been reading too many dirty books, Charles. Things like that just don't happen in the real world. Not to dudes like us.'

'You wanna bet.'

'Sure.'

'I bet you a hundred dollars that I get laid tonight and you don't.'

'You got a deal, Chuck.' Malcolm knew Charles hated being called 'Chuck'.

Louisa arrived with the drinks.

'This round's on me, guys – I hope it makes you feel better.'

'That's mighty kind of you, Louisa – here's to your good health.' Charles eyed Malcolm with an 'I told you so' look. Malcolm just ignored him.

'How long are you in town for?' It was the perfect lead-in question. Charles answered – the others were just spectators at this point.

'Oh, only for tonight, I'm afraid. Well, not even that – we have a minibus in the parking lot that's got to be back by morning. It's only a couple of hours drive so we thought we'd break the journey with a little partying.'

Partying. There was the magic word Louisa was looking for. The universal code word for having too much fun in too short of a space of time. In this case she was sure it meant sex.

'Well, I'm sorry that it's pretty dead around here, but I'll do my best to entertain you.'

'Whooo weee – that sure is nice of you, pretty lady.'

'Why, thank you for the compliment.'

This time as Louisa got up she made sure that Charles got an extended full-on frontal right-between-the-eyes panty covered beaver shot. She even paused and looked right at him as he stared at her cunt. He looked a little surprised to be confronted with such a forward gesture. Louisa just smiled back, a look that told him he'd get more than a look if he played his cards right.

Louisa was intrigued by the prospect of fucking a black man. She'd just never had the chance for no reasons in particular. It's just not the thing that occupies a young girl's mind − thinking of all the various groups of people to fuck or not to fuck. It just happens − you get fucked. But now that she was so randy, and there was readily available and apparently willing representatives in attendance, this was the perfect opportunity to experiment and see if there were any differences as the graffiti in the women's bathroom claimed there were. She wasn't too keen on fucking the whole team, especially the shithead Malcolm, so her biggest challenge turned out to be how to get Charles alone.

It turned out not to be a problem. Just before last call Charles walked up to Louisa at the serving station.

'Where's the bathroom, please?' He knew very well where it was, having already been twice.

'Just round the corner, to your left. It hasn't moved.'

He hesitated, knowing Louisa knew that he was making conversation. Louisa waited for the opening. It came very quickly.

'Say − I was wondering if you'd like to have a drink with me after you get off work. The guys are going to eat in your restaurant here, so I'll be all on my own in the mini bus. I ate already.'

'Sure − I'll bring a couple of drinks out there, right about two-fifteen.' Louisa tried to appear none too excited. She always had to have the upper hand when it came to men.

Charles didn't even bother to go to the bathroom. Instead he headed back to the guys to try and convince them that they wanted to eat in the restaurant and not leave right away.

Malcolm was argumentative.

'How'm I gonna know you're really gonna be fuckin' her if I'm stuck in the damn restaurant eating fried chicken?

'I'll leave one of the blinds open so you can come out about two-thirty and watch my ass going up and down on her sweet cunt. And you can give me my hundred bucks shortly thereafter – sucker.'

'I'll be there to watch you pump your own meat and pay me for the pleasure of watching you do it – sucker.' After that little discourse Charles retired to the parking lot and the others situated themselves in the restaurant to drink coffee and see if there were any likely female prospects having a late night snack.

There weren't. So they just sat around and talked about fucking while waiting for Charles to put his money where his mouth was – so to speak.

Charles sat in the back of the minibus biting his nails. He really had no idea whether Louisa would show – she could have been bullshitting him – but then again, she did flash him her cunt real good. But you never could tell with girls like that . . .

His worries were ended by the sight of Louisa, large drink glasses in hands, wearing a floor-length white raincoat, walking quickly across the parking lot. Even her step indicated what was on her mind and in her body. To Charles it was obvious. The click of her Pumping Station five-inch high heels on the asphalt of the parking lot tapped out s-e-x, s-e-x, s-e-x, just like in Morse code.

Charles opened the door of the minibus and invited Louisa in. The drinks she carried permeated the air with alcohol. They had been made especially strong.

'What have we here?'

'Well, this is a Long Island Iced Tea – it's my favourite drink. I brought that for you. And this is something new that I thought I'd try tonight.'

'Smells strong – and sweet. What is it?'

'A chocolate banana. I can't wait to get my lips around it.'

And with that Louisa stuck her tongue into the foamy drink and swirled it around, curling the very tip back into her mouth.

'Hmmmm – I think I like this chocolate banana. I want more.'

Charles was about to burst his elasticated sweatpants. He couldn't stand any more suggestive teasing. It was time.

'Aw sheeet – to hell with these drinks. Let's fuck, mama.'

'Well, I never. And I thought you were such a gentleman.'

'Yeah – and you such a lady showing off your cunt to me.'

'Did you like what you saw.'

'It was sweet – very sweet. Only I'd like a close-up.'

'Only too happy to oblige, Charles.'

Louisa shook off her raincoat to reveal her Pumping Station uniform minus the dress – red suspender belt, fishnet stockings, red lacy panties, high heels, firm high tits jutting forward with distinctively hard nipples leading the way. She'd added one item that made the outfit perfect. In addition to the mandatory pearl choker she'd donned a huge string of pearls that dangled all the way down to her knees. She twirled them in her fingers seductively.

'Are you just going to look – or do you know how to fuck?'

Louisa hooked the pearls around Charles' neck and pulled him towards her as he struggled with his clothes. It was difficult to get his trousers off over his huge inflatable-soled basketball pumps. He stumbled onto his knees, his face inches away from Louisa's red-lace covered cunt. Louisa laughed at his predicament.

'For an athlete you sure aren't too coordinated.'

'I'll show you my coordination.'

'Oh do – please do.'

Charles gripped the thin side straps of Louisa's red panties and with one quick tug snapped the thin band of material that held them together. The diaphanous material fell away, releasing a musky odour into the cramped confines of the minibus. Louisa enjoyed the display of force. She could feel her sex getting wetter and wetter. Charles, his face only inches from Louisa's smouldering cunt, could taste the thick smell of cunt in the air.

'I'm gonna eat your pussy.'

'Don't talk about it – do it!'

Charles buried his face into Louisa's snatch and gobbled

148

away with lustful abandon. Able to steady himself against Louisa's pubic mound, Charles freed his hands from her hips and wrestled his sweatpants over his giant feet. Louisa lay back on the bench seat and toyed with her nipples, thinking of the fucking to come. Charles was not too sophisticated when it came to cunt-licking, preferring to slobber and munch like a starving beggar. Louisa wriggled her ass to move her swollen clitoris against Charles' lips. From side to side she vibrated, catching the sensitive bud on the basketball player's slobbering mouth. Every uncertain moment, following no apparent logic of movement, huge shivers of intense pleasure shot up Louisa's spine, causing her to arch her back and open her moist opening further to Charles' oral fumblings. The art was all Louisa's – Charles just provided a firm tongue, a ready supply of suction, spit and all the rabid enthusiasm of an excited dog in heat. Louisa used her body to direct Charles' movements. Her silky thighs gripped his head tightly and by flexing her legs up and down she was able to make his tongue thrust in and out like a small and incredibly agile penis. Her gyrating hips added the extra dimension of sensation to her excited button, bringing her all that much closer to the brink.

Louisa could have kept this up all night, but she wasn't interested in a marathon session. She'd wanted sex all evening, and was in no mood for patience. Louisa was on a *blitzkrieg* mission of sexual exploration. She'd had better oral sex – it was a cock she wanted now.

'Fuck me with your black dick, Charles. Give it to me – grind it into me.'

Charles couldn't hear a word. His ears were muffled by Louisa's thighs, and his own frantic cunt licking. It was then quite a surprise when he felt Louisa's hands on his shoulders tugging at his body. He looked up, cunt juice dripping from his face, to see her resolute stare.

'Get on your back, Charles. I'm going to grind that dick of yours into minced meat.'

His eyes widened with shock and surprise, and he readily complied with eager anticipation.

It was this portion of the fucking that Louisa had been

craving all night long. Louisa loved this position more than any other for there were no sensations like the truly exhilarating feeling of mounting a supine man's frame and riding him into ecstasy. Louisa's love of fucking in this position had something to do with a need to feel in control, and the purely practical consideration of it being the best way for her to get off. She didn't have to rely on a man to fuck her in just the right way. She was in control – and Louisa always fucked the right way.

Charles lying on his back, naked except for his pump-up basketball shoes and socks was a sight to behold. His ebony skin rippled and twinkled in the dim light of the darkened minibus. He was in excellent shape. Long, lean and in perfect tone, he looked like a Greek god carved in the darkest of marble. His eyes were closed and he was moaning soft encouragement to Louisa.

'I want your sweet cunt to sit on my dick, baby. Ride me like a horse. I'm your stallion, and I'm gonna buck you and fuck you good.'

'That's what I like to hear.'

Louisa took his cock in her hand and straddled his thighs. His dick jutted forward between her legs such that it almost looked like it belonged to her. The optical illusion was not lost on Louisa.

'This is mine – all mine – and I'm going to do thing to it that aren't very nice.'

Charles moaned again and covered his eyes with his arms. He was enjoying this fuck much more than the usual on-top-in-and-out-yo-mama screws that came his way. He knew he was in the hands of a real expert and he was going to enjoy every minute of it. The realisation that he'd probably come too quickly haunted him. He tried to think of basketball to take his mind off of the swelling feeling in his cock – but it didn't work. He kept visualising himself flying through the air and slam-dunking the ball into the hoop, and just when he'd think he was safe from coming he'd flash back to a scene in his mind's eye of him flying through the air again with a big old hard-on and slamming it into Louisa's wide and willing cunt-hoop. It was just too damn bad that he hadn't thought to wank off earlier in the evening to prevent him from blowing his wad too quickly under Louisa's delicious prompting. Oh well, not to worry, he rationalised. He'd never expected anything like this — and to think he was going to get $100 off Malcolm for the pleasure of fucking Louisa. He couldn't stop himself from smiling. That was why he covered his face. He didn't think it too complimentary to be seen laughing in such a position as he was in right now.

Charles needn't have worried. Louisa didn't look at his face. She was concerned with a totally different head altogether. She held Charles' black rod against her pale skin and marvelled at its lustre. It didn't look real at all. It didn't feel real. Even in the darkness she could make out the different shades of purple, blue and black of his swelling that gave the dick an appearance of being some exotic and rare carving. With her bright red nails she raked the foreskin completely back to uncover the bulging cockhead. It gleamed a lighter purple and glistened from the juices her touch was causing it to emit.

Once again Charles moaned and this time he shook from Louisa's nails invading such a tender spot. In response she wanked his dick hard with an extremely tight grip. His dick was not massive, nor small but just average — if such an inadequate word could be used to describe such a fine specimen of male pride.

'I think this meat wants some cunt sauce — don't you Charles?'

'Most certainly Louisa — I want to fuck your little cunny till it can't take no more dicks.'

'If that be so then this had better be good. Is it going to be good, Charles?'

Louisa was squeezing his balls and running her fingers through his tight black pubic hair. It was coarse and sticky from sweat and other fluids.

'This will be the best fuck of your sweet life.'

'I can hardly wait.'

Louisa raised her lovely frame on her knees, arching her back so Charles could see just how perfect the swell of her tits were. Reaching behind her she grasped the throbbing shaft in her hand and guided it between her ass cheeks and lower to her cunt opening. Without warning she collapsed her knees so that she fell upon the dick impaling herself and taking the wind out of Charles.

'Whoah – take it easy mama!'

'The hell I will. Hold on big boy – I'm going to fuck you so that you can't take any more cunt.'

Charles moaned deep inside, wishing more than ever that he'd had a pre-fuck wank.

Louisa bounced up and down on her knees almost lifting herself off his pulsing dick with each stroke. The sight of her sexual athleticism was enthralling. Charles was hypnotised into a stupour by the lovely bouncing gymnastics of Louisa's titties. They seemed to have a mind of their own, pirouetting around her body, describing complex figures in the air with her hardened nipples. Charles reached to the nipples and held them between his thumbs and fingers, rolling the pulsating knobs hard and painfully to and fro. Louisa did not slow her fucking motion because of a slight amount of pain. It only excited her further, making her content to have her tits held by the nipples and bounced around by her own violent motions.

Every few thrusts, Charles would completely enfold Louisa's tits with his huge hands as if they were small basketballs. He squeezed them expertly with a grip that he'd practised on the court millions of times, only now it seemed a much better use of his hands to be mangling these lovely white breasts. His rough play pulled Louisa forward so that her clit rubbed into his coarse pubic hair as she thrust up and down. She almost screamed with the intensity of orgasm that welled within her and flowed from between her legs.

She steadied her quaking body by placing her hands on Charles' chest. His nipples were hard to her sweating palms, causing her to focus on the tiny brown points during her shattering climax. She pressed his chest as hard as she could and gripped his buttocks with her thighs. Her head and its blonde adornment flowed back, straining every muscle in her neck. Her tits stretched tight – her chest heaving as she let her juices drown the ebony cock within her. Under such nourishment it seemed to grow inside her with every undulating moment. His thrusting dick seemed to expand in all possible directions so that every nook and cranny of Louisa's cunt was filled with his dark meat. She visualised the scene inside her as a hot spray of semen sputtered forth and oozed throughout her sex. Charles was rolling his head and beating on the sides of the minibus with his huge hands. He felt unable to contain the rush that began and ended at the tip of his dick but travelled throughout every nerve of his body on its way into Louisa's thighs. As he came he felt like the blonde bombshell above him was turning his whole body inside out as though his face, his head, his mind were being pulled by the sex-crazed woman through his body and out of his cockhead.

Neither Charles nor Louisa dared to stop their thrustings and buckings. Neither cared to admit defeat at the other's urgings, desperate to continue fucking at all costs. Charles' orgasm took Louisa higher and higher, to a sexual plateau where existence was one long continual rolling orgasm. To come was to flow as if she was pissing all over him. As far as she knew she could have been. At this point Louisa had no control over her body or its functions. As Charles' dick began to loose its erectness, she too folded, becoming as limp as his cock. Nothing could hold her come-drained body together after the release it had suffered. Her final pleasure was to collapse all over his body as his dick squeezed out of her still swollen and sodden cunt.

Somewhere in the blackness of her exhaustion she could hear the muted sound of Malcolm's jive and the rest of the team's retorts. It mattered little to her. She'd seen them staring through a gap in the mini-bus blinds and figured why not let them enjoy themselves? She wasn't going to let some hard-up basketball players spoil her fun. It even made her try harder to destroy Charles' manhood knowing that she had a jealous audience to entertain.

Finally woken by the other players' poundings on the minibus door, Louisa hadn't bothered to dress before exiting in front of their drooling stares. She couldn't resist dishing out a few

153

well-chosen jibes directed poignantly at the grinning Malcolm.

'I hope you enjoyed the view – cause that's the only pussy you'll get tonight,' Louisa paused. 'Oh, sorry – I lied. My torn and soaked panties are still in the bus – you can sniff them or eat them if you like. Stuffing them in your mouth and shutting you up would be a good use for them.'

Malcolm was at a loss for words and $100. He pushed his way into the bus, followed by the jeers of his fellow players. Charles walked Louisa to her car. She didn't bother to put on her coat, feeling refreshingly free now that the evening's sexual tension had been released. She sat in her car revving the Mustang's engine whilst Charles did his best to say goodnight. It was difficult for him to concentrate on Louisa's face when he could sense and see just a few feet away from his body the cunt that had held him so tightly. Sitting in the car seat, naked except for her suspender belt, stockings and high-heeled shoes, Louisa was causing Charles' beaten penis to stir once more. He forced himself to think of details in an attempt to keep his brain occupied on other things than the sexy sight in front of him.

'Can I have your phone number?'

'I don't give my phone number out to people I meet at the Pump.'

'But how will I get in touch with you?'

'Look, it was a great fuck – but don't go falling in love. And if you are in town again and want to do it again – you know where I work. And if I'm not here, then I'm not available.'

'Just like that.'

'Yeah, Charles – just like that. I'm a cocktail waitress. I've heard every line in the book and a few that haven't been written yet. Right now you're thinking with your dick. It's a nice dick, but it doesn't have any brains. Use it for what it's best at – fucking. Leave the thinking to up here.'

She touched his head, and he gently kissed her hand as she backed the car away from him and into the night. As she pulled out of the parking lot and into the Silicon Valley night Louisa thought to herself that there was no difference between

154

black men and white men in bed. She smiled wickedly to herself. A guy could be purple with green spots and pink hair, but if he knew how to handle his dick, his mouth, his hands and his brain he'd be worth his ugly weight in gold to Louisa. Oh well, she thought, at least she now knew that the graffiti in the bathrooms was wrong.

As the lights of the cars flashed by, Louisa also pondered how like little schoolgirls all men were. It was a myth that it was the woman who fell deeply in love after one roll in the sack. Now it was the man who wanted to have a lasting relationship and own a woman after just one bonk. She thought back over what she'd said to Charles and sighed. She hoped she hadn't hurt his feelings but she just wasn't going to get involved after one quick fuck. Sometimes she worried that she was getting too hard — that she'd scare off Mr Right whenever he came along with her Teflon attitude. She quickly put such sentiment out of her mind. Fuck 'em and forget 'em — that was Louisa's motto.

Little did she know that her credo would soon be put to the ultimate test, and she would be giving herself somewhat the same lecture as she'd given Charles, over and over again, under very different circumstances, in just a few weeks time.

And trying desperately not to believe it.

10

Lady be Good

Mix

1½ oz. Brandy
½ oz. Creme dc Menthe (White)
½ oz. Sweet Vermouth

Shake with ice and strain into a cocktail glass.

It had been a bad few weeks for Officer Norman Moore. The waking nightmare started that night that he'd overstepped his authority and got a truncheon up the bum courtesy of Louisa Hampton. Since that fateful evening when he'd been discovered by what seemed like half the population of Silicon Valley in a somewhat compromising position in the back of his police cruiser, life had been a living hell. He'd become the butt of numerous police jokes from his so-called colleagues. There had been a few unsavoury newspaper articles written, and at least one television exposé of so-called police perverts. He'd been 'transferred' indefinitely to traffic duty. His wife had left to get a divorce, crying that she wasn't going to stay in the same house as a pervert. And to add insult to injury it had taken him all this time to get over the physical pain of having such a large and nasty object stuck quite rudely where the sun rarely shined. He hadn't been able to sit down normally since.

Even now, three weeks later, he still had a bit of a limp, but even worse than the physical reminders of that fateful night was his inability to get that feisty little blonde out of his mind. He'd become obsessed with his sexual nemesis. That she had beaten him at his own game filled him with an admiration that now bordered on infatuation. He'd thought about the sordid situation all of those nights that he couldn't sleep – lying there on his stomach unable to roll over. He was sure that after what they had gone through together they should be the best of friends. Surprisingly he felt no animosity towards her, but rather a deep desire to spend the rest of his life with her. He had convinced himself that Louisa Hampton would feel for him as he now felt for her. And now that he was finally able to walk like a man again he'd summoned up enough courage to visit the unwitting object of his desires.

Officer Moore finished directing traffic at the local high school at four p.m. He'd checked at the Pump and found that Louisa started work at five. He'd spent the waiting hour sprucing himself up. He'd put on his best suit, a liberal supply of aftershave lotion and even had time to purchase a dozen roses. He arrived in the Pump's parking lot at one minute past five. His heart skipped a beat as he saw Louisa's telltale red Mustang. The top was down and Norman paused by the car, recollecting that sex-filled night. He remembered looking up Louisa's skirt as he leaned in the car. He could still clearly see the curve of her breasts peering at him from her seductively open leather jacket. These views had haunted him all these weeks. It was all he had thought of. The memories of her body, her smell, her sex had nursed him back to health − and now it was time for more than fond thoughts. He was here to claim what he was sure was rightfully his.

Or at least that was what he kept saying to himself as he walked into the darkened bar. His eyes rapidly adjusted to the dim light because he had been wearing his regulation police issue dark glasses outside in the bright sunlight. In a move that was best described as suave, he removed the shades with daring aplomb, careful not to drop the roses or scratch his head on the thorns. The bar was quite empty except for the bartender and Louisa. They were chatting together casually. Louisa was smoking a cigarette, which she held between her fingers, resting her slim hand on the subtle curve of her hips. As she turned her eyes focused on the expectant figure of Officer Norman Moore.

'Oh shit.'

Norman did not hear her exclamation across the bar.

He quickly advanced on Louisa. She appeared to be confused as if not knowing which way to run. Norman had practised his opening line for weeks.

'Hi – remember me?' He thought it had just the right combination of casual disregard and humour. He wasn't prepared for the answer.

'No – should I?' Louisa was lying – she was trying to buy herself time whilst she figured out what the hell to do about Officer Moore.

'Officer Moore – Norman. We, er, spent some time together several weeks ago in the back of my car late one night after you'd got off work.'

'Oh, yeah. No – I see so many guys in the back of their cars – I don't really remember you.'

Norman swallowed his pride and figured he'd go for the brass ring.

'Look – these are for you. I want to see you again.'

Norman handed Louisa the roses. She didn't take them, but stepped back a few paces.

'I can't accept those.'

Norman kept his arm stiffly outstretched. He advanced towards the retreating Louisa whilst Arnold Rimskikoff, the bartender, looked on in amazement. Arnold wasn't sure what to do. He entertained vague notions of defending Louisa, but thought better of it. She seemed to be doing just fine.

'Look – I want you to know I forgive you for what you did. I've left my wife so we can be together.' Norman was lying. His wife had left him, and it was she who had filed for divorce. But he felt the need to try and impress Louisa with his determination to remove all obstacles between them. He was getting desperate. Things weren't going quite as planned.

Louisa grabbed at the flowers and threw them vindictively at Norman's vulnerable form. Rose petals flew everywhere. Norman was covered in a snowstorm of red foliage. The thorns scratched his skin, raising small droplets of blood on his cheek, but it was Louisa's words that stung harder.

'I don't know who the hell you are or what you think I am to you, but just fuck off. You'll get me fired. I don't care if you've left your wife. I wouldn't go out with you if you were the last person on earth. Just get out of here. Go on – leave.'

161

Louisa screamed the last word and pushed Norman towards the door. In a daze he limped a retreat out into the parking lot, stumbled to his car and sat there crying behind the wheel.

'Who the hell was that?' Arnold was understandably curious.

'Oh, some asshole who thinks I'm his true love. Never seen him before.'

'He looks familiar – I think he's a cop. I'm sure I've seen him in the restaurant, eating doughnuts, drinking coffee.'

'I don't know who he is. I probably served him a drink sometime and he fell in love – you know how they are. One tip and they think they own you.'

Louisa and Arnold laughed the incident off. Secretly Louisa was glad to have gotten out of the situation so lightly. It had been a spur of the moment thing to pretend not to recognise Officer Moore. Louisa patted herself on the back for successfully dodging yet another one of life's little bullets, but deep inside she kept telling herself to be more careful. Her conscience kept whispering to her that one of these days her fast life was going to catch up with her, and somehow she knew that little voice had a point, and sooner more than later there was going to be one of life's little bullets she wouldn't so easily evade.

Arnold wasn't the only one of the Pump's employees to recognise Officer Norman Moore for being a member of Silicon Valley's finest. Annie da Pheelanupe was leaving the Pump after working a rather boring day shift in which she'd only managed one hand job on a fat salesman during a rather slow lunch hour. She didn't like working days, but the odd day shift once in a while did give her the night off for the pursuit of more lucrative activities. She was walking through the parking lot when she saw Officer Norman Moore covered in rose petals crying his eyes out in the front seat of his car. Having activities that weren't strictly too legal, Annie made it a point to know all of the local police by sight. It was a precaution that made for no embarrassing and potentially costly mistakes. Thus, when she saw one of the Silicon Valley police force in obvious distress her immediate thought was

162

that here was a golden opportunity to score a few points that may one day come in useful.

Annie approached the car. Norman continued to bawl his head off.

'Why sugar, can I be of service to you? Is there anything wrong?'

Annie realised what a silly thing it was to say, but she really couldn't think of anything else. Norman didn't clearly hear her, but he did sense her presence. In response, Norman just looked up and stopped sobbing momentarily. Rose petals fluttered off of his head and onto his lap. Without explanation he covered up his eyes and started crying again.

'Oh honey, it can't be that bad. Tell Annie all about it. Y'all will feel much better.'

Annie opened the car door and motioned for Norman to slide on over onto the passenger side. She got in and sat down behind the steering wheel.

'Now – my name's Annie. What's yours?'

In between sobs Norman spluttered out his moniker.

'Please ta meet ya, Norman, Now what's got ya'll so riled? Woman trouble, is it?'

Norman spewed forth his womanly travails in staccato sentences punctuated with teary sobs. 'She's left me ... doesn't want to see me again ... won't even talk to me ... even brought her roses ... threw them at me ... after all we've been through ...'

Annie added friendly consolations not knowing Norman was talking about her cocktail-waitressing colleague Louisa. And Norman seemed unable to mention Louisa's name. It was always 'she', or 'her'. Once he started to say 'Louisa,' but he sobbed and started over again and burst into tears so the name came out sounding like Lulu.

Annie knew well the signs of rejected love and also knew the best cure for it.

'Norman, honey, I know how to make you forget this Lulu chick. I'm taking you home, sugar.'

Annie started up Norman's car and drove quickly to her apartment before he could regain his senses. Norman sobbed and sniffled all the way, but he didn't object. Safely inside the comfortable abode, Norman sat on Annie's couch still sobbing.

'Here sugar, drink this. Y'all will feel much better.'

'Ttth – th – thank – y – you.'

Norman cradled the huge goblet of warm amber liquid and gulped down a major slug of brandy. He coughed roughly, but immediately downed the whole snifter. His sobbing became a minor sniffle. Annie poured him a refill and herself a small one. They clinked glasses.

'Well, here's to brighter times.'

'Thank you, Annie.'

'Now you just sip your brandy and relax. Let little old Annie here make you feel right at home.'

Annie was skilled at making nervous men feel like skilled Romeos. She knew how to soften the firmest of resolves and weaken the stiffest of inhibitions.

'Why don't we loosen that stuffy old tie?'

Annie pulled the knot until the constriction released itself. Skilfully she used her long pink nails to pop open the buttons of Norman's starched white shirt. She stopped just above his belly button and slid her silky hand inside the crisp material. Norman's skin tingled at her touch, but he resolutely kept sipping his brandy, each gulp further removing all thought of Louisa from his crazed brain.

Annie's palm brushed across Norman's sparse chest hair and came to rest on his nipple. Using her delicate fingers and long pointy nails she flicked the end of his tit to and fro, pausing to fondle and squeeze his chest every few moments. It was during one of these lulls in her actions that Annie reached over and intercepted the brandy snifter on its way to Norman's mouth. She placed the glass on the coffee table and pulled Norman towards her.

'I want your lips on mine.'

Norman felt unable to speak as the gulf between their bodies narrowed. Annie expertly cradled his head with her hands while pulling his willing body towards her, careful to massage the sensual area just below Norman's hairline. Her soft pink lips paused ever so slightly before kissing him so that she could rake her nails through his hair. Their eyes met as Annie gently closed hers, careful to flutter her lashes as their lips met. Annie's tongue gently parted Norman's lips and travelled around the terrain of his mouth. She twisted her agile lips against his as their tongues entwined. Norman could taste the perfume of pink lipstick in his mouth. It was as intoxicating to him as the brandy he'd just drank.

Their first kiss lasted a long time. Annie knew that the longer she held Norman in this first embrace, the easier it would be for her to thoroughly seduce the policeman. Norman would eventually be putty in her hands, but this initial instant was the critical juncture in their embrace. In her sexual career, Annie had seen many men on the retreat from relationships who desired release with an intimate stranger, only to turn tail and run away after a small kiss tinged their guilt ridden consciences. She really needn't have worried about Norman. In his emotionally charged state Norman was easy prey for Annie's gifted charms. He wasn't going anywhere. He was determined to lose his wretched life amidst the lovely flesh that so willingly offered itself to him.

As they kissed, Annie rolled on top of Norman and straddled his body. With both hands she held his head to hers and continued their initial kiss. Under her insistence Norman's body slid fully onto the comfortable couch so that her crotch could oscillate up and down over his growing hardness. Finally, confident in her conquest, Annie pulled her lips away from Norman and sat erect on top of his body. No words were spoken – only their eyes communicated the lustful thoughts that flowed between them. In a slow dance of enticement, Annie's pink nails unbuttoned her light blue silk blouse to reveal a temptingly firm set of tits encased in a pretty lavender lace bra. The pink gloss of her nails contrasted provocatively against the light purple of the flimsy material, focusing Norman's rapt attention at the protruding darkness of her nipples as they peaked innocently through the inadequate camouflage of the bra. Her breasts strained through the lace, begging to be touched. Through the flimsy barrier of the lavender material Norman boldly cupped the warm tit flesh with his hands as Annie reached behind her to unclasp the bra's catches. The lace cascaded away into his grip, and Annie clasped her arms together so he could pull the seductive garment free of her body. Stripped bare, Annie's proud tits jutted firmly forward, her hardened nipples, like those of some sculptured beauty defying gravity and piercing the anticipation filled air. As she pulled aside Norman's shirt, Annie once more latched their lips together, careful to grind her tits into his chest. Her nipples felt like small bullets against his body as her tits pressed against his own. As their tongues flicked playfully, Annie let out a small moan that reached inside of Norman's brain and unleashed his closeted libido. The moan was not a lusty sound but more one of feminine submission − an indication of the willingness of this woman to do whatever he wanted her to do.

And in consenting so, Annie knew that she would do whatever he wanted. She was letting her well-oiled defences down. This was no longer business but something much more personal. Strangely enough, it filled Annie with intense excitement Annie to be fucking someone on a completely friendly basis. It hadn't started out that way. She had decided to fuck Norman because it might help her to have a friend in the police force, but she didn't view the action as a business transaction any more. This was how sex used to be for her before it became a moneymaking proposition, and the feelings she felt ignited intense passions within her. Her body quaked with the desires to please Norman.

As their second kiss ended, Annie stood up by the side of the couch and unzipped her jeans. Form-fittingly tight they were, but it didn't stop her from wriggling seductively out of them to reveal a pair of lavender lace panties that matched the bra she'd shed just a few minutes before. Hooking her fingers into the sides of the fancy garment, she stepped out of the lace panties and dropped them on the floor. They fluttered just inches away from Norman's face. He watched them fall to the ground and then made his move. He stood up and gripped Annie's naked body by the shoulders. With an urgent kiss to her neck he guided her to the couch and undressed before her as she slowly undulated on the soft cushions. His cock sprang free and jutted forward leaking its urgency in small sticky drops as it bobbed about. Annie

166

reached forward and grasped the hard cock between her fingers and pulled Norman Moore on top of her.

'Please fuck me, Norman. Please don't wait any longer.'

Annie hadn't felt such urgency for fucking since her earlier years. She wanted to feel a nakedly hard penis inside of her straining in and out, pushing against the walls of her cunt and spraying forth its come inside her body. She wanted to squeeze her thighs against Norman's buttocks to give him the ultimate pleasure of her soft flesh against his. She wanted to slide her cunt against his pubic mound to titillate her throbbing little bud to the brink of release. She wanted to feel his teeth on her tits as she came. She wanted to wait no longer for these pleasures, even though their lovemaking to this point had not been too prolonged. Annie was not just thinking of this evening's passions. She was mindful of all the nights that she'd taken in a cock and thought of only the dollars that had been building in her bank account. And now that she felt the rough pleasures of fucking for fucking's sake once more, it was like all those other nights were just so much more teasing foreplay.

Her urgency burst forth in her forced speech.

'Stick it in me, Norman — make love to me.'

Annie's experienced hand guided the tip of Norman's cock to the moistness of her cunt opening. Norman did the rest with a heave of his wanting body. Annie's insistence created confidence within him just like old times.

'Is this what you want?'

It was a rhetorical question. Still Annie answered it with both speech and the thrustings of her hips.

'Yes — yes — I want your dick. I want to be fucked by you.'

Norman complied, being unable to do much else. Under his weight, Annie thrust her cunt at him and pulled it immediately away in a manner that matched Norman's own motions. They fucked in such exquisite coordination like some intricate ballet.

Each millimetre of Norman's hard dick tingled as he pushed his throbbing member deep inside Annie's cunt. As his cock drove deeper and deeper Annie gasped with delight as the head banged against the confines of her pussy. She could feel his erect penis pulse under the delicate squeezes of her cunt muscles. With sexual elegance she rippled her cunt along the length of Norman's cock as it slid its full length in and out of her. With each thrust she grew wetter and wetter. She could feel her juices flowing down between her legs, past her ass and soaking the couch. Her tawny pubic hair tangled with Norman's darker mass spreading her juices over her pussy mound. She could hear the scratching sound that their entwining made as he ground his dick inside her. No longer pulling his cock in and out, Annie was gripping his buttocks with her legs wrapped around him and latched at her trim ankles. Norman was unable to thrust but was forced to wiggle his cock inside of Annie's pussy. The resulting grinding motion squeezed Annie's engorged clitoris better than her own hand could. The feeling was luxurious, as if Norman's entire weight was being forced on to that one delicate spot. The contact was continuous and pressing − the throbbing clit was forced in small circular motions, unable to escape the orgasm inducing pressure. Annie continued to gasp with each high that peaked deep inside her. Norman was aware that he was being used as a fucking machine, but had no objections. He was secretly relieved not to be ramming his tender shaft inside Annie. The last time he'd had sex had been with Louisa, weeks ago, and so his body had built up a massive reserve of sperm that his dick found hard to contain. The grinding motion that Annie was directing, although supremely erotic, gave him the breather he needed so that he could continue fucking without the worry of coming too soon.

Annie came in a long slow rush that felt as if she was ice cream melting on Norman's hot dick. She didn't gasp or scream but let out a soft sigh and released her legs from around Norman's ass. Her hands, latched behind his neck fell away, as every bone in her body seemed to dissolve. She felt as if she was flowing amidst the very fibres of the couch, melting like a snowman on a warm winter's day.

Norman, released from the grip of Annie's long legs, began to thrust hard once more. Annie immediately gasped as her come-racked cunt was hit with the full thrust of Norman's body. It was as if her rolling orgasm had suddenly crashed upon some hidden rocks, dashing its smooth progress into a million rivulets of foaming intensity. Each one of those small eruptions itself became an orgasm threatening to tear apart Annie's small body. With each hard thrust she thrashed about on the couch as if some massive electric shock was jolting her form. Norman was unaware of the emotion he was unleashing, as his own orgasm was perilously close to blowing the head right off of his cock. As he came into Annie's thrashing body he rammed his dick fully inside her drained cunt and held it there by gripping her lovely firm bottom with all of his might. He lifted her off the couch and pulled her rag-doll like form firmly against him as he collapsed into her.

Moments later the only sound to be heard was the pounding of their hearts doing their very best to convince their respective hosts that they were still alive.

Officer Norman Moore had never been a real die-hard sexual athlete. Usually it was all over once his cock had blasted away his orgasm into whatever willing receptacle he could find. He'd usually fall asleep right away, content in the knowledge that he had done his manly duty. Only this time something was different. As he'd come he'd grabbed Annie's bottom and pulled it tight towards him. After a momentary rest he'd realised that he still had his hands latched tight on those firm cheeks. Inside Annie's cunt, his cock was losing its firmness, so by simply shifting his weight he let it slip sloppily out and leave a slimy path down Annie's thighs. Still, his hands gripped Annie's bottom tightly as he slid to the side of her collapsed form. It was then that Norman Moore got a very naughty thought. Somewhere deep in his disturbed psyche two got added to two and his shocked brain came up with what appeared to be four. There in his hands was a very delectable-looking ass. Annie's tousled blonde hair reminded him of that night not so long ago when another blonde-haired woman had drained him dry. His ass, not used to the exertion his still healing body had just undergone, reminded him of what had happened to end that night a few weeks ago. His dick started to grow hard at what he was thinking.

He rolled Annie over, who was only too happy to comply.

169

She still felt like a straw scarecrow who was losing a little stuffing. She was glad Norman was taking charge. On her stomach Annie felt relaxed and perfectly at ease. She didn't mind feeling Norman's body on top of her. His weight forced her further into the couch. The pressure on her back felt good. Even when he took his hand and slid it roughly inside her cunt she didn't care. The feeling was pleasurable. She was happy. It didn't cause her a moment's hesitation as she felt his finger smear their mingled juices over her bottom and up her anus. In her thoroughly relaxed state he was able to gain easy entry with his finger. She didn't mind. She knew what he was going to do. He was going to fuck her in the ass.

As his cockhead forced its way into the button-sized opening Annie cried out with a little pain. She'd had sex this way several times before, but never regularly enough to make that first moment of entry pleasurable. Her long nails gripped the couch as he slid what seemed to be a huge object in and out of her tight bottom. In her cunt his dick hadn't seemed that big, but now in this tighter cavern, his member assumed mammoth proportions.

'Oh – oh –' Annie couldn't speak. The pain was too intensely pleasurable for her to do anything but moan. Norman grunted as he rutted away. His eyes could not shake the image that dominated his view of Annie's ass shaking under his thrusts. He continued to grip her bottom pulling the delectable morsel on to his throbbing dick. He'd never felt such pressure on his cock. Her ass-opening was so tight it threatened to choke off his cock at the very root of its stem. All Norman could do was grunt and exorcise the demons within.

Annie began to feel the throes of another orgasm building as her cunt was rubbed on the couch by Norman's pushing and pulling. Her cuntlips were being spread on the soft material of the cushions and her clitoris pummelled under Norman's weight. She forced her hand underneath herself and slid a finger deep within. From within her cunt she could feel his cock sliding in and out of her ass, but it didn't distract her from the main focus of her attention – her cunt and the throbbing knob guarding her juicy opening. With one long finger she fucked herself and with the nail of another she frigged her clitoris as Norman's once slow ass-fucking motions now became more rapid and forceful.

Norman came first without any real warning. He didn't expect the onrush nor the violence of eruption that the tightness of Annie's sphincter exerted on his swollen dick. He thought for one moment that he'd caused the woman to explode as he gushed inside her. He began to collapse but Annie interrupted his body's decline.

'No – No – don't dare stop – keep fucking.'

Underneath Norman she bucked into him with all of her might as she brought herself off. Inside her bottom Norman's cock filled her with a delectable fullness that seemed to permeate through her cunt as she fucked herself. With Norman lying inert on top of her she arched her back and thrust her ass into his pelvis and her fingers did the rest to her beaten cunt.

It was almost an hour later when she awoke with Norman still on top of her. His cock was still erect from the constriction of her bottom. Gingerly she freed herself and made her way to the bathroom. A little while later she returned with a blanket and covered the apparently sleeping Norman with it. She crawled in next to him and snuggled against his dozing form. She felt comfortable and satisfied that sex could still be new and exhilarating. As she fell into a never never land of sleep she kissed Norman on the cheek.

'Sweet dreams – y'all have sweet dreams indeed.'

Norman was having anything but sweet dreams. He really wasn't asleep. He was concentrating with his eyes tightly closed as if to shut out the real world. Norman's sexual excesses had served to uncage monsters that had remained hidden throughout his recent ordeal of a few weeks ago. Deep in his disturbed subconscious he was conjuring up nasty plans for the woman who'd rejected him and caused him to act like a pervert.

Once Annie was soundly asleep Officer Norman Moore got up, got dressed and quietly left the apartment. He had plans to implement, people to see. There wasn't a moment to lose. He now knew how to get his revenge on Louisa Hampton.

171

11

Silk Stockings

Mix

1½ oz. Tequila
1 oz. Creme de Cacao
1½ oz. Cream
1 dash Grenadine

Shake ingredients with crushed ice.
Strain into cocktail glass.
Sprinkle cinnamon on top.

*L*ouisa stood next to the waitress's serving station watching the last few customers dawdle out of the Pump. She was emotionally drained. It had been an eventful night's work for Louisa. Her rollercoaster emotional ride had started out with the unexpected visit of Officer Norman Moore who Louisa had ceremoniously dispatched into the parking lot. The up-and-down ride continued soaring from the depths of Moore's visit to the high of one of those exceedingly rare occurrences – a really attractive male customer who didn't try to pick up on her – but did pour his heart willingly out to her. And Louisa willingly listened.

The Pump wasn't overly busy so Louisa was able to strike up more than just a passing conversation with the chap. He was Australian it turned out, visiting America on business from England where he now lived. His name was Sydney Nats and he was a lawyer. And his interest in Silicon Valley wasn't totally professional. Over the summer in England he'd met a young American law student from Silicon Valley University who was reading law at Oxford University. They had a wonderful affair amidst the dreaming spires of that sleepy town, and he'd come to America ostensibly on business, but his real purpose was to renew his love with the budding American lawyer.

Only it hadn't worked out that way, and Sydney found himself inside the Pumping Station needing a drink and a shoulder to cry on. Louisa was able to provide both in adequate supply. After a few casual remarks she'd taken her dinner break with him. She'd snacked and he'd drank, and the story he'd told caused even her to catch her breath. At first he'd been reticent to give anything but the sketchiest of details, but Louisa had pressed.

'Oh come on now, Sydney – this girl must have been pretty special to get you to come all this way.'

'Oh, she was special all right.'

'In what way?'

Sydney fell silent again.

'Was it her personality, her looks – her ...?'

'It was all of those things and more. It was the most captivating sex I'd ever experienced. I felt totally bewitched.'

'You're kidding.'

'Oh, I wish I was. She was a modern-day siren luring an unwitting lawyer to crash upon her most attractive rocks. The things she did – the things she could do ...'

The metaphor was lost on Louisa who hadn't dabbled in mythology. Still, the way this really attractive man was espousing this woman's talents intrigued her. She had to know more. It was kind of like throwing down the gauntlet to her, to talk about someone with such legendary sexual capabilities to a person who considered herself an expert on such matters. Louisa kept pouring drinks and encouraging Sydney to pour his heart out. Suddenly, Sydney drew in a deep breath.

'Well, all right Louisa – if you think you can handle it – I'll tell you the full story.'

'No sweat, Sydney. Fire away. I'm all ears. Go right ahead. No sweat at all.'

It took the rest of her dinner break for a rather drunken Australian lawyer to tell his remarkable story. And its telling did cause Louisa to do a lot more than sweat. His soft voice caressed her curiosity, and his bold delivery of such randy acts disarmed her usual stonewall defences. She became putty in his hands. He began slowly at first – probing to see how far he could go with his verbal advances.

'I'd been staying at Magdalen College in Oxford for a legal conference. It was July, the hottest English July in decades. There's a river that runs past the college, with a path

176

following it, circling a small island. It was on this path that I first saw Catherine. She was walking toward me. I could see her off in the distance as she approached, her form seeming rather curvaceous from far away, even more so up close. As we passed, we both looked politely and shyly away, hello-ing to each other under our breath. Once we were well clear of each other I boldly turned to admire her figure — her legs, long but not unusually long, though perfectly proportioned from ankle to calf, to knee, to thigh, to ... well, obviously I couldn't see any further than that. Her bottom curved just like you'd imagine it would, sensually and firmly. Her back, what I could see of it, was smooth and flawless. Of course, by the time I got through staring at her legs and ass, she was too far away to be seen in any detail.

'As happens in all the movies, I went back to where I'd met her — the river path — the same time, next day, in hopes of seeing her. Of course, she wasn't there. I eventually did see her, though, the next evening. I'd been playing tennis with a friend from the conference, and my shirt and body were sweat-soaked. It was one of those warm summer nights, just at twilight, so I took off my shirt as I walked home down the river path. I was thinking about nothing in particular when I looked up to see her standing off the path several yards in front of me. She seemed to be looking for something, so I took the opportunity to be the perfect gentleman by offering her my assistance. She said she'd lost her shoe the night before somewhere by the river's edge, when she'd been frolicking around with someone in the black of night. This night she was wearing a thin summer dress, and against the last light of the sun I could see the silhouette of her body through the thin fabric. I could see how flat her stomach was, and I imaged how she would look sitting naked on top of my cock, tight stomach connected to tight cunt, decorated with rich brown pussy hair. Within moments the sun was completely obscured by the hills, and the clear image of her nakedness disappeared.'

Louisa swallowed at Sydney's graphic use of the English/Australian/American language. It took all of her composure to not appear shocked. It was a new feeling for

177

her — she was usually the one doing the shocking.

Sydney continued, unaware of the effect he was having on Louisa.

'I guess I had been staring at her, because the next thing I remember she was saying, "Excuse me, but I think I see my shoe. Sir, are you OK?" I instantly cleared my head of those lascivious thoughts and ventured down the embankment to fetch the elusive footwear. Unfortunately, in all my nervousness I lost my balance and collapsed into the mud of the riverbank. You can't imagine how embarrassed I was. I did, however, retrieve the shoe. I couldn't believe my luck when this pretty young woman next asked me if she could repay my kindness by fixing me a drink and throwing my muddy tennis shorts in the washer. It's the least she could do, she said. I had nowhere I had to be, so I took her up on her seemingly innocent offer.

'It turns out she was staying in the building just across the river from where we were. After a short walk back to the college, we entered the building. Her room was one of two on the bottom floor. It had two tall, tall windows, facing out onto a deer park. Downstairs were several reclining chairs and a small, uncomfortable-looking couch, along with a refrigerator. Up the spiral staircase was a loft bedroom, small but cozy. The bedroom overlooked the downstairs area, separated only by a metal railing. I guess she had been doing laundry that day, because all colours and styles of lingerie were hanging on the railing to dry. Without staring I managed to catch a glimpse of a demure, white lace bra, a pair of powder-pink stockings, a sheer white g-string, two pairs of red seamed stockings, a red and black satin bra, which from this perspective seemed terribly low-cut, a black and copper coloured suspender belt, and three different attachments for a vibrator. Of course there were lots more, it's just that that's all I could see without making it obvious I was looking at her underclothes. I must admit, I was curious about the vibrator attachments, sitting proudly erect on the railing in the various shapes and sizes. One of them, as I recall, was long, with a bulbous, round, prickly end, and my mind mulled over the possibilities of how this intriguing female

178

in front of me used such a device.

'This time I was so careful not to get caught staring. However, she noticed right away that my attention was not on her offer of a drink and a clean towel to wrap myself in while she laundered my clothes. She seemed embarrassed about me seeing what I saw. She laughed nervously, but with that mischievous smile she has said, "Here's your drink − I hope you like mint juleps. They're real refreshing on a warm night like this." With that, she handed me my drink and my towel, turned around in the skimpy dress she was wearing, so that her back was towards me, and said, "All right, lose the shorts." I was mesmerised by her, not knowing whether she wanted me there for sex, or whether she was just a carefree young woman, on vacation, toying with whomever she met, or whether she was just friendly and was really grateful that I rescued her shoe. Modestly, I wrapped myself in the towel, took off my clothes and handed them to her. She spirited out of the room, presumably toward the laundry.'

Sydney paused to take a long drink.

'I tried to make myself comfortable staring out of the window and sitting on the old couch, but the sight of the lingerie and sex toys on the railing kept calling me. I was dying to get a closer look, so with the excuse that I wanted to see what the upstairs view looked like if I was caught, I walked up the spiral staircase with all the nonchalance I could muster. As I walked towards the bedroom I let my hand fall on each item of clothing that was hanging up. A multitude of silk, lace and satin textures met my touch. Then I reached my true goal, the sex-toy attachments. For a moment I stood there, looking out of the window so I could use my excuse should I be caught. I sat on the bed and stared at the rubber objects directly in front of me. With a sudden pang of guilt, I turned my attention elsewhere. My eyes were instantly glued to a pair of black stockings with gold threads running through them and a seam up the back. I tried to imagine what those stockings would feel like if Catherine were wearing them and rubbing her foot against my cock. My imagination, however failed me. Glancing over the railing to see that no one else was looking, I reached out to feel the stocking. At that

179

moment, however, I also heard the outer door to the building open, so I grabbed my drink and rushed downstairs, unknowingly pushing the stocking over the edge of the loft, down on to a chair below. I reached the bottom of the staircase just in time, before the door opened.'

Louisa breathed an unconscious sigh of relief. Like watching a good movie, she was getting caught up in the progress of events unfolding.

'In came Catherine, that mischievous smile on her face once more. She told me that my laundry was well under way, and would be finished shortly. With that, she pulled herself up onto one of the oversized windowsills and leaned back, drink in hand. The thought of getting caught in her bedroom ogling her lingerie had given me an incredible thirst, so I fixed myself another drink on her invitation. We chatted for a while, about nothing in particular. By then I was more comfortable being around her wearing just a towel. She was obviously more relaxed as well, because she pulled her knee up to her chin, resting her foot on the windowsill, her calf and ankle enticing me. Something else enticed me too. For the way she was sitting, her dress fell open enough for me to get a clear view of her pussy. She was wearing some kind of light-coloured panties, a sheer material, I could tell, because I could clearly see her darker pussy hair beneath. The effect of the drinks and this sight kept me spellbound, and I'm afraid my body was showing how much she enticed me. I had to readjust how I was sitting in order to hide the raging hard-on I had underneath the now inadequate towel. Luckily for me, Catherine arose at that moment and left the room to check on my clothes. I tried to clear my mind of thoughts of her cunt, but found it difficult to look at where she was sitting without remembering with perfect clarity the place between her legs.

'Catherine returned, my erection still fully on-duty. She retook her place on the windowsill, again pulling her knee up to her chin, foot resting on the ledge. I forced myself not to look, but looked anyway. At that moment Catherine casually informed me that she had had some other laundry to do, and would I mind if she had thrown it in with mine?

Of course, I said no. For that other laundry, from what I could tell, was those thin panties she had been wearing only moments earlier. Her cunt now stared at me fully unobscured, dark hair veiling the pinkness of her insides. She reached down with the hand that held her iced drink, and set the glass down between her legs. She shivered and spoke very quietly, just loud enough for me to hear, "Mmmmm, this will cool me down." If only I could have been one of those icecubes at that moment. To be that close to such a hot cunt. It took great restraint on my part not to leap up from my chair and bury my face in between her legs. A moment later she removed the glass from its warm resting place. She purred in a girlish voice, "I'm so cold now, I should do something to make my cunt hot again like it's supposed to be." She reached down, this time without the glass, and caressed her nakedness. Then she took her middle finger and let it slide up inside her. The way it slid so gently, I could tell she was dripping wet with her juices. Meanwhile, unbeknownst to me, the towel I was hiding my body with had come open from the force of my hard-on. I certainly didn't notice, and it seemed to me that she didn't either. She was too busy with her cunt.'

Louisa tried to picture the scene in her mind. This gorgeous man, naked and hard, sitting on a couch. She imagined how beautiful he must have looked, and she wished he was sitting here, now, next to her, naked and hard, just like in his captivating story. Sydney continued, disturbing Louisa's fantasy.

'As I recall, she reached behind her and produced a vibrator, one of those forked ones with two shafts coming out of a common base, sort of shaped like a very narrow V. She turned it on, and pushed one of the fake dicks up her cunt. Pulling it out, she then slowly lifted it to her lips, and pushed the dildo into her mouth just as she had inserted it elsewhere seconds ago. Her lips and tongue lingered on the toy, long enough for her to transfer the taste of her juices into her mouth. Then the toy was put back in its normal place – her hot, wet pussy. For the time being she left the second dick of the vibrator well enough alone. Just watching her push and pull the vibrator, in and out, in and out, in and out, in

181

and out..., it was absolutely transfixing. Every once in awhile she would let the tip of the pseudo-cock buzz against her clit, at which point she would let out a gasp of delight. Then it would be back inside that cave of hers, pumping away.

'Without missing a beat, she pulled the vibrator all the way out of her cunt and stuck the other shaft inside her. This one had one of those long, straight, prickly attachments on it. She seemed to really like the change in sensation. She almost had a look of pain on her face, from the sharpness of the prickles. For a moment I considered getting up from my couch and licking her cunt juices off the now-free alternate vibrator dick, but of course I stayed where I was, both shocked and transfixed. For awhile, she alternated dickheads, from the smooth one to the prickly one, fucking herself and teasing her delicious pussy bud – her clitoris. Sometimes she would use her hands too, stroking herself in the way that only adept fingers can. Despite the hum of the sex toy, I thought I could hear the sound of her cunt juices against her fingers as she fucked herself. It was clear that she was as wet as a woman can possibly be. That amount of wetness that only a really experienced, desirous woman can get, when she can play with herself or be played with so much and for so long before giving in to the relief of final orgasm.'

Louisa felt like interrupting that she knew all about that state – she was starting to approach it quite rapidly. She didn't dare slow Sydney one little bit. This was a new kind of sex for Louisa – and she was totally captivated. Never before had she realised how exciting hearing such a story, told in such a sincere and honest manner, could be. Sydney continued, as if reading a bedtime story to a child incapable of sleep.

'At this point Catherine had had enough preliminary foreplay. The next time she slid the smooth, now slippery cock out of her flowing cunt, she twisted the vibrator around 180 degrees, and simultaneously pushed the prickly end up her pussy, and the smooth end up her ass. She let out a moan, whether of pleasure or pain I could not tell. I imagine it was probably some of each. The juices from her erupting cunt

182

dripped down on to the cock that was fucking her ass, keeping it slippery for the intruder. By now she had both feet on the windowsill, her back against the wall, her drink perched precariously on the ledge. She fucked herself more insistently as she went, her body bucking as much as possible from that position, alternately moving toward and away from the buzzing dicks. Her free hand worked away at her clit. The combination of sensations from being fucked in both orifices at once was too much for her to oppose. With a final frenzied movement, she forced both cocks inside her as far as they would go and teased her pussy into a thunderous orgasmic spasm. Her cunt and ass squeezed hard on the dicks as her body tensed beyond control. Her left foot jerked almost imperceptibly, knocking her drink onto the floor, the shatter of the glass in unison with the moan escaping her throat.'

For several moments Sydney said nothing, reliving the passion of the moment in his mind. Louisa wanted to say, 'And then, and then . . .' but she dared not interrupt the spell that had been cast over them.

'She sat sprawled on the ledge, her breathing fast and short, emitting little noises of exhaustion and elation from time to time. Surprisingly, I had done nothing more than play with myself absent-mindedly throughout Catherine's performance. I was so taken by her passion that I didn't pay attention to the desires of my own body. Now, however, nature took over, bringing me back to my normal awareness of the state of my cock. My dick was, in fact, straight upright, throbbing intensely. But being a true gent, I went to the rescue for the second time that day. I walked up to Catherine, careful to avoid the broken remnants of her drink, lifted her into my arms and carried her up the spiral staircase to her bed. As much as I wanted nothing more than to fuck the daylights out of her, it was clear that her energy was sapped for the time. So instead of satisfying my own lust, I simply covered her with a cool sheet, sauntered back downstairs and cleaned up the glass shards. Because my clothes were in a washing machine located god knows where, I could do nothing but wait for Catherine. I considered wanking off by myself, but somehow that just wouldn't be right after the tremendous events of the evening. I would just have to wait until a more appropriate opportunity presented itself.

'To relieve the tension that wracked my body I took a cool shower, followed by a warm bath to relax me. I sprawled into an easy chair, finished off my third drink, leaned back, and drifted off to sleep. I remember that I was dreaming of being by the ocean, Catherine in that almost sheer summer dress, the wind blowing the fabric taunt against her breasts, her nipples prominent.'

Sydney suddenly stopped and focused on Louisa rather than the imaginary space on which he'd been concentrating.

'Oh dear. I hope you don't mind me telling you all this — only it is essential for you to understand how I feel. I have to tell someone.'

'Oh please continue — please do — I'm fascinated. And don't worry — you can't possibly offend me. Remember, I'm a cocktail waitress — there's nothing I haven't heard.' Louisa didn't bother to add that she was exaggerating a little — she'd never heard anything like this — but she didn't want Sydney to stop his tale out of some misguided concern about her tender ears.

'Thanks — you're a real sport. The next part of the story I only know because Catherine told me about what happened much later, when we were down in the catacombs of a tube station somewhere beneath London. I remember her laughing in that naughty way that she has, conscious of the effect the breeze from the oncoming trains tantalisingly lifting the hem of her skirt had upon me. Apparently after my bath I'd dozed for quite some time. Meanwhile, she had woken up, and was disappointed to think I had left. She was getting dressed for a meeting she had, when it struck her that there was no way I could have left her room without my clothes. Knowing now that I was her captive, she left for her appointment.

'She returned shortly to find me still dozing, sleepy from the alcohol and the effects of the bath. Walking over to my makeshift bed, she reached across the chair and removed the damp, soft towel from my body, my flesh warm from the heat of the night. She removed her conservative grey business suit jacket and opened her blouse, revealing an amazingly unconservative portrait of lingerie and flesh intermingling. Her silk stockings brushed against my thigh as she rolled me from my curled up position onto my back. She leaned down and kissed me gently on the lips, her tits, encased in a sheer black bra, dancing across my chest. Down my body she moved, leaving a trail of hot, wet kisses and sensations of skin on skin.

'Reaching my lower body, she took my balls in one warm hand and my cock in the other. With her tongue she began to tease me, starting at the tip of my cock, now beginning to awaken due to this unexpected stimulus, travelling down to my balls, which she sucked and squeezed in that way she has. She stopped a moment to look at my face, but that portion of my body was still oblivious to her touches. While she admired my thin, muscular body, her hand unconsciously snuck between her legs, insider her panties, inside her cunt – hot, wet, soft; tight, dark, slippery. That delicious place from where hours earlier so much tension had exploded. Not until well after she began caressing her clit did she realise she had been neglecting me, her unwitting plaything. She removed her hand from the wetness and traced a path of her juices over my cock. Leaning over me once again, she licked the trail of female liquid away, surprised at how I could sleep throughout this entire time. Frankly, I'm surprised too. And disappointed. I would give anything to have a woman lick her pussy juices off my cock, then kiss me passionately, the thought of us both enjoying her at once bringing us to even greater heights of ecstasy.'

Louisa wished desperately that she could take notes, but thought it obvious and impolite to try.

'Catherine went back to playing with herself again, this time straddling my body, her legs on the arms of the chair, her cunt lightly rubbing against my cock. My dick jerked unconsciously with the unbearable pleasure of such stimulation.

'Then with sudden inspiration she stood up, gently moving my legs to one side, keeled down in front of me and began to give me one of those blow jobs I'll always remember her for. She has this way of starting off easily and lightly, building a cock into an uncontrollable climax. Lots of women start

185

off the same way, but the key is that Catherine knows that there's more to a good cocksucking than mere slurpy tongues and lips. There's the way she holds my balls, first in her hand, then taking them into her mouth, sucking, rolling them around, enjoying the sensation of having something like that in her mouth. Then there's the exact pressure she uses to squeeze my balls with her hands. It's enough to take away my breath, without causing unbearable pain. After she's done paying so much attention to that portion of my anatomy, she lets her tongue slide down to that little place something like a bridge, that separates balls from ass. There's nothing more sensual than to have a woman lick that small area of flesh and touch-sensors. From my experience with other women, I don't think many people know how erotic that little place can be. By now, of course, I was waking up. I was still a little fuzzy-headed and it wasn't until her mouth was fully over my dick again that I began to realise the position I was in. For Catherine's sake, I didn't move. I didn't want her to become self-conscious by knowing I was awake. In retrospect, though, I don't think it would have disturbed her at all. Still, it was so relaxing to enjoy such an expert blow job as this one, just like a dream, that I'm not sure I wanted to fully awaken anyway.'

Once again Sydney paused, as if in a trance.

'Now we come to the other part of cocksucking that Catherine is so good at. For a short time she continued the light licks and touches with her tongue, just to get the rhythm going again. She then brought on the big guns. With her mouth she increased the pressure of her lips around my cockhead, paying particular attention to the sensitive area where the head meets the shaft.'

Here Sydney gestured to Louisa, as if to draw in the air the exact place on his cock he was talking about.

'Her tongue danced around, circling my cock, assisting with the stimulation the lips gave. While this went on her one hand continued to squeeze my balls, while the other encircled the base of my cock. Working firmly and determinedly with both her hands and mouth, Catherine brought my raging erection to its pinnacle.

'While any good blow job can achieve this, it was other things about Catherine that really made her performance stand out. Hot from her exertions, she had somewhere along the line removed her skirt and blouse. As she sucked me her tits knocked against my leg. I could sense the various textures of damp, warm flesh, and some flimsy, filmy material they make those sexy black see-through bras with. Her panties were the same material embellished with a vivid mint satin, the colour reminiscent of the mint juleps I had been drinking earlier. I imagined that her panties must have been soaked through with her juices. Her suspender belt was of light blue satin, an innocent colour to contrast with her obviously unchaste ways. All in all, a perfectly delectable combination.'

Sydney's eyes twinkled with approval.

'So — as her tits slapped my leg, as she sucked my cock and squeezed my balls, she gradually rotated her cunt around until she was practically fucking my leg. She rubbed her pussy up and down on me, just as if my calf was another cock for her to play with. I decided to help her out some by rubbing my foot against her ass, right between her crack in another one of those sensitive areas. She responded to that by taking the hand that was squeezing my balls and with it undoing the ties on her panties. Catherine is one of those women who always dresses conveniently for fucking. Once she had removed her cunt-wrapping she lowered herself down onto my big toe, my other toes teasing her ass. I had never had my toe inside a pussy before, so I wasn't exactly sure what to do. That didn't matter, though, since Catherine did everything. I'm not sure it felt really wonderful to her, but clearly the thought of being fucked this way while sucking a cock was enjoyable to her. So between her fucking herself using my body anyway she could, her lingerie exciting me visually and physically, her tits knocking against me, and of course her hands and mouth giving me the most professional blow job I've ever had, it was all I could do not to come in her mouth there and then.'

Louisa wondered to herself whether her cocksucking efforts had ever been this successful. Sydney's spellbinding voice continued the story.

'Even if I'd wanted to, Catherine wouldn't have let me come. She slowed down the oral fuck she'd been giving me, and within moments the door opened. In walked a man, tallish, good-looking, wearing only a bathrobe. Catherine kept on with what she was doing, stopping only briefly to tell this man to be quiet and sit down. He did both. I did the first one. I closed my eyes, thinking I might lose my hard-on if I thought about the other man in the room. Catherine removed her pussy from around my toe, and her mouth from my cock, replacing it with her hand. She straddled me, bringing her mouth close to my ear, and her sultry voice whispered, "Let me keep fucking you. Please, Sydney, just pretend he's not here." My confidence in my erection had returned. She continued, "I knew when you saw me fuck my ass and fuck my cunt earlier that you liked to watch. How would you like to watch a man come on my tits? You can do it too. Both of you can come all over me at the same time. Whaddya say, Sydney? For me? Please?" The way her hand was moving on my cock I could hardly say no. I would've said yes to anything, as long as she didn't stop what she was doing to me.

'Catherine told the other man to get over here. He stood in front of her. She turned her back to me and sat down, her cunt encasing my cock, my cock ripe for orgasm. She didn't move around much, just sat there. Which, if I had to wait to come, suited me fine. The feeling of being warm and hidden inside a pussy, I find, is somehow therapeutic. And just sitting there quietly gave me a chance to calm down so I wouldn't shoot my load inside her yet. She put her hands on the other man's hips and moved him directly in front of her. His cock, at this point, was definitely ready to be sucked. She began her manoeuvres on him, just as she had done with me earlier. She apparently knew his legs would soon be tiring, so after a few minutes of giving him her best, she told him to sit in the recliner next to my chair, which he did. For a moment she ignored him. He protested in his posh English voice, "Catherine, my dear, come fuck me. It's been an eternity since you left me earlier tonight. And I didn't even get to fuck you. You're lucky I found you here, or I might

188

never have forgiven you for leaving me orgasmless after watching you writhe on the bed and fuck yourself like you did.''

'I began to get the picture, as they say. Catherine's thrill was to get men's dicks hard beyond belief, then bring them all together to come on her at once. While I have no bisexual proclivities, the thought of this fantasy of Catherine's caught my interest, so I went along with it.

'This is how it went: Catherine sat on the floor in front of us, legs spread wide — she had been a gymnast or a dancer and could do the splits if she wanted — hands moving all over her body. She touched her tits, her ass, her cunt, everywhere, fondling herself into ecstasy. I had the feeling she'd never been able to pull this off before, because she was so turned on by just thinking about her fantasy come to life. The other man and I were wanking off individually. Luckily for our deeply heterosexual male minds, the arms of our chairs hid our enraged cocks from each other while we got ourselves back into peak condition for coming. Catherine, meanwhile, was squeezing her tits in the most engaging way. "Sydney," she said, "fuck me with your hand, please now." Her request was tainted with urgency. I obliged, tempted to stuff my dick up her cunt while I was at it. "You." she said to the other man, "kneel down and put your cock where I can suck it." This he did willingly. She sucked his dick and fucked my hand. A few minutes later she continued her orders. "Now, both of you stop what you're doing, kneel next to me and jack off on me. In my hair, my mouth, my tits, my stomach. Anywhere on me. But don't come till I say." I swore to myself to follow her directions and not to come a second sooner than she wanted.'

Louisa leaned forward in anticipation of what was to come, and Sydney refreshened himself with another gulp of his drink.

'Catherine pulled out a vibrator, this time with an attachment that resembled a very large dickhead. She put the vibrator on top speed and fucked herself furiously. The sight of such desperation almost drove me wild. The sight of the three of us urgently and passionately fucking ourselves

189

almost sent me over the edge. But what finally did it was the other man's come. It shot from his cock unexpectedly. The first bit, due to bad aim, hit my leg. Catherine moaned in ecstasy at this. Most of it, though splashed on Catherine's chest, some smothering her lips, and the last little bit squirting onto her tits and her hard nipples. That was it for me. And that was it for Catherine, too. "Now, Sydney, now!" she screamed and moaned at once, as my come came bubbling through my cock like hot lava. With precision I managed to cover the rest of Catherine with my spunk, trails of it streaming through her pussy hair, lines of it hitting her stomach, and the rest splashing onto her cheek. Catherine writhed and moaned, making the vibrator finish the last necessary pumpings to complete her orgasmic play thoroughly. As she came she released the fake dick, which, saturated with pussy juices, slipped quickly out of her cunt. This final, sensual movement across her over stimulated pussy brought an involuntary moan from her throat and she squirmed from the touch.

'When I awoke who knows how long later, I was alone. My clothes were neatly laid out for me, with a note from Catherine. In the note she told me that she had to see me again. We got together twice more after that, once at the college and once in London. The times we had – I was sure this was the woman for me, the woman of my dreams. And I thought she felt similarly about me. As if we were a match made in heaven, and all those other clichés. Anyway, she left to come back to America once her course was over. We wrote several times and I decided to surprise her by magically appearing ready to resume where we left off. It was a big mistake. She is engaged to be married, and from what I gather leads a very prim and proper existence over here. I guess she was unleashing all of these deep sexual inhibitions when she was away from her home environment. I really don't understand the full story – she even pretended she didn't know who I was.'

Louisa suddenly felt very guilty about her treatment of Officer Moore earlier. The thought snapped her back to reality. She'd taken an hour dinnerbreak and the bar was full

f very thirsty people and an angry bartender. She excused
erself from Sydney and told him she'd be back as soon as
he could get caught up.

Whilst she was picking up bar supplies from the rear store-
oom Sydney Nats left the Pump. At first she thought he
night have gone to the bathroom, but he'd signed his charge
nd left a small note that just said 'Thank you, Louisa —
hope I haven't been too forward. Sydney.' Louisa was in
ome small way heartbroken. She'd taken quite a liking to
he quiet and soft-spoken Australian who had a very definite
vay with words. He hadn't even tried to get her number.
sn't that the way it goes, thought Louisa. All the losers in
he world that she's fucked who would readily follow her to
he ends of the earth, and the one guy she actually fancies
oesn't even try to pick her up. What a night, thought Louisa
- what a night.

It wasn't over yet.

As Louisa pulled her car out of the parking lot of the Pump
he was surrounded by the flashing lights of many Silicon
'alley police cars. *Dèja vu*, thought Louisa, and then it
awned on her that this must have something to do with
)fficer Norman Moore.

It did.

'Could you step out of the car, miss?'

Louisa knew better than to argue. She was being set up.
)eep inside she knew there was no dodging this bullet. She
ot out of her car and offered her driver's licence to one of
he officers.

'Had anything to drink, miss?'

'No — I've been working all evening.'

'Why didn't you stop at the stop sign?'

'I did.'

'I'm afraid you didn't — would you mind taking a few tests
or us?'

'I did stop. Now what are you guys up to?'

Over her shoulder she saw two officers going through her
ar. One of them was Officer Norman Moore.

'Just step to the side, miss, while we call in your licence.'

Louisa complied realising that she was about to be fucked

– but not in the usual way. The feisty little blonde couldn't resist playing with the police. If you were going to go down you may as well go in style, thought Louisa.

'Don't you want to kiss me?'

'Excuse me, miss?'

'You see I usually get kissed before I get fucked – so I wondered if you wanted to kiss me before you fuck me over.'

'I don't know what ...'

The officer detaining Louisa was interrupted by the two officers in her car having a heated discussion. In the still night air their words were clearly audible.'

'I thought you said it was under the seat.'

'I did – it was. You must be blind – let me look.'

There followed a few moments silence followed by a loud 'shit!' Officer Norman Moore came storming over to Louisa.

'What did you do with it?'

'With what, Norman?'

That the blonde referred to Norman by name caused his two colleagues to cast inquiring glances at each other.

'You know damn well what – now it will be easier on you if you cooperate. Or else we'll tear that car apart.'

'For the second time tonight I really don't have any idea what the hell you are talking about.'

There were more glances from the other two officers. They were beginning to realise that Norman hadn't told them the full story about his 'hot tip' on a major drug deal going down at the Pump.

Officer Moore took a threatening step closer to Louisa but was interrupted by the appearance of Sydney Nats.

'What seems to be the problem here?'

'Who the hell are you?'

'I'm Sydney Nats – I'm Miss Hampton's attorney. Now what seems to be the problem?'

Officer Moore was seething. He kicked the tyre of the police car and stomped off to the other cruiser. One of the remaining officers took charge. Retreat seemed the best way to avoid a nasty lawsuit.

'Oh, no problem, sir – just a routine traffic stop. Now drive carefully, miss. Good evening.'

As the police cars pulled off, Louisa turned to Sydney and smiled. This time she had a superman to thank for helping her to dodge one of those little bullets.

'I guess I owe you some thanks – but would you mind telling me what the hell is going on? And where did you disappear to?'

'No problems. After I left the bar I sat in my car for a while wondering whether I should go back in and ask for your number. You were so good about hearing my story – you were amazing – but I think I was a little embarrassed that I actually told you all that stuff. I was upset and I'd had a bit too much to drink. So, sitting there in my car summoning up my courage I was just about to venture forth when in my rear view mirror I saw this character lurking around the parking lot. I thought he was going to break into a car or something, so I crouched down and watched him. He went over to your car – I remembered you saying that you had a convertible red Mustang – and I watched him stuff something in your car and run off. Strange, I thought – so I waited and investigated. This chap – who happened to be the officer who seemed a bit out of sorts a moment ago – had stuffed about a pound of cocaine in your car. Now for all I knew you could have been a dealer and this was your drop – but it seemed like a set-up to me – so I put on my driving gloves and took the coke and stuck it into the garbage dumpster where it would be safe if you really needed it, and then I waited around and watched. It seems I made the right decision.'

'Boy, did you ever.'

'So why are the police out to sink you?'

'It's a long story'

'I see – I guess we've had enough of long stories tonight. Well, someday maybe you'll tell me what a nice girl like you is doing mixed up with guys like that. But it's late and I have an early morning meeting, and I've already taken up too much of your time.'

Sydney hesitated and then continued.

'Since I'm now your attorney you'd better have my card. I've put the number where I'm staying if you'd like to get a hold of me. And I'd be careful if I were you. I don't think they'll stop here — although that officer is going to have quite a bit of explaining to do about how he lost all those drugs.'

They both laughed uncomfortably.

'Well — I'll say good night, then.'

'Hey, wait a minute — didn't you ever make up your mind?'

'About what?'

'You said you were coming back into the Pump to ask for my number — but the cop distracted you.'

'Oh, yes — well, can I have your number?'

Louisa was overjoyed that he'd finally managed to pop the question she'd been dying to hear. He'd been able to tell her all of these intimate details but seemed nervous to ask for her number. It made him all the more appealing.

'Certainly, Sydney — here, let me write it on one of your cards. I have a machine if I'm not home.'

Louisa wrote her number on one of Sydney's cards and handed it to him.

'Thank you — I'll call you.'

'And thank you for saving me from a fate worse than death.'

Louisa reached over and gave him a peck on the cheek leaving a figure-of-eight red lipstick stain. She was going to wipe it off, but Sydney backed away, appearing a little embarrassed.

'I'd best be going then.'

'OK. Well, thanks — and call me.'

'I will — and drive carefully home.'

'Don't worry. I'm not taking any chances.'

And to her great surprise Louisa didn't speed like she normally would. She didn't even turn on the radio. And it was only days later that she realised that she hadn't even thought of all that coke going to waste in the dumpster.

It just wasn't like her.

She had other things on her mind.

One thing in particular.

His name was Sydney Nats, and Louisa couldn't wait for the phone to ring.

12

Legspreader

Mix

1½ oz. Courvoisier Brandy
1½ oz. Hot Water

Pour brandy and hot water into snifter.
Add lemon twist.
Drink while hot.

*T*he sign on the door of the Pump read 'Closed for Private Party.'

Was it ever.

To celebrate the closing of his biggest deal, Arthur Wize spent an undisclosed sum of money to take over the Pump on what would normally have been a quiet Tuesday night. Word of Arthur's celebration had reversed that sleepy-night trend in a real hurry. The Pump's phones were ringing off of the walls and the managers' desks. In response, all of the Pump's employees were called in at the last moment to deal with the expected rush. A ticket to the party was the most sought after perk in Silicon Valley. There were even news crews with minicams lurking at the front door interviewing those lucky enough to have an invitation and seeking nasty comments from those that didn't.

It had been earlier in the day at the elegance of the Regency Hotel that Phuc Yu's takeover of several Silicon Valley companies had been officially announced, thereby surprising the three or four people that hadn't heard about it through the gossip grapevine. Phuc Yu had made a few patriotic statements, and was followed by Janet Hodges giving some of the more involved details. Arthur Wize closed the press conference with an off-the-cuff reference to tonight's party at the Pump. Arthur couldn't resist letting the world know that by the Valley's usual standards of success he'd finally made it. Behind his joviality was the unmistakable and unsaid gloating that those that had laughed at him in the past could now wait in line for an invitation to his celebration. No one had ever closed the Pump for a private party of this nature. Arthur Wize was definitely sending a message that he had firmly arrived at the zenith of his not-so-illustrious career.

To close the Pump and issue invitations to the private party was truly a precedent-setting move that anyone who thought themselves to be a mover and a shaker in Silicon Valley would have to top if they were ever going to outdo Arthur Wize.

And Arthur Wize was doing his fair share of topping and moving and shaking in the third stall of the Pump's women's bathroom. The object of his affections was the twenty-two-year-old wife of one of his most hated competitors. She'd begged Arthur for an invitation, and he'd been his usually blunt self.

'The only way you'll get in is if I get in'

Mrs Treadwell was not very insightful. It was well known in the Valley that Harry Treadwell did not marry her for her brains, and she had not married the sixty-nine-year-old company head for his good looks.

'Excuse me, Arthur. It's your party — of course you'll get in.'

'That's what I wanted to hear my ever so bright darling. Now wear something sexy and be nice and wet so I can stick my dick right up your tight little cunt. Harry tells me you have quite a box.'

'Arthur! Harry would never say something like that — and anyway, how would he know?'

Arthur's belly-laugh could be heard in every men's lavatory in the Valley.

'Just joking — Harry and I never talk any more. But seriously Mrs Treadwell, there will be an invitation waiting for you at the door, and I'll be waiting to take a poke at you if you fancy the services of a younger, more successful man.'

Mrs Treadwell laughed girlishly at Arthur's brazen attitude, and them immediately went to her wardrobe to find just the right thing to wear. She chose something that had been custom-designed for her natural assets.

Arthur sincerely appreciated her sartorial effort as he lifted up the hem of the skin-tight pink dress. It was made out of that type of material that appeared to have been poured on and left to dry on every telling contour. Julie Treadwell's ample breasts were covered — if that is the right word — by the same material. Only her tits weren't really obscured at all. The dress designer, in a perverted departure from the expected form of the dress, chose to radically alter its profile. In what more rational minds could only describe as 'pure genius — sheer adulterated genius', the designer reduced the tightness around the bosom just millimeters past the horizon of the wearer's erect nipples. The effect was lewd beyond belief. The perfectly sensual arc of the lower portion of her tits was revealed with skin tight x-ray clarity. The fullness of their form was encased in the pink second skin pulled edibly tight at the budding nubs of her nipples. Then, like a cascading waterfall the material lost just the right amount of tightness to reveal completely to anyone interested in taking even the most marginal of peeks, the full, uncensored details of the women's breasts. Even the slightest of dips, bends or coughs made the dress's upper contents jiggle as if they were desperately trying to escape the lower-than-the-nipple-line constrictions of the pink glovelike dress.

From purely convenience and practical points of view, Mrs Treadwell had decided against wearing any undergarments. A bra was right out of the question — it would have thoroughly destroyed the uncaged effect her ample bosom enjoyed. And besides, she really didn't need any further support. The lower portions of her tits were cradled by the tightness of the pink material lifting those firm breasts higher than nature would normally allow — just as if she were wearing a corset or Victorian-style bustier. Below the waistline anything next to her skin other than the pink dress would have created unsightly lines and made bathroom fucking just that dash more difficult. Without stockings or tights, Mrs Treadwell felt the need to accentuate her incredibly long and tanned legs with tiny pink lace ankle socks that contrasted intensely with her spiked black high heels and her shiny pageboy-cut black hair. The combined effect of the dress, the socks, the shoes and Julie Treadwell's body was simply — in a word — stunning. It was an outfit to be worn by someone with a body which should really require a licence to walk down the street.

Julie Treadwell had just those kind of looks.

And Arthur Wize was ravishing them against the bathroom stall wall with all the might that his massive form could muster. The tight pink dress hem was forced over the golden curve of Julie's hips. The oh-so-loose top of the dress was stretched below her bouncing tits. And yes, they were bouncing incredibly high as Arthur Wize's blood-engorged penis battered its way in and out of Mrs Treadwell's cunt. The bathroom stall shook with the vibrations of their lust even more so than when those pesky earthquakes jolted the Silicon Valley area with their ever increasing regularity.

The engaging scene must have looked something like a pornographic version of beauty and the beast. Julie Treadwell – her short black hair bobbing up and down, her breasts jiggling frantically, her long tanned legs lifted off the ground, her slim lace-covered ankles wrapped around the thrusting hulk of Arthur Wize's ass, – his gray pinstriped suit trousers around his ankles, black bikini underwear, which really belonged on a younger and thinner man, around his knees, pulsing dick sticking out from underneath his starched blue and white shirt, red tie thrust over his shoulder. It was sublimely tawdry.

In his leaning position and in her resulting raised state, the average bouncing motion of Julie Treadwell's tits brought them every few seconds into Arthur's face. It was a simple matter for the married lady to arch her back and subsequently batter Mr Wize about the head with her creamy white jiggling globes. It drove the heaving hulk of a man wild. Her extremely pointy nipples slapped hard against his nose, or occasionally one would hit him right in the eye, or if he was lucky he was able to wrap his lips around one as it flew by and have a good old suck.

'Oh yes, Arthur – please bite my titties.'

'Hmmmpherumph.'

It was difficult for Arthur to talk with his lips firmly wrapped around one of Mrs Treadwell's nipples, but his grunting was sufficient to drive the supercharged lady to add her own efforts to those of Arthur. With her long fingers she grasped Arthur's head and pulled it firmly into her milky

200

white bosom — thereby smothering the humping giant.

'Splutterumphherrump.'

Arthur was blowing a warm breeze into the excited lady's cavernous cleavage having broken away from the gnawing of her nipple. She was kissing his forehead and biting his ears. The image of two dogs playfully nipping at each other ran through her mind. She did feel like a bitch in heat — and Arthur Wize was the randy old bulldog having his lascivious way.

'Oh God Arthur, when you blow on my boobs I could scream . . . they feel like they might . . . you feel like your dick is going to poke right through my cunt and fuck my tits . . . you really do have such a good cock . . . I've wanted it inside of me for so long . . . please keep that up . . . just like that . . . more to the right . . . harder . . . harder . . . oh . . . I can feel your balls banging on my thighs . . . you're hung like a bull . . . you're such a stud to fuck me here in the bathroom . . . everyone must be listening to you grunt . . . and to me moan . . . they must be so jealous . . . knowing your big dick is up my cunt . . .'

Arthur wished she'd shut up and come because he wasn't going to last too much longer. Providing such aural stimulation, albeit a little irritating, Julie Treadwell's high pitched baby-doll voice played on Arthur's raging libido. It was like fucking a randy schoolgirl. And with that thought titillating his cock, it didn't take Arthur Wize too long to climax. He forced every inch of his trembling cock inside her dripping little pussy. The force of his entry made her slide up the bathroom wall. Arthur stood on his tiptoes looking up at her tits and at her head lolling from side to side. He bellowed like a wounded bull moose.

'I'm coming . . .'

It was a bit of a redundant statement.

'Oh yes Arthur — yes — you're so much bigger than Harry — you can come more than him . . . you are so much of a better fuck than him . . .' Mrs Treadwell was skilled in stroking the egos of Silicon Valley executives. She'd fucked enough of them — and they were all the same. They were all convinced that they were better than the other guy, and they all longed to hear it confirmed by a pretty woman.

She felt herself reaching climax and decided to take control. Julie pumped Arthur's shoulders harder, bashing her breasts violently on his sweating face. The resulting slapping sound emerging from the stall sounded like someone having a jolly good wank.

From Arthur Wize's point of view that was just what he was doing. The moment he'd finished shooting his angry load inside of her he'd let the good lady down and thanked her for being so accommodating. A little put out by the letdown – she had been quite close to getting off – Julie pulled down her dress with a delightful wriggling motion of her hips that betrayed her continued fuckability; pulled up the top of the pink garment to cover up her jigging breasts; smoothed her hair with a quick combing of her lovely long fingers; and opened the stall door to let the waiting audience of Silicon Valley femme fatales catch full view of Arthur Wize sitting exhausted on the porcelain throne. With his trousers around his ankles and a rapidly deflating cock pointing into the toilet he looked anything but like the new King of Silicon Valley business. Julie couldn't resist a parting shot heard by all the inquiring female minds.

'Well, I think I'll go find that Phuc Yu. I hear he has a tool big enough to satisfy me.'

And with that Mrs Julie Treadwell sauntered out of the bathroom to the dying admiration of her audience. It didn't phaze Arthur Wize one little bit. He nodded his head at the attentive audience and burped a one-syllable response that summed up the attitude he best thought fitted his new-found status.

'Nexxxxt . . .'

And as two rather adventuresome secretaries that had been on someone's guest list tip-toed giggling into the stall, Arthur asked the remaining audience of ladies-in-waiting for a slight favour.

'Say – if you're going to watch – could one of you ladies be so kind as to get me a drink?'

And one of them did.

Several times . . .

As hard as she searched. Mrs Treadwell couldn't find the well-hung Korean. With good reason. Phuc Yu was pursuing his latest passion in the privacy of the Pump's female employee's changing room. He was completely naked. His partner wore the undergarments of a Pump cocktail waitress. The slinky black dress lay on the cold tiled floor. Mr Yu sat on the wooden bench, his mammoth dick straining skyward.

'This is the most I've ever enjoyed sex. I have found my true delight.'

'I enjoy it too, Phuc.'

'Ah, but Hazel, it is so kind of you to use your beautiful breasts to give me so much pleasure. You have no idea how exquisite they feel on my dong.'

'Tell me, Phuc – tell me how good my titties feel on your dick.'

Without pausing in her motions, Hazel poured more moisturising lotion between her tits. A rude squelching noise emanated from her huge cleavage as Yu's dick penetrated the tightness between her compressed flesh.

'When I stick my penis between your breasts it is like – it is like – I am having every possible kind of sex at once. Does that make sense?'

'Yes, darling, but tell me more.'

Hazel had her hand between her legs casually stroking her clitoris hidden in the plumpness of her cuntlips. Phuc Yu's descriptions of her abilities excited her. It was flattering to hear such compliments about her body.

'Well – how should I say? Your tits are better than any cunt I've ever fucked. They are tighter and conform to the little ridges of my dick better than any pussy ever could. They grip the entire length of my shaft – and quite a length it is – no pussy can ever hold it all. And the same goes for bottoms. I've never found one – not even the whores in Bangkok – could take my dong up their asses. The same with their mouths. They couldn't get their lips around it so they just masturbated me whilst kissing my cock slit with their nimble tongues.'

Hazel thought how nice it would be to have the nimble tongue of a Bangkok whore doing just what her own finger was doing at this moment. Phuc Yu continued his musings.

'Fucking your tits is even better than playing with myself. The cream, the lotion, it softens the skin making every touch of your breasts — your titties as you call those huge pleasure globes — like a thousand hands. I feel like I have many young girls and boys wanking me off, as if I am some holy figure whom they worship. And my cock is their altar. They crave to touch my dick with their little fingers.'

'I worship your dick, Phuc. I'm praying to it now.'

'Well, your prayers will be answered with manna from heaven, my dear. Soon — very soon.'

Hazel admired Phuc Yu's control over his body. He continued to talk as his dick slid in and out of her greased-up mammaries, almost as if she was doing nothing more than giving him a great back massage. But his words — his body movements — betrayed the rapture he was feeling. His commentary served to excite her with its calmness. It was like someone was watching them and describing their antics.

Which no one was, since Bob Vest had the security system on normal operations because of the crowd in the parking lot. Phuc and Hazel were safe from his prying video eye.

'Hmmmm.' Phuc moaned the deep throaty sound that gave warning of his impending eruption.

Deep inside his balls Hazel could feel the juices begin to stir. His testicles were squashed against her chest — mashed with every stroke between her creamy tits so she could feel even the slightest of pulses, of stirrings deep inside her body. His swollen sperm-filled sacks were pushed together and forced through the cuntlike gap that Hazel formed by compressing her boobs with her arms. It was if he were fucking a woman who had the unique ability to open her cunt just a little to let his balls inside of her, and then close the juicy opening tight on his gonads with an exquisite rush far better than the usual hand underneath his ass grabbing at his hanging jewels.

'Hmmmm.'

'Phuc — baby — I'm going to catch all of your come in my mouth. Don't spare a drop — let it all out into me. I want to drink . . .'

'Hmmmmmmmmmmmmmmmmmmmmmmmmmmmmmoooooooohhh-hhhh!'

Hazel didn't have time to finish her encouragements as Phuc Yu shot his creamy load into her mouth. It splattered around her lips and nose making her cough. Hazel ground her body on her finger until she began to feel herself flow. It began slowly at first but burst violently as she rubbed herself backwards and forwards.

Impaled on her finger, she kept his dick between her tits and kissed his cockhead. The swollen slit was sensitive and caused Yu to shudder as if a cold wind had blown through the humidity of the small room. He held her head between his hands and controlled her motions with all of his limbs. She felt completely in his control and had no cause to object when she heard the Korean say, 'You are mine – all mine – forever. Ever since that mystical night high above my Silicon Valley – when I first felt your marvellous breasts on my flesh – I have known that you belong to me.'

Another relational by-product of that opium-inspired orgy at the gorgeous penthouse suite of the opulent Regency Hotel was progressing well. Since that night Kerry had spent many hours denying to herself that she was a lesbian. She told herself that she was simply fascinated by the feelings, and the lack of pressure she felt when she was in Janet's embrace. She rationalised the whole affair as just a phase she was passing through no doubt caused by the strange situation at the Pump, and her unfortunate involvement with Bob.

He'd been furious that she'd not showed up at his apartment on the night that she was busy at the orgy. Bob was so incensed at being stood up that he hadn't wanted to hear any of her excuses. He'd practically accused her of incest, sodomy, child abuse, necrophilia and a few other perversions known only to residents of the Hollywood hills. She'd told him that he was acting like a jealous ex-husband, and he'd told her she had no right to fool around. She'd promptly reminded him that they'd only been seeing each other for about three weeks, and further he had no right to act like he owned her. There had been much subsequent

205

shouting and general accusatory speeches from both camps. An icy truce had been declared, but to say that the situation was strained was putting it mildly.

While at work at the Pump Bob hovered over Kerry looking for the littlest thing to criticise her over. He particularly hated it whenever she seemed to be enjoying herself with a customer. Bob was jealous – and it showed. He'd fallen head-over-heels in love with Kerry Farnum and felt betrayed by her apparent disregard for their relationship. He'd never bothered to ask her if she felt the same. He'd just assumed that she did. He'd come to treat Kerry as a little girl needing protecting, and it had been quite a shock to learn that the little girl had grown up.

And in all of his self-pity and hurt he never bothered to think of the times that he'd spied on her in the changing rooms, and had disabled her car just so he could appear like the hero and fix it and fuck her in the process. And then he'd told her not to mention their relationship at work, ostensibly because employee morale might be affected, but really because he didn't want anyone – especially the really cute new food waitress – to think he was attached. None of these love-life double standards entered into his hurt maelstrom of emotional turmoil.

Such was the resilience of the male ego.

Bob leaned over and whispered in Kerry's ear as she was talking to Janet Hodges.

'Don't you have some glassware to put away?'

Bob was being nit-picky. He didn't like the way that Kerry was talking to the little English blonde that had been in the fight and had been nursed back to health by Hazel. From his videodisk recordings he knew exactly what Janet's persuasion was, and it irked him to think that Kerry might be offing him for a woman.

Such was the frailty of the male ego.

'No, Bob – I'm all done with the glassware.'

'Well, there are other customers.'

This time he whispered his gripes loud enough to be heard by Janet.

'Oh don't worry, Mr Vest. Mr Wize – who I'm sure you

know is paying your salary this evening – has said that Kerry is to be solely concerned with serving Mr Yu's party. At the present time I am the only member of Mr Yu's party here, and Kerry is doing her wonderful job of looking after me very well – so there is no need to worry.'

Bob stumped off in a huff to find a busboy to yell at or a food waitress to hassle.

'Janet, you shouldn't have – he's mad enough at me as it is.'

'Oh, Kerry – I don't know why you bother.'

Janet put her hand on Kerry's shoulder. The soft touch of skin on skin was comforting. It spoke of deeper pleasures. Janet continued.

'I shouldn't be telling you this because Mr Yu wanted to approach you directly, but I really can't stand by and watch that brute Bob Vest abuse you. There really is no need to put up with this life, you know.'

Kerry began to object, but Janet waved the engineering student-cocktail waitress to be quiet.

'I know all about you needing money to finish university – but you do have another option. Mr Yu is very impressed with you and is willing to hire you as his personal assistant reponsible for his Silicon Valley operation.'

Kerry stared at the petite Englishwoman in amazement.

'The position will pay very well. You won't need to go to graduate school – you'll start right at the top – and there will be lots of fringe benefits.'

'There has got to be a catch.'

'No catch – you know what Mr Yu is like. The same thing happened to me. I was a bright and up-and-coming engineering student at Cambridge when I ran into Mr Yu at a university garden party. He offered me the job and I never looked back. Now I run his European operation. The same thing could happen to you, only here – in Silicon Valley.'

'I don't know what to say.'

Kerry wondered just what sex orgies had gone on at the university garden party and whether part of Janet's job description involved her continued participation in such activities. After the other evening at the Regency, Kerry was indeed very much aware what Mr Yu was like. Would similar evenings be required of her? Would she recruit bright young things for Mr Yu to enjoy? Would she . . .

It was clear to Janet that Kerry was deep in thought. She thought it wise to bring her back to this planet.

'Well, don't say anything when Mr Yu formally approaches you. He likes the ceremony of being the one to announce important things − so act surprised. And say yes. Just think of the fun we can have. You can visit England − and I'll have someone special to see when I come over here.'

'I just don't know what to say. It's so sudden. There's so much to think about.'

'Well, just be glad I gave you a head start. That way you can be prepared to negotiate with Mr Yu when he approaches you. He likes to take people by surprise, thereby getting one up on them. So you'll have a little advantage. The first of many.'

Janet patted Kerry on the thigh. Feeling no resistance she slipped her hand up the mesh of the fishnet stocking and met that delectable transition from taut nylon to silky flesh. Inching her way up Kerry's suspender she brushed her pubic mound. Janet leaned over and gently kissed her on the lips. Kerry responded but appeared stunned. As their tongues touched Janet pulled aside the elastic of Kerry's panties and gently slid one finger inside her cunt. Their lips parted, but Janet kept her finger deep within the waitress's cunt. She spoke softly at Kerry.

'Please say you will. We can talk more about this later tonight, once this party is over. Why don't we spend the night at the Regency − just you and I?' Janet pulled her finger out of Kerry's pussy and licked its full length. The effect was very wicked.

'I think I need a drink.'

They both laughed and Kerry took the opportunity to excuse herself. She nodded and said she'd be right back with a real drink for Janet. Kerry's world was spinning − she needed to think. She was glad of Janet's warning. The head start would help her collect her thoughts. But how the hell was she going to do any work this evening with all of these conflicting emotions rushing around her brain?

For very different reasons both Louisa and Annie had similar dilemmas. Neither one of them was concentrating on their cocktailing jobs. Louisa was rushing to the phone every chance she could get to dial her answering machine to see if Sydney Nats had called yet. Tonight was to have been her first night off and she had planned to sit by the phone in case the Australian lawyer called. She was afraid that he might not leave a message if he called and got her machine – or worse – that he'd call and say that he was going back to England or even Australia and wanted to see her tonight – and because she wasn't there she'd miss him. So she dialled her machine religiously and polled her messages – all the usual crap – but nothing from Sydney so far. Then it was back to cocktailing and messing up people's orders because she was thinking about what might happen with her and Sydney.

Annie was similarly 'out to lunch'. She was caught between the proverbial rock and the hard place. Here she was in the midst of at least a hundred celebrating men who would pay dearly for her talents – but somehow she couldn't get into the groove. She hadn't turned a trick since that night with Norman. She didn't know whether she really fancied him – or even if he had the hots for her. Was it just a one night fling or could it mean something more? He didn't have her number, and she hadn't got his, so the only hope was that he'd come into the Pump when she was working. Annie didn't know that there was little chance of that happening, but until she satisfied the questions that were haunting her every moment she didn't feel like having any form of sex – for money or pleasure. Her legendary randiness had gone on strike, and consequently so had her cocktailing abilities. She just didn't want to be at the Pump, and hadn't relished being called into work at such late notice – especially since it was a private party and there was little chance of Norman showing up.

Lester Byron had a little different dilemma that was making it very difficult for him to concentrate on pouring drinks. He wasn't waiting for that someone special to phone, and he certainly wasn't in love. Phuc Yu hadn't offered him a job or anything like that. Oh no. His quandary had nothing to do with Phuc Yu. Well, circumstantially it did. In a very roundabout way, Lester Byron owed his current good fortune to Phuc Yu. If Phuc Yu hadn't have retained Arthur Wize to act as his business broker, then Arthur Wize wouldn't have rented out the Pump and Julie Treadwell wouldn't have begged for an invite to the private party, and because she couldn't find the well-hung Korean she'd settled for giving Lester a blow-job underneath the bar. She figured it would pass the time whilst she waited for the Korean to emerge.

Lester the Molester couldn't have cared less about Mrs Treadwell's motives. He couldn't even believe his good luck. This really foxy babe (Lester's own words) with bitchin' hooters had positioned herself at the end of the bar and asked Lester if he knew where Phuc Yu was. She'd leaned over the bar when she'd said those magic words and Lester was able to see all the way down her cleavage to her belly-button. His perverted eyes bugged out as he leered at Julie's nipples, and the way the soft flesh of her breasts rippled in front of his bulging eyes.

'I said do you know where Phuc Yu is?'

'I'd love to.'

'What?'

'Fuck you.'

'No way – but I will give you a blow job. If you can tell me where Phuc Yu is.'

'He's upstairs – I'll even let you back there if you'll suck me off.'

'Okay – a deal's a deal.'

And with that Mrs Treadwell dropped to her knees and crawled underneath the counter to position herself for the administering of a good sucking. She was expert at such things, having to perform it nightly for Harry Treadwell. It seemed to be the only kind of sex Harry enjoyed. Once it was over he'd roll over and go to sleep, so Julie had become an expert in bringing him off in double-quick time. Firmly positioned beneath the counter, Julie Treadwell reached up and unzipped Lester's trousers. His raging boner popped right out at her because Lester wore no underwear, a fact which struck Julie as a bit strange. Lester liked the way the rough material rubbed on his cock – he'd even been able to bring himself off just by walking down the street behind schoolgirls, such was the intensity of feeling that the friction between polyester, cotton and dickskin created.

Gripping the base of Lester's hard-on with her right hand and cupping his tiny little balls with the other, Julie Treadwell slipped the pencil-like dick between her pouting lips. As her mouth travelled down his shaft she jerked his cock with her hand and began to squeeze his balls with the other. As his dick slid down her throat she pulsed her tongue along the quivering length. Alternating her tongue into different shapes she matched the motions of her hand. Relaxing her lips ever so slightly she let her saliva trickle down his cock where she rubbed it heartily into his scrotum.

Lester had only ever dreamed of such things as this. And even when he'd dreamed of them he'd always wake up in a sticky mess, so it was difficult for him to concentrate on anything other than blowing his wad into Julie Treadwell's warm throat. At the bar he just stood with a glazed expression on his face, propping himself up on the counter by his elbows. Two of Mr Yu's Korean helpers were trying to place drink orders, but Lester looked straight through them. Much to their consternation he gave them glasses of water and a smile.

Mrs Treadwell knew all of the tricks that she'd learned in her intensive training as a young bride. As Lester's cock became more and more sensitive she raked her teeth along its length, careful not to inflict injury, but very careful to inflict just the right amount of pain to make Lester want to come in bucket-loads. Her experienced fingers changed their grip from a clenched fist to more of a pinch and then back to a clenched fist. Her tongue slid purposefully along the little slit at the top of Lester's dick flicking away the telltale juices that were emerging. And as Lester's balls began to contract she pumped each one in her palm and squeezed the come out of them. His dick reached the stiffness of cold rolled steel and spit its load into the back of her throat. With two quick swallows she destroyed all evidence of Lester's orgasm.

It was only as she crawled out from behind the bar that she turned to see that she hadn't put Lester's dick back in his pants. The rapidly softening penis was dangling out of its hide-out for all the world to see. She was about to say something to Lester when Phuc Yu emerged from a side door. All thoughts of Lester's little one were eclipsed by the prospect of Phuc Yu's reputed dreadnought. She left Lester behind the bar pouring drinks with his dick hanging out.

She wasted no time in introducing her willing body.

'Mr Yu – I'm Mrs Julie Treadwell. My husband owns Treadwell Technologies. Is there somewhere we could go and talk a little business? I may be able to make your empire a little bigger.'

The *double entendre* was not lost on Phuc Yu, who motioned Mrs Treadwell to follow him to his limousine which was parked next to the Pump's back door. He'd been careful to make sure Hazel was occupied with Janet before he'd made his exit. He didn't want to do anything to jeopardise the availability of his tit-fucking specialist, but this was a unique business opportunity that had presented itself – herself – to him. He could already feel his empire growing.

With Hazel back on the floor from wherever she'd been, and Annie and Louisa somewhat doing their jobs, Kerry decided to take a short break. She needed to collect her thoughts. If what Janet said was true, and there seemed no reason to doubt it, Kerry had a few major decisions to make. Amidst requests for gin and tonics, screwdrivers, beers and all sorts of wines, Kerry had barely functioned. She looked forward to her thirty minutes of peace and quiet, so it was with a little shock that she was assailed by a very drunk Arthur Wize in stall number three of the women's bathroom. Kerry had thought she would just shut herself in a stall and think about the decision she'd have to make – to be or not to be Phuc Yu's assistant, and all that stuff. She hadn't expected to run into Arthur Wize practically passed out in the bathroom in a somewhat embarrassing state of undress. Bobbing out from beneath a rather nastily stained shirt was a very battered looking penis. It was all red and puffy, just like Mr Wize's eyes and his tie.

'Kelly – how nice to see ya.'

'Kerry, Mr. Wize.'

'That's what I said, didn't I – Kelly?'

Arthur Wize was slurring his words, but for the sake of clarity here, the slurs will be omitted.

Kerry just nodded and motioned to walk away. She didn't particularly enjoy staring at Arthur's one-eyed trouser snake.

'Don't rush off – I want to apologise.'

'It's all right, Mr Wize. This is your party – you're entitled to a little fun. And by the way, congratulations. You must be proud of what you've done.'

'I am – but that's not what I meant.'

Arthur was beginning to get earnestly sincere in only the way that really inebriated people can. He stood up and stumbled. He'd forgot that his pants were tangled around his ankles. Kerry helped him to his feet.

'Thank you, Kelly. No I meant about the other night – behind the dumpster. It was nice of you to be such a sport about everything.'

Kerry's brain started churning – nasty thoughts began to worm their unsettling way to the surface. She thought it best to encourage the drunk's confession so she just smiled and didn't say a word. She wasn't sure what to expect, but she had a feeling that it wasn't going to be pleasurable.

'Yeah – he didn't know it was you at all. He thought it was Annie. She'd been turning tricks back there all night long for me, you know, to help clinch the deals, and I'd told him to go back there for one for the road. You just happened to be in the wrong place at the wrong time, and then when you struggled and knocked yourself out on the dumpster – well, I was so worried.'

Arthur Wize plopped himself back down on the toilet. In his stupor he hadn't realised how pale Kerry had become.

'Old Phuc doesn't really remember a thing about it. He was drunker then than I am now, but it was really nice of you to keep quiet. You could have nixed the whole deal – if you'd gone to the police and created stink, we'd have never closed those deals. I guess I really owe you one.'

'I guess you do.'

'Say – would you like a little now in the way of a down payment?'

Arthur fondled his battle-scarred penis hopefully. Kerry

213

was amazed at Arthur Wize's resilience. He'd fucked god knows how many women this evening and still wanted more. It was all she could do from kicking him in the balls, but she remained composed. There were other ways of getting even. And she now had the ammunition for doing just that.

'I think you've had enough, Mr Wize.'

And Kerry just shut the stall door without further ado. Within seconds she could hear his grotesque snoring rattling the stall partitions that his fucking excesses had previously loosened. Kerry stared at the bathroom mirror, even more confused than ever. Life had been so simple before she started being a Pump cocktail waitress. Now – now it was so damn complicated.

Staring in the mirror she could see in her mind's eye the visions – the images – that her shocked brain had sought to hide. The fat fingers with the rings holding her shoulders down – the feel of that massive cock inside of her. 'Later,' her brain had told her that night of the opium orgy – 'Later.'

'Later' had finally arrived with all the violent inevitability that fate has a cruel way of mustering. Gazing at her pale reflection in the mirror Kerry began to calculate just what her response would be. She was not panicked, she was not flustered, she did not feel like she had been raped. She really didn't blame Phuc Yu. Annie da Pheelanupe had a few things to answer for, but Kerry didn't really blame her either. Kerry was just overwhelmed with all of these shocking items of information. They were like raw precious stones that she had to polish for them to reach their full value as priceless jewels.

In the background she could hear the so-called King of Silicon Valley business snoring off his evening's amorous exploits. A plan began to formulate in her mind. She now knew how she'd handle Phuc Yu and his offer of employment. She smiled to herself – if someone like Arthur Wize could call himself the King of Silicon Valley business, then why couldn't a twenty-two year-old engineering student and part-time cocktail waitress be crowned Queen.

Why not indeed?

13

Sex on the Beach

Mix

¾ oz. Chambord
¾ oz. Melon Liqueur
3 oz. Pineapple Juice

Pour over ice.
Fill the glass with cranberry juice.
Garnish with fruit.

*T*he sleepy unsuspecting Pacific coastline of Northern California, just due west thirty minutes on a good day from the frenetic pace of Silicon Valley, was the site of the Pumping Station's annual employee end-of-summer beach picnic. Miles of sprawling beaches with such names as New Brighton, Capitola, Aptos and Santa Cruz were the traditional escape targets for the millions of burned out high-tech workers of the Valley. The surprisingly icy coolness of the Pacific Ocean, the heat of the California sun, a relatively lazy drive through picturesque ancient redwood forests to get there – all were guaranteed to soothe even the most harrowed high-tech brow.

The Pump's annual beach picnic was something of a Valley tradition, attracting not just the Pump's employees but also the complete spectrum of hangers-on. The afternoon of sun, sand, sex, drinks, barbecued food and more sex usually produced enough gossip to keep the wagging tongues of Silicon Valley going for at least the next month. And with all the recent goings on at the Pump, this year's picnic promised to be extremely fertile ground for the blossoming of a rich crop of juicy stories.

Phuc Yu's stretch limousine stood parked on a hillside gleaming black above other fine automobiles like the head of a wild animal herd looking down upon its fold. Mr Yu had brought Janet, Hazel, Kerry and Arthur Wize along in the spaciousness of the car. Kerry planned to specify her terms to Phuc today at the beach, but as she walked passed the gleaming chrome and steel trophies of success to get to

217

the beach she began to feel the apprehension of doubt creeping into her mind.

Fancy automobiles weren't the only vehicles occupying spaces in the parking lot. Littered amongst the chariots of the Silicon Valley gods were the more humble cars of the worker bees. Louisa Hampton's bright red Mustang was there – as was Syndey Nats' white rental car of generic Japanese origin. He'd finally gotten up the nerve to call Louisa and she'd wasted no time in inviting him to the picnic. If all went well they'd be together, walking hand in hand down the beach as the huge orange sun set below the rolling surf. The setting would be postcard romantic – who knows what might happen, thought Louisa whilst doing her very best to convince herself that she couldn't care less about the extremely dishy Australian lawyer. Louisa had fought for so long to remain independent and free from emotional entanglements that now that there was the potential for a real, honest-to-goodness love affair, she was caught in a mighty dilemma.

And Sydney wasn't about to make it easy for Louisa to ignore him. He spared no expense in putting together a picnic basket full of the very best in romantic foods – French champagne, oysters, caviar, strawberries and cream – and there were always the barbecued hotdogs if that combination didn't do the trick. And like Louisa he'd been telling himself to take it easy. He knew that his experiences with Catherine had left him vulnerable – fools rush in where angels fear to tread and all that stuff – but there was something captivating about this feisty blonde cocktail waitress that brushed aside his inhibitions. He had only ten more days left in Silicon Valley before having to return to England, and he didn't want to leave behind more memories than when he'd arrived in search of the elusive past.

Noticeably absent from the beach parking lot was Annie's car. She'd called in sick to the Pump for the last week and no one had seen nor heard the slightest titbit about her. Everyone had expected her to show up at the picnic with some truly amazing story, but so far there was no sight of the Texas belle.

And some people hadn't bothered to drive. Mrs Treadwell, fresh from her by now notorious experiences at Arthur Wize's party, had used her husband's helicopter to make a spectacular entrance on the beach – emerging from the cloud of blowing sand in just ten square inches of fluorescent pink material covering the barest minimum of flesh. Like some powerful magnet atracting a storm of iron filings, Julie Treadwell was besieged by every free male on the beach. All the regulars – Fred, Basil and Larry – were there, hoping for some of what Lester had told them about.

Lester was doing his best to appear nonchalant, but had to go and stand waist deep in the cold ocean water to quench the raging hard-on he'd developed in just seeing the lovely Mrs Treadwell. Lester had paid a high price for his sucking off at Arthur Wize's private party. Julie Treadwell had left Lester's dick hanging out of his pants, and in his euphoria he'd forgotten to put it away. His cock was sopping wet after her delicious sucking, and Lester had gotten the shock of his life – literally – when his exposed dick had brushed by an electrical outlet. Luckily for him it had just been the merest of contacts, but the resultant burn had caused many tender nights and even now the slightest tingling of an erection caused untold pain. The sting of saltwater didn't help much, but at least the coolness of the ocean waters did make the throbbing dick shrivel rather quickly. Lester's inferiority complex wasn't helped by his embarrassing accident, and its rather painful consequences. He hoped that no one had noticed his evasive actions. He was quite wrong. Lester's plight had been thoroughly enjoyed by the guffawing forms of beer swilling Bob Vest and Don Palumba, both of whom had the misfortune to have to administer emergency first aid to Lester on that fateful night.

And so here they all were, the key and not-so-key players in Silicon Valley, gathered at the beach amidst the framework of women in bikinis, men in various versions of what passed for bathing suits, eating and drinking, some playing ridiculous beach games as the grander game of life evolved around them.

To get away from all the enforced jocularity so prevalent

at events such as annual beach picnics, Sydney and Louisa went for a walk. They'd consumed the contents of the picnic basket, and the resulting amorous aftereffects of champagne and fine food had convinced both of them of the need for a cooling-off walk. Only it wasn't turning out that way. Their hands touched with all the static of restrained lust. Every little brush of skin seemed to invite further, more prolonged encounters. It seemed that it was just a matter of time before their bodies were to be writhing together in the sand.

After many teasing touches and the occasional playful chases that ended in brief bouts of intimate wrestling matches, further down the beach they came to the remains of an old pier. Many of the timbers had collapsed inward, forming a hidden shelter into which a bold wave sometimes lapped. Sydney stepped inside.

'Come on in, Louisa − I won't bite.'

'It's not you I'm worried about. There might be things with big snappy jaws in there.'

'I'll protect you. I'll be your knight in shining armour with my trusty lance − ready to fend off anything with big snappy jaws.'

'Sure . . .'

Despite her reluctance, Louisa entered. The place smelled secret as though it had been expressly designed for furtive encounters of the sexual kind. Tentatively she entered. A strange type of milky-soft light illuminated the darkness. Through beaming shafts of half-light she could easily distinguish Sydney's well-proportioned form.

'Now why would you ask a girl to come in here if your intentions weren't strictly dishonourable?'

'And why would you come in here wearing that extremely sexy bikini if you weren't out to seduce a poor unsuspecting Aussie lawyer who'd lost his way?'

'From what you were telling me the other night, you're neither unsuspecting nor have you lost your way.'

Suddenly Sydney became deadly serious. He put his hands on Louisa's shoulders.

'Look Louisa − I've really got to apologise for that. I was drunk, upset, and I let myself get carried away. I should never have told you such things. I don't know what you think of me.'

'Don't be ashamed. It was the nicest thing anyone has ever said to me. It was the most original come-on I've ever heard, and you weren't even trying to pick me up or anything like that. It was as if you were trusting me with your deepest secrets – and I loved it. And as for what I think of you, let me show you ...'

Sydney just stared at Louisa. Her breathing quickened perceptible. Louisa continued.

'And I must be honest – even though you didn't mean to, you really turned me on – hearing about you and Catherine. I didn't realise how exciting mere words could be. Maybe it's your accent – but for days after that night while I was waiting for you to call, I closed my eyes and thought of you doing those things to me and talking to me while you did them. And I touched myself while I thought those things. Right here – and here – I touched myself until I shook so violently I couldn't keep my fingers on my body.'

In the semi-darkness of the collapsed pier, Louisa had let one of her hands slip inside the taut elastic of her bikini panties and the other toyed inside the cup of her bra. She leaned back against the fallen wood and continued revealing herself to the amazed Sydney. He began to wonder what it was about him that attracted such bold women who were willing to bare much more than their souls. Louisa continued with her dialogue, as if she were confiding deep dark secrets to a dear friend ...

'It was so different for me. I've never wanted or lacked for people to fuck, but now, after that night of hearing you and what you did with that woman, I suddenly wanted you and only you. I played with myself, hoping that in my rubbing I could cause you to appear like a genie out of a magic lantern. And you would have your way with me. And perhaps you'd tell someone else all about our sex, some night in a bar somewhere. Only I'd never make the mistake that Catherine made. You'd talk about me not out of regret but out of longing for when you and I met again.'

As Louisa talked she fingered her cunt in front of Sydney.

His eyes darted from watching the material of her bikini panties contort as her fingers danced seductively underneath, titillating her clitoris in the process, to the revealing way in which the hardness of her nipples protruded through the silky material of the bikini top.

'I want you to fuck me Sydney, but I want you to talk to me while you do it — tell me everything you're doing — just like the other night. Only do it with me. Now. Here.'

'All right.'

Sydney swallowed — the words barely escaped his throat. What else could he have said to such an invitation? He wasn't prepared for this kind of play, but the sight of Louisa's beautiful and willing form writhing just inches away from him squashed all inhibitions. He thought back to all those randy novels he'd read while waiting for planes or sitting in steamy train stations. His mind raced and he began to prepare a fantasy that was, like the best of fantasies, partially true.

'The first thing you should know, my dear, is that I planned for this to happen.'

As he spoke he removed his small running shorts. His dick sprang free, attracting Louisa's heaving attention.

'All the food and champagne — I hoped it would get you randy. And I can tell by the sounds you're making with your cunt — and the smell of your juices — it worked.'

'Yes — yes — what does my cunt smell like? What do you think of when you taste me in the air?'

'The scent is heavy and musky like something that has been forever living in the dark. It smells like a perfume so concentrated that one drop would drive men wild. It is driving me wild. See — you can tell by the way my dick climbs towards you.'

Louisa leaned further back against the wood as if backing away from Sydney's member. Telegraphing her true intent she let out a deep guttural groan that coincided with the noise of the crashing waves. She closed her eyes to deny herself a vista of impatient cock. She wanted these moments to last, and she wanted to hear every word. By closing her eyes she sacrificed one sense for the intensity of another. Louisa was not disappointed. Every syllable stung exquisitely like the

222

delicate lash of a playfully wielded whip.

Sydney continued his 'bedtime' story. He became more insistent as his confidence grew and his erection strained for the gentle caress of warm female flesh.

'Now I want you to take off your bikini – but do it slowly – strip for me – striptease me. Here in this darkness. Dance for me.'

'Tell me what to do – please?'

'Stroke your tits and your cunt on the outside of the material. Yes, that's right. Now move and act like the shafts of light are spotlights in a smoky nightclub. Don't forget to arch your back as you dance. Fuck me with your movements. Make me think that I am on top of you and you are writhing underneath my thrustings. Play to me, for I am your only audience, and the sight of me sitting here with a ripper of a boner excites you terribly. And as you dance for me – and as you strip – I'm going to stroke my throbbing cock. You watch me very carefully, discovering which of your moves get me the most turned on.'

Louisa shook her body like a sleazy stripper. The crashing waves were like cymbal crashes, the seagull cries were like the wolf-whistles of an imaginary crowd, and just as Sydney had said, the shafts of light were like theatrical lights.

'Now turn your back to me and get ready to take off your top – that's right, shake your pretty blonde hair – unclasp your top, turn away from me, show me your lovely back and those statuesque shoulders. Arch them inwards so your top falls away, hold the bra in your arms, lean forward jiggling your ass, drop the top on the floor, let your hair fall forward, that's a good girl – now turn around shaking your tits. Yeah, that's the way – slap 'em around a bit. Straighten up and bounce them as you take off your bottoms. Yeah – you've done this before, haven't you? You naughty little girl. Now turn around – point that pouty little ass at me – jiggle it – walk over to me and let me kiss it. First on this cheek – then that one – and then right here in the middle.'

Louisa couldn't decide what was more erotic, the actual events or the hearing of her actions being described to her. Sex before had always been so clear cut and simple. It had been fun, but now there was a new element. And in many ways it was more filthy than anything she'd ever done. And she didn't need to be drunk off her feet or high as a kite to enjoy it.

'Now I want you to lie down – here in the sand – right here. I want you to feel the water come up your legs as you get fucked.'

Louisa sprawled on to the moist sand. In the darkness of the collapsed pier the dampness of the sand was extremely cold to her warm skin. Her body shook as the heat of her cunt and her ass sank into the ground, and then with a sinister trickling the ocean waters invaded and splashed up to meet her own juices. Louisa screamed in shock. She went to close her legs, but was stopped by Sydney's calming tones and the insistence of his hand.

'Now, Louisa, you wouldn't want to do that. This is part of the fun. Let me tell you what it will be like if you do exactly as I say.'

Louisa nodded. She was shivering both with cold and with eager anticipation. Sex had never been this charged before.

'In a very short while I'm going to take the head of my cock and place it right here.'

Sydney touched the opening of Louisa's cunt. After the briefest of touches he inserted his finger all the way in.

'Now just imagine that this is my dick. It will be much bigger than this – but I'm sure you have a good imagination. I'm sure you know what a dick looks like – and feels like.'

Louisa nodded, her head rapidly digging a small depression in the soft sand.

'As I fuck you – you know – slide my dick in and out of you very slowly – you'll get really excited. With every long stroke of my cock you'll want to scream, and very quickly you'll want to come all over my throbbing flesh. It is possible that you might even pass out with the intensity of your release, so the ocean has obliged us with a regular cooling splash of ice cold ocean water. As I fuck you, every seventh wave will crash on the beach and its foremost front will penetrate up between your legs along with my cock. You'll have the heat of our sex and the coolness of the ocean.

The one will raise you up to new heights of ecstasy, and the other will momentarily cool you down so that the next thrust of my cock will feel that much better. That is what I'm going to do to you. Assuming of course that you are ready for my dick. Let me see . . .'

Sydney withdrew his finger and tasted it like he was scooping up a dollop of rich jam. Louisa's juices mingled with the saltwater to make a tasty concoction.

'Very tasty, but perhaps . . .'

'No, Sydney – fuck me now. And don't stop talking.'

'As you wish, my dear. Is this what you wanted?'

Sydney kneeled over Louisa's submissive form and let his erect cock brush over her intimate parts. He toyed with her cunt, almost entering her – but not quite. Her body strained to take his cock fully inside her, until Sydney could resist no more.

'Ohhh. Yes – yes – I have you now – quick – tell me what you are doing.'

It was getting difficult for Sydney to comply with Louisa's heated requests for continuous commentary. The tightness of her cunt gripped his shaft with a violence he hadn't expected. She quivered noticeably with the opposing sensations of cold water against hot thighs. Sydney too felt the contrast deeply. The cold ocean water almost burned on his balls. He could feel grains of sand sliding between their bodies and rubbing on their skin as they fucked. The feeling was uncomfortable – but exciting at the same time. He forced himself to talk to Louisa.

'In the darkness I can see your breasts shake with each thrust of my dick. The nipples are very hard and inviting. I can tell you want me to bite them, but if I did I would stop talking to you, so I decide not to. I know what excites you the most. You can squeeze your tits for me. Let me watch you do that. Pinch your nipples for me.'

Louisa complied, rubbing rough grains of sand on her breasts. She pulled the nipples taut and rotated them amongst her fingertips. The flesh of her tits stretched under her manipulations.

'Like this, Sydney – like this?'

'Yes, that is the way I like to see it done. Ohhh ...'

Anther wave crashed and found its way to their entwined sex. The effect was exhilarating. It made their bodies thrust and buck at each other to get away from the cold water and to generate as much heat of their own.

'You can feel my dick getting harder with each thrust. You know that you are going to milk it very soon so you quicken your own pace. You rub your little clit on my body, letting the grains of sand stimulate you even more. You pull my body into you and grind your cunt around my cock. You wrap your long legs around my ass – you want more of my cock in you – you want ... ohhhaaahh.'

Once again the water hit between their legs, cooling down the bubbling cauldron of Louisa and Sydney's fucking. It was an enforced teasing that only the most excited could ever endure. It was as if they were reaching orgasm just as the waters crashed on their heaving bodies, thereby cooling them down for further fucking. It was agony. It was almost unbearable. And still Louisa wanted to be talked to.

'Come on Sydney – keep – talk – please – tell me dirty things – don't stop – it – excites – god – I can't – don't – say something filthy – to me.'

Sydney was exhausted. It seemed as if they had been fucking for hours. He knew that his body desired release, but there was something magical in each thrust that begged not to be extinguished. He fought on giving up his body to whatever forces controlled such motions. He collapsed against Louisa – his body thrusting in short stabbing motions. His head rested on the sand. He turned and whispered into her ear.

'And you are going to come as I come – as a wave splashes up our legs – all over my balls and up against your cunt – you are going to come. And I will fill you with my come and the ocean will fill us both. You can't stop it. You must not try. Open your legs – open your cunt – let yourself fuck all over me ... feel my dick it's – it's – exploding –'

Sydney began to burrow his body furiously into Louisa who wrapped her legs tightly against him. They rolled to and fro in the damp sand, coating each other with eternities of pleasure. They became as a single fucking creature rolling on the beach in an intricate erotic dance. Wave after wave of salty water lapped their bodies as their orgasms soaked each other's desire. Their moans cheated the seagulls of centre stage. The small things with snappy jaws crouched safely in the darkness staring at the strange many-limbed creature that had invaded their private domain. It appeared to be dying, because its movements became more desperate – more forced – as if great energy was required just to survive.

'And now I'm going to pass out in your arms,' was all Sydney could add before a blackness much darker than the shadows of the collapsed pier claimed him. Louisa smiled back, already in that comfortable place. Arms wrapped tightly against each other they stayed, oblivious to the continual lapping of the patient ocean currents.

Another Pumping Station couple were doing their best not to ignore the waves, but to create a few of their own. Roughly several hundred yards offshore, precariously balanced in a small rowing boat, rocked to and fro the well-endowed forms of Hazel Heyes and Phuc Yu.

Just like Sydney, Phuc had plied his partner with fine champagne and richly decadent food. They had consumed their picnic bobbing up and down on the ocean's currents, feeding the occasional scraps to the ravenous seagulls. And now another ravenous scavenger was being satiated.

It was time for Phuc's regular afternoon tit-fuck. Although tit-fucking in a rather unstable rowing boat could hardly be called 'regular'. The act took quite a bit of ingenuity.

Phuc sat on the small rowing seat with his swimming shorts around his ankles. Hazel knelt on a pillow on the floor of the boat and wrapped her tits around Yu's enormous erection. With sun tan lotion and sweat as the lubricant she bobbed up and down wanking off Yu's dick. The hardness of her bullet-like nipples rubbed on the inside of his thighs driving him wild with every stroke of her tits. He lay back trying to prolong the moment, cushioning his neck on several towels that they had brought along in case they'd gone swimming. Hazel had to be very careful not to rock the boat. To say that the small craft was top-heavy was a bit of an understatement.

'How does it feel, Phuc baby?'

'How does the sun feel shining on my body? How does the water feel supporting our lovemaking? How envious are the birds that I have the tastiest morsel? I feel much better than any of them. I am much luckier to have such a gifted woman as yourself willing to satisfy my unusual desires.'

'You're so sweet, Phuc. You know I'd do anything for you?'

'Ah – I believe you would. So perhaps you might try sucking my dick as it emerges from the caress of your bosom.'

'Of course – I'd love to.'

Just as Mr Yu suggested, Hazel, by tilting her head down and sliding further down his cock, was able to give Yu an additional bonus to the tit-fucking – he was also getting a bit of a cock-sucking. Hazel wasn't able to get her mouth fully over Yu's massive dickhead, but she was able to latch on to the sensitised knob and suck firmly on it while sliding her tongue over the slit at the end. Yu was in heaven. The full length of his cock and balls were being stimulated in one form or another. No part of his priapic equipment received any respite from sexual stimulus. No sooner had his dick emerged from the confines of Hazel's well greased tits than her mouth latched on to Yu's cock and pulled it upwards with her suction. It didn't take much of this activity to start Mr Yu's come bubbling from deep within his balls up to the opening of his cock. He came just as Hazel was sucking hard on his dickhead. At first she thought she may have been hurting him, but concluded it was understandable for him to scream so. Hazel sucked even harder, as though she were trying to pull Yu's internal organs out of the end of his penis. Gasping, Yu broke off their embrace, clutching at his dick.

'Oh – that was – that was – fucking brilliant.'

Hazel laughed. She'd never heard Mr Yu swear. Upon seeing her reaction, Yu laughed as well. He was quite aware that his quite large vocabulary had failed him.

'Now please, lie down – I have a surprise for you.'

Hazel complied wondering what the Korean was up to. At first she thought he was just being playful as his hands wandered over her cunt.

'I wish to make you very happy – to give you some of the pleasure you feast upon me.'

'Oh please do, Phuc baby – please do.'

Phuc Yu pressed his pudgy ring encrusted fingers between Hazel's legs. Each finger kneaded the pump cuntflesh like a baker preparing dough for the oven. Hazel closed her eyes and lay back against Phuc's lap. He cradled her with his body and toyed with her cunt. His fingers slid up and down the folds of the labia, gradually moistening her crevices, producing that deliciously slippery sound of finger and juices. One bold finger found its way underneath the shroud of skin that protected the most sensitive of spots from all unwelcome visitors. The bud quivered at the finger's insistence and danced eagerly around the intruder. Wetter and wetter Hazel's cunt got until the slippery opening begged for a finger to be inserted. Phuc Yu was only too glad to oblige – slipping the fattest of his digits into Hazel's musky cunt. Slowly he penetrated her as his other fingers danced their wicked dance in and around Hazel's pubic mound. As he quickened his finger-fucking, his other fingers added a teasing dance around Hazel's thighs, pinching at the soft flesh, raising small welts and large moans from the supine woman.

Hazel was most definitely overdosing on this pampering. It was quite unlike Phuc to be so attentive to his partner's needs. He was usually so concerned about his own feelings and fantasies that he rarely demonstrated the caring that he was now dishing out in giant-sized portions. Hazel's sexual preferences meant little to her in the condition she was in. She languoured in the mush of contentment that having her most intimate parts played with underneath the hot beating sun, rocking gently backwards and forwards in a small boat on a very large ocean produced within her. She was lost to the real world, carried away into the land of dreams on the wings of Phuc's fingers.

He would let his fucking finger slide deliberately out of her and pull it all the way up between her fleshy lips. In doing so he'd smear her juices all over her cunt, especially compressing her clitoris in shock waves of pleasure. Hazel was lifting her ass off of the boat and pulsing her hips to his urgings. The smell of her cunt oozing forth its golden nectar was palpably sexual. She felt as if she had fallen overboard and was drowning in a sea of fondling hands. As she clamoured for air, wave after wave of pleasure sucked her under and claimed her for the deep. She was in an abyss of desire, her nipples erect and pointing skyward, her dark brown surrounding aureoles swelling with each sigh as if being forced outward by the welling rush inside her body. She could not contain her orgasm any longer – it was cruel to try. She gave in to her body's wishes and let the tension flow in rushing torrents – staccato moans issued from her mouth in machine-gun like bursts of sound. The small boat was in danger of taking on water as she shook so violently. Phuc Yu held her tightly. Through a dense sexual fog she could hear his calm voice.

'It is all right, Hazel, you will be fine. Please open your eyes – I have something for you.'

He repeated himself several times until she drearily blinked into the bright sun. She could see he had placed a small box between her breasts.'

'What – what – is – it?'

Sensing her confusion, Mr Yu snapped open the small velvet covered container. Bright shafts of light immediately danced around her eyes.

'My God – what – why – I – I?'

'Ssshh – be still, my dear. It is an engagement ring. I want you to marry me. You please me like no other woman has, or ever could. And you will see in the box there is another ring. It is a key ring with a key attached. You may recognise the key as being to the front door of the Pumping Station. I've bought the bar where you work, and where we met. I purchased the Pump from the Nevada holding company that has owned it for the last few years. And I am giving it to you as a wedding present – should you accept my offer of marriage. Let me add, before you answer, that I also know of your sexual preferences and have no concerns that they will conflict with mine. To be quite specific, I do not mind you having girlfriends as long as the same goes for me.'

Hazel couldn't say yes. She couldn't say anything. Her vocal chords seemed to have short-circuited. She definitely didn't want to say no. She just started crying and blubbering something that sounded like 'oh, Phuc Yu' over and over again. She was overcome with emotion. She had no idea that Phuc Yu cared for her so.

'I take that as a positive answer, Miss Heyes.'

'Oh yes – yes – yes – Mr Yu.'

Anyone on the shore with binoculars observing the scene would have seen the ample outlines of the boat's occupants slide down below the hull. The shorebound voyeur would have had to surmise what happened next. He would have most probably been wrong, assuming that the couple would be fucking merrily away. Far from it. Under the heat of the glittering sun, Phuc Yu and Hazel Heyes talked dreamily of the future and fell into the kind of deep, deep sleep that comes from absolute contentment, sexual exhaustion and emotional fulfilment.

Back on the shore even more shocking announcements were being made. As the second round of hot dogs were being barbecued, the unmistakable form of Annie da Pheelanupe came tottering out of the beach haze. Addressing the throng of Pump people she sounded purposeful, as if she had planned a speech and waiting for everyone to assemble could throw off her timing.

'Where is everyone?'

'Hazel's on a boat with the Korean dude and Louisa went off for a walk with some Australian dude.' Lester was trying to act real cool, but his limp gave away his discomfort.

'Well, y'all will have to give them my regards and my news. I don't have much time.'

In the distance everyone could hear the honking of a car horn as if someone's patience was wearing thin.

'Look y'all – I'm quitting the Pump. That's the bad news, I guess. The good news is, I'm getting married. I'm marrying a guy I met who used to be a Silicon Valley cop, but he got transferred to El Paso in Texas – my home state. He starts Monday so we're driving down and stopping off in Las Vegas to get married. It all happened so sudden, I don't know what to say.'

There was a stunned silence broken finally by Arthur Wize.

'Well, let me be the first to congratulate you, Annie – my dear.'

Arthur hugged the small woman to him, theatening to squeeze the life out of her. In her ear he whispered, 'Does this mean you're giving up the game?' Annie just nodded back affirmatively. Arthur thought for a few seconds then added in full earshot of everyone, 'We'll miss you, Annie.' And then everyone was around her hugging and kissing her and saying goodbyes. After a few more car honks Annie finally broke away and waved goodbye.

'I'll miss y'all. Say hello-goodbye to Louisa and Hazel and Mr Yu for me.'

Everyone said they would be sure to pass on the news – knowing full well that any innocent passers-by might get trampled in the rush to pass on this titbit of gossip. As she walked away, Don Palumba asked the question that everyone else had seemed to forget.

'So what do we call you – Annie what?'

As she walked away she shouted back her answer.

'Annie Moore – Mrs Annie Moore.'

The Pump beach picnic was rapidly taking on a grandiose atmosphere. After Annie's surprise announcement, Phuc Yu had rowed ashore to top that with the announcement of his engagement to Hazel and that he had bought the Pump for her as a wedding present. In celebration of her agreement to take his hand in marriage he had closed the Pump for two days so the picnic could go on through the night. There had been much whooping and singing of 'For he's a jolly good fellow', especially after he'd added that no one would lose their jobs and that everyone would receive a ten per cent pay raise as a token of his gratitude for bringing him and his intended together. In between all of the congratulations Kerry thought that this was as good a time as ever to deliver her response to Phuc Yu's offer of employment.

They walked down the beach, silhouetted by the setting sun. Phuc Yu pretended not to notice the three men that were

232

jacking off on the prone body of Mrs Treadwell. She was moaning something about getting their spunk all over her sun-burn or something like that. 'It's very good for the skin,' she yelled at Phuc and Kerry. They walked by without acknowledging her greeting, apparently oblivious to the decadent scene. Out of the corner of her eye Kerry noticed that one of the men was Bob Vest. He had sneered at her as he pumped his dick at Mrs Treadwell. The pitiful sight was just the tonic needed for Kerry to swallow her last-minute nerves and get on with the job of carving out a future for herself. It was fitting in some small way that Bob, who thought he was so superior to Kerry, should be wanking off on the likes of Julie Treadwell, whereas the woman he thought he once owned was in the process of taking a very giant step forward. The thought made Kerry determined to succeed. Mr Yu broke the spell of her mental meanderings.

'I take it you've reached a decision.'

'I have.'

'Well?'

'I wish to accept your offer on the following terms. The salary is far too low. I want at least twice what you offered me, and I want to start drawing that salary immediately and continue to do so while I finish my university education. I will be able to work for you part-time while I complete my studies. I am willing to take on any assignment you give me. And I also want a stock-option plan. You are well aware how good I am at everything I do. I am worth it. That is my response.'

'And why should I agree to such terms?'

'Simple. I have already demonstrated my loyalty to you – far beyond what you might expect as the normal call of duty.'

Kerry paused letting her words sink in. Phuc showed no sign of recognition. Mr Yu defined the term 'poker face'. Kerry continued, not being bluffed by Yu's lack of response.

'I don't blame you for it because you were quite drunk, but I was the woman behind the dumpster that you fucked that Sunday night many weeks ago. If I'd gone to the authorities I could have created such a stink that you'd have never closed those deals.'

Yu stopped dead in his tracks. He was visibly shaken. He had not expected anything like this. He had negotiated the sale and purchase of billions of dollars worth of assets and was well attuned to all of the negotiating ploys used by highly trained men in suits. But this was different. Here stood an extremely attractive young woman in nothing more than a few inches of bathing suit effectively blackmailing him — with all of his power and money, he was helpless. He was honour bound to accept her proposal.

'You — I see — now I remember. I thought you were someone else — but no matter. Now I know why I was so fascinated by you. I had but a small taste of your sweetness. You are right — I do owe you a great debt.'

Phuc Yu paused as though thinking. Kerry was about to interrupt when he raised his hand to stop her.

'I agree to your terms. With this action all of our debts are cancelled. We start our new relationship with a clean slate.'

'Certainly, Mr Yu.'

Phuc Yu walked away to find his bride-to-be and Janet Hodges. They would probably be together somewhere celebrating his engagement.

Kerry stared out at the last few gasps of the eventful day's sunlight. Maybe it was her imagination, but it did seem that as the huge orange disk fell below the horizon it winked at her.

The new Queen of Silicon Valley business had been crowned.

14

Mimosa

Mix

**Equal Parts of
Chilled Champagne
with
Fresh Orange Juice**

Serve chilled in a stemmed goblet.

*L*ying on her back on a small folded open sleeping bag, Louisa was naked underneath the fading stars of a very special Silicon Valley night. Her only covering was the equally naked body of Sydney Nats. The pre-dawn air was chilling in the hills overlooking the technologically magical valley, but the cold had little effect on the couple's urgent lovemaking.

'Make love to me, Sydney. Make love to me tonight, before the daylight comes. Make love to me now,' Louisa had asked of Sydney as they lay naked in each other's arms. And their sex − their fucking − their lovemaking − had been special. Since that time on the beach just a few days ago, Sydney and Louisa had shared each other's bodies at every opportunity. They fucked a lifetime in the blink of an eye, but tonight they made love. They had to.

Sydney Nats was to be at San Francisco International Airport at five p.m. later that same day to take his first-class seat on British Airways flight 286 to London's Heathrow Airport.

Sydney was going back to try an extremely important case that he was pivotal to. Neither Louisa nor Sydney had talked about his leaving during their brief time together. It was mutually understood to be taboo. But as the metaphorical eleventh hour approached, they sensed the need for something special. When Louisa left the Pump after work the night before they had driven aimlessly until her red Mustang seemed to migrate towards the hills. They'd parked off the road and walked to a secluded bluff overlooking the twinkling lights of the Valley below. Their breath condensed as they talked about nothing in particular, daring not to mention more serious matters. They undressed and wrapped themselves in an old sleeping bag of Louisa's that had seen better days. Gently kissing each other rather than talk, they sipped coolly refreshing Mimosas from plastic cups and said goodbye to the stars as the cruel dawn chased the protective night away.

It was then that Louisa had said, 'Make love to me, Sydney. Make love to me tonight, before the daylight comes. Make love to me now.'

And if ever two people could have made love, Sydney and Louisa did.

Their bed was the sleeping bag covering a mattress of fallen pine needles. It could hardly have been described as comfortable, but neither Louisa nor Sydney cared.

As she spoke her words to him Louisa reached down and gently caressed his stiffening cock. She fell gently backwards pulling Sydney towards her. His lips covered her mouth and his tongue gently probed around her own, stroking it as she stroked his cock.

There was no question of foreplay. The last ten days – the last ten years – their whole lives had been preparation for this moment. It couldn't be rushed, it couldn't be slowed – it just happened at its own inevitable pace.

Sydney broke away from kissing Louisa and gently nibbled at her ear lobe. He flicked her flesh around his mouth occasionally applying a soft biting pressure. Louisa arched her neck as if to break free, but she really didn't want to. With his tongue, Sydney traced a yellow-brick-road path down Louisa's neck, passed her shoulder blades down to her cleavage. He paused there momentarily to blow-dry the wetness he had created with his tongue. He cocked his head first to one side and then another, directing the soft breeze onto Louisa's hardened nipples, making her shudder in the cold twilight of the sun's first few rays.

All this time she had been holding Sydney's cock in her hand, gently stroking and coaxing the member to new heights of stiffness. Her touch had been both gentle and firm as she let her long fingernails feel every throbbing inch of Sydney's shaft. She wanted to know his cock well. She and Sydney had fucked many times, but she didn't feel as if she knew every small bump, every little ridge, every bulging vessel, every tiny hair as intimately as she desired. It was as if she were blind and touch was her only sense, and in her mind the radar of her fingers described a phallus of utterly beautiful form. The straining curve of its erectness followed some perfect proportion that in her hands felt as natural as the petals of a rose. Sydney's cock fit in her long fingers like a glove.

Louisa wanted that statuesque cock inside her. It belonged there as much as it belonged in her hand. Her cunt was its cradle, her hand its carriage. With a sweeping movement of her thin wrist she guided the penis deep within her. At first there was a slight resistance as her cunt opened to greet the welcome intruder. With help from Sydney's thrusting buttocks, the resistance was easily overcome and fountains of lust began to flow. Louisa's cunt dripped — it sweated forth a golden nectar in which to bathe the pulsing cock. Louisa tried to ignore the sensation, but it had felt remarkably like she began to climax the moment Sydney's dick entered her not-quite-ready cunt. And now the climax feeling wouldn't stop rolling through her body, melting every sinew and sapping her consciousness.

Sydney had his arms wrapped tightly around Louisa as he used the natural arch of his body to move his penis in and out of the orgasming woman. He could tell she was feeling intense emotion for she had that far away look on her face that even the morning light could not tame. He wanted to say something that couples at such moments of rapture were supposed to say, but words would have been cheap at such a time. Their bodies spoke to each other in a language that only lovers could understand.

Sydney kissed her quivering forehead, blowing gently on her closed eyelids. With one free hand he swept away the unruly blonde hair that was matting with sweat to Louisa's face. Almost immediately she turned her head from side to side, once again covering her love-racked visage with her hair as fast as Sydney could brush it away. She began to chew on the soaked blonde strands. Sydney kissed her lips and licked Louisa's sweat-soaked hair with her. The effect on her was electric — she raked her nails along his back and reached underneath his bucking form for Sydney's balls. Their bodies locked together, mouth on mouth, chest to breasts, stomach to stomach, sex to sex, they attained a state of lust-induced rigor mortis. Sydney's cock didn't so much as move in and out of Louisa's pussy as merely pulse under her constricting muscles.

Sydney muffled his orgasm-cry with a mouthful of Louisa's hair. He had been perfectly still inside her, locked statically together when the sheer tautness of her contracting cunt had brought him off. The closest thing to the rush of intensity he felt was as a teenager having a wet dream. He remembered those adolescent halcyon days when in a dream world he'd imagined himself involved in some fantastic sexual escapade like fucking the neighbour's wife or the cute little English teacher with the big breasts. He'd always wake up just instants before coming, unable to stop his perfectly still penis from spraying all over his bed. His body had been on erotic autopilot with a license to roam free, and he'd never experienced anything like it ever again. Until now, when Louisa's cunt had performed her magic on his dick.

'Please eat me. Taste me. Drink me. Please me.'

Sydney thought he might have been having a wet dream. A wet dream to end all wet dreams. But the cold morning air on his sweaty bottom convinced him that he was lucky enough to be in the here and now. And here and now Louisa was whispering in his ear those words. She appeared to be in some sort of trance, as though she were reciting a mantra. She kept repeating the words over and over again as Sydney disengaged himself from her arms and complied with her wishes.

Louisa's thighs were soaked with his come and her juices. He licked gently at her milky-soft thigh flesh, his breath misting in the cold air. Still she chanted her incantation.

'Please eat me. Taste me. Drink me. Please me.'

Sydney covered Louisa's puffy cuntlips with his mouth and drank deeply of her moistness. His tongue lapped inside her and rippled through every crevice of her soaked cavern. She gripped his head with her thighs, threatening to do him bodily injury. Through the mufflings of her flesh he could hear her continue to moan ...

'Please eat me. Taste me. Drink me. Please me.'

Sydney felt himself begin to stir. The smell of Louisa's come-soaked cunt permeated his brain and brought forth a throbbing erection just moments after he'd expelled himself into her. It was as if drinking their combined orgasms was replenishing his cock. He felt ready for more sex with every lick of Louisa's pussy. He slid his tongue in and out of her opening like some small dexterous cock. He lapped at her clitoris like some thirsty beggar guzzling wine. Sydney lifted Louisa's bottom off the ground to give himself the deepest possible penetration he could muster. It was as he was sucking away, latched onto her swollen cunt that he realised that she'd stopped her verbal encouragements. Indeed, Louisa's body had stopped to function in the waking world, giving way to the deepest possible of sleeps.

It was immensely satisfying to Sydney to have shared in such intense lovemaking. He gently placed Louisa's bottom back down on the ground and pulled the sleeping bag around her. He had but one thing to do before he too could join her peaceful rest. His cock was pulsing with a ravenous desire to come. He felt a perverse pleasure at the prospects Louisa's slumbering form offered him, when out of the corner of his eye he caught sight of the perfect means of relieving his straining erection. He and Louisa had tossed their clothes to one side rather quickly in the early morning darkness. Now as the stark morning light illuminated the scene, Sydney could see Louisa's silky black nylon tights lying strewn across his crumpled jacket. She'd worn the kind of nylons that are all-in-one sheer panties and tights cut enticingly in the sexiest French lace. He picked them up and marveled at their extreme softness. He smelled the nylon and inhaled Louisa's perfume. He tasted the crotch and smiled – Louisa had been quite wet before she'd taken these off. The sweet smell of her body and its juices was supremely intoxicating. He cuddled up to Louisa and wrapped the tights around his

241

throbbing cock. He nestled the pulsing instrument between the cheeks of her ass and gently stroked his cock up and down. Louisa did not stir, so deeply was she asleep. That she did not respond excited Sydney even further – the feeling of silky black nylon on his dick was unimaginable. Louisa's bottom provided just the perfect pressure on his cock forcing the nylon to rub ever so gently on his straining shaft. He reached under her ass and squeezed his balls, milking them free of their heavy load. He soaked Louisa's tights with his orgasm and smiled at his perversion. It was a fitting end to a truly magical evening.

Before dozing off, modesty forced him to put the soaked tights into his jacket pocket. Something deep inside Sydney's mind told him that a souvenir of the night's varied lovemaking was in order – and he could think of nothing better than Louisa's love-soaked black nylon tights. He fell asleep cuddled closely to Louisa – like two spoons they rested while below them the inhabitants of Silicon Valley were beginning just another business day.

It was the sound of traffic on a nearby highway that woke them. The sun was high in the sky, betraying the lateness of the hour. Sydney and Louisa rapidly dressed and rushed to the waiting red Mustang without exchanging even the smallest of pleasantries. Louisa never mentioned her missing tights and Sydney was too rushed to notice the bulge in his jacket pocket. It was already two p.m. In three hours he had to be at the airport, and with traffic the way it was in Silicon Valley, he would be lucky to make it. He and Louisa had left the car with his packed bags in the boot parked nearby to the Pump. Since Louisa was due at work at four, they decided to go directly there.

They were both taciturn as the Mustang carried them onward to their inevitable goodbye. Sydney felt like he should say something, but with every onrushing mile it became more difficult. As they rounded a curve in the road he was just about to open his mouth, but an exclamation from Louisa halted him flat.

'What the hell is that?'

A pall of acrid looking smoke hung over the Valley.

'God knows – one of the high-tech plants must have gone up in flames.'

As they neared the Pumping Station the traffic got heavier and heavier until it finally reached a standstill. Louisa wasted no time in resorting to the skills years of driving in Silicon Valley's heavy traffic had nurtured.

'I know a back way to the Pump – through a couple of parking lots. We can't have you missing that plane because of a little smoke and fire, can we?'

Bouncing over speed bumps the Mustang rounded a corner on to MicroProcessor Way – the street the Pumping Station was located on. Louisa screeched to an eye-bulging halt.

'Oh my God – Jesus-fucking-H-Christ.'

Louisa looked at Sydney in horror. Sydney wasn't sure what to say.

'Oh my God.'

Louisa appeared dumbstruck. It was understandable. The Pumping Station lay in rubble. Huge flames leapt skyward from a gaping hole in the ground. Oily black smoke billowed forth in mushroom-like clouds. The whole devastating scene looked like something out of a nuclear war.

Stunned, they parked the car and walked down to where Sydney's car had been left last night. Large boulder-sized debris had just missed the rental car, but smaller chunks of rock had peppered the bodywork. Standing off to one side behind the police line were Hazel and Phuc Yu. She was crying and he was doing his best to comfort her. Louisa walked up followed by Sydney.

'What the fuck happened. Is anyone hurt?'

Phuc responded – Hazel just kept sobbing.

'The situation is a little unclear – but it appears that when Hazel closed the Pump last night she forgot to turn off the fire-pit bubbling fountain. Ordinarily this would present no problem – it is on after all throughout the evening – but it seems that the Pump was built on the ruins of an old petrol station that had failed many years ago. The fire department says that the station owners never removed the petrol storage tanks – and over a period of time the fumes just built up until a leak developed and – boom. We are lucky it occurred when the Pump was unoccupied. It appears no one was hurt. Now that you are here everyone is accounted for. We were quite worried about you.'

'It's all my fault,' Hazel sobbed, almost in hysterics. She felt as if she had failed Phuc by destroying his wedding present to her. She was mumbling things about bad omens and things not meant to be.

Mr Yu took charge as he was accustomed to doing.

'If you will excuse us – I think it best that Hazel rest now that we know you are safe. It has been a very trying time for her.'

Sydney watched them walk away. He suddenly felt impulsive.

'Louisa, you obviously don't have to work this evening. There's still time to catch the plane. Come to England with me.'

'What – I'm sorry, I wasn't listening?'

Sydney Nats repeated himself. Louisa breathed deeply. She didn't look at him – she stared instead at the devastation that used to be the Pump. She'd hoped he wouldn't ask her. There was a time, quite recently, when she might have accepted his offer – but not now.

'Look, Sydney, I'm a cocktail waitress first and last. That is what I do. You'd quickly grow tired of me. I wouldn't live up to your expectations . . .'

Sydney tried to interrupt, but Louisa wouldn't let him.

'You are a lawyer and I'm a waitress. No matter what pair of rose-coloured glasses you wear it wouldn't work out. We had great fun and I'll never forget last night, but real life can't be like that all the time. You'll get over me – look how quickly you got over Catherine.'

Sydney was about to say something like that was different but realised it was futile. Louisa continued her denials.

'I don't have the time to go jetting around the world. Right now I have to find another job.'

'What will you do?'

'Cocktailing – what else? There are always plenty of jobs for good waitresses. I'll just look in the paper.'

Louisa picked up a paper that was laying amidst the rubble.

244

She opened the burned remnant up to the Classified Advertisements section and mumbled to herself . . .

'Cocktails . . . cocktails . . . cocktails . . . there's plenty of jobs. I'd better get on the phone, and you'd better get to your plane.'

'Just like that.'

'Yeah – just like that. Let's leave it with good memories. There's no reason to make it something it was never meant to be.'

Sydney turned and walked to his dented rental car. He was secretly glad that she'd decided to stay in Silicon Valley. He'd looked back to wave goodbye to her. He'd hoped to see her, perhaps a tear in her eye, waving farewell to him. It would have been dead romantic – the way a sad movie might have ended. Sydney should have known better – in the mood she was in, Louisa was more like romantically dead. Framed against the rubble of the Pump, backlit by the flames and smoke, Louisa wasn't even looking at him. She was too busy with her head buried inside the paper looking at the cocktail-waitress job listings. She didn't even wave goodbye.

Louisa had gotten off the emotional roller-coaster she had been riding for the past few weeks. Sydney Nats had touched her in ways she thought impossible to reach, but last night had dramatically shown her the difference between what was and what was to be. With Annie and Hazel rushing off to get married, and Kerry quitting for such a good opportunity, Louisa had gotten caught up in the possibilities of life beyond cocktailing. Louisa and Sydney had enjoyed a wonderful 'holiday' romance. They had both taken leave of their normal reservations and enjoyed a momentary flirtation with the frivolity and vulnerability of love. The holiday was over for both Sydney and Louisa. Sydney was returning to England to be the calculating lawyer he'd been trained to be, and which he was exceptionally good at. It was time too for Louisa to go back to work – and even though she didn't have a job, Louisa's vocation was clear in her mind. She was a cocktail waitress. She served cocktails and sometimes the promise of much more to her customers. And she was damn good at it.

Sydney Nats couldn't have agreed more.

245

The Boeing 747 rose thunderously skyward and banked to the east. Far below the massive jetliner, Sydney Nats could see the receding sights of Silicon Valley. By following the unmistakable snake of Highway 101 due south from the airport he was able to locate the still smouldering rubble of the Pumping Station. There were still a few fire engines parked nearby. Sydney imagined that he caught sight of a speeding red Mustang, and it was then that he felt the dampness of the souvenir in his coat pocket. He had forgotten that he had secreted away Louisa's dampened tights in his pocket earlier that morning. Tears welled up inside him and made the harrowing journey down his face. He wiped them away with the silky black nylons. It was the wrong thing to do. Louisa's perfume, the smell of her body mingled with the scent of his desire, filled his nostrils, flooding his senses with regrets of what might have been. He put the tights back in his pocket and closed his eyes, willing the Silicon Valley terrain to be obscured by clouds.

'Cocktails, Mr Nats?'

'Pardon me?'

It was a perfectly trim and proper British Airways' stewardess attempting to calm an apparently distraught traveller with a little pampering and a stiff drink.

'Would you care for a drink? Something to help you relax. Champagne? A cocktail perhaps?'

It didn't take Sydney long to respond.

'No, thanks — I'll have a cup of tea.'

Order These Selected Blue Moon Titles

Souvenirs From a Boarding School $7.95	Shades of Singapore $7.95
The Captive $7.95	Images of Ironwood $7.95
Ironwood Revisited $7.95	What Love $7.95
Sundancer $7.95	Sabine $7.95
Julia $7.95	An English Education $7.95
The Captive II $7.95	The Encounter $7.95
Shadow Lane $7.95	Tutor's Bride $7.95
Belle Sauvage $7.95	A Brief Education $7.95
Shadow Lane III $7.95	Love Lessons $7.95
My Secret Life $9.95	Shogun's Agent $7.95
Our Scene $7.95	The Sign of the Scorpion $7.95
Chrysanthemum, Rose & the Samurai $7.95	Women of Gion $7.95
Captive V $7.95	Mariska I $7.95
Bombay Bound $7.95	Secret Talents $7.95
Sadopaideia $7.95	Beatrice $7.95
The New Story of O $7.95	S&M: The Last Taboo $8.95
Shadow Lane IV $7.95	"Frank" & I $7.95
Beauty in the Birch $7.95	Lament $7.95
Laura $7.95	The Boudoir $7.95
The Reckoning $7.95	The Bitch Witch $7.95
Ironwood Continued $7.95	Story of O $5.95
In a Mist $7.95	Romance of Lust $9.95
The Prussian Girls $7.95	Ironwood $7.95
Blue Velvet $7.95	Virtue's Rewards $5.95
Shadow Lane V $7.95	The Correct Sadist $7.95
Deep South $7.95	The New Olympia Reader $15.95

Visit our website at www.bluemoonbooks.com